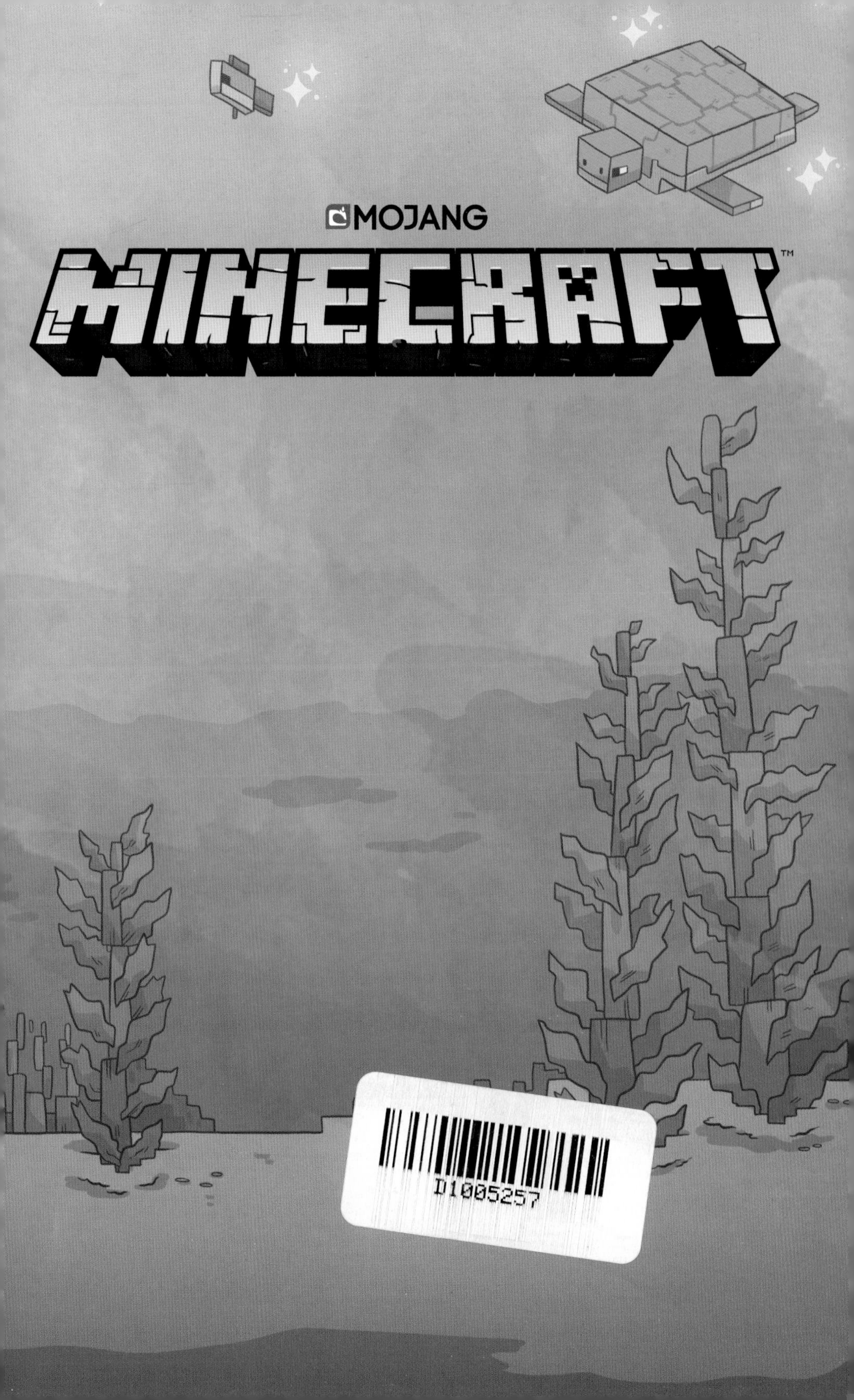
MOJANG
MINECRAFT™

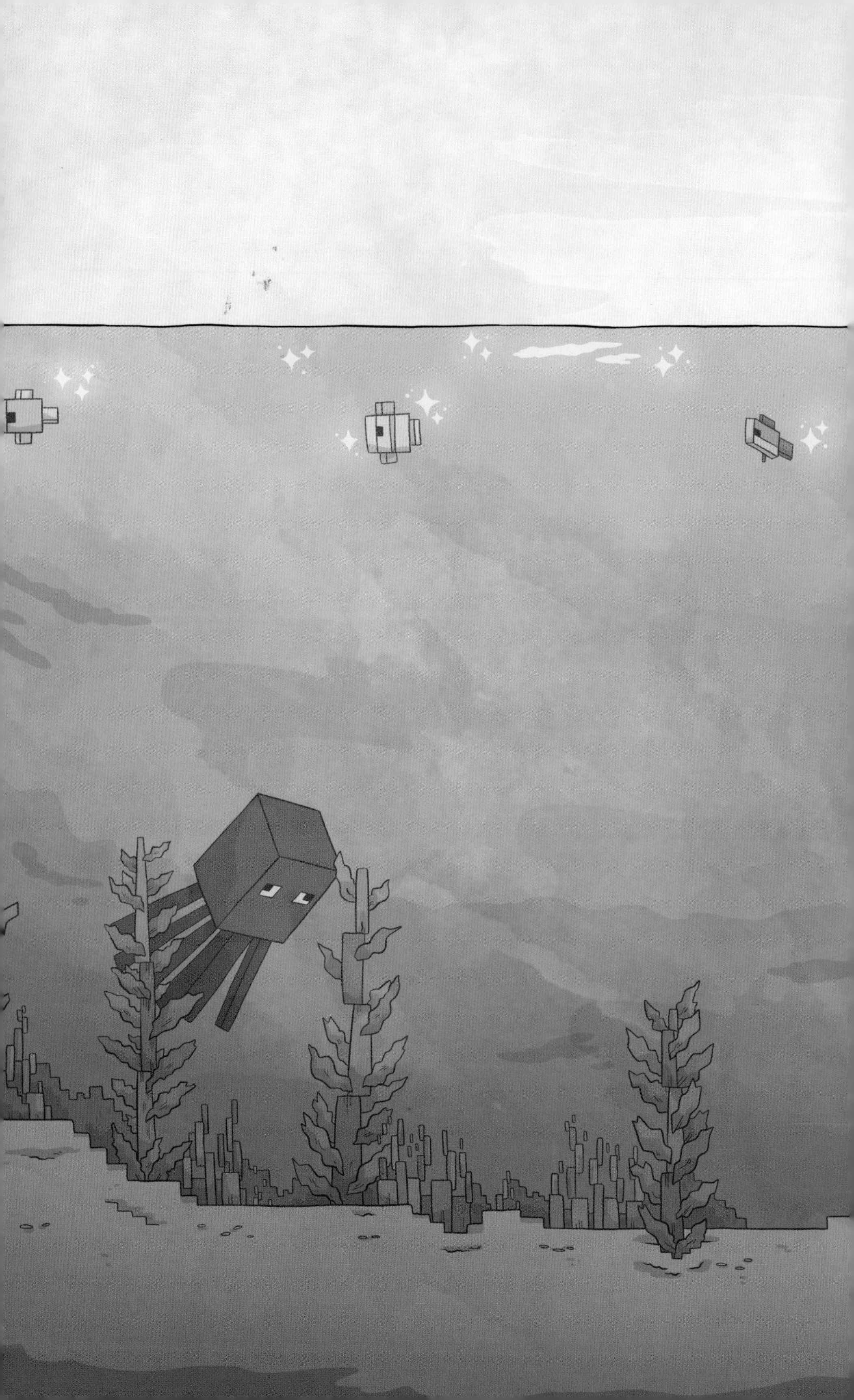

MOJANG

# MINECRAFT™

WRITTEN BY
## SFÉ R. MONSTER

ART AND COVER BY
## SARAH GRALEY

COLOR ASSISTANCE BY
## STEF PURENINS

LETTERED BY
## JOHN J. HILL

DARK HORSE BOOKS

PRESIDENT & PUBLISHER
**MIKE RICHARDSON**

EDITOR
**SHANTEL LaROCQUE**

ASSOCIATE EDITOR
**BRETT ISRAEL**

DESIGNER
**KEITH WOOD**

DIGITAL ART TECHNICIAN
**JOSIE CHRISTENSEN**

SPECIAL THANKS TO
**JENNIFER HAMMERVALD,
ALEX WILTSHIRE, KELSEY HOWARD,**
AND **SHERIN KWAN.**

Published by Dark Horse Books
A division of Dark Horse Comics LLC
10956 SE Main Street
Milwaukie, OR 97222

MINECRAFT.NET
DARKHORSE.COM

To find a comics shop in your area, visit ComicShopLocator.com.

First edition: October 2020
Ebook ISBN 978-1-50670-865-2
Trade paperback ISBN 978-1-50670-836-2

10 9 8 7 6 5 4 3 2

Printed in China

Library of Congress Cataloging-in-Publication Data

Names: Monster, Sfe R., writer. | Graley, Sarah, illustrator. | Hill, John
  J. (Letterer), letterer.
Title: Minecraft / written by Sfe R. Monster ; illustrated by Sarah Graley ;
  lettered by John J. Hill.
Description: First edition. | Milwaukie, OR : Dark Horse Books, 2019. |
  Series: [Minecraft ; volume 1]
Identifiers: LCCN 2019000776 | ISBN 9781506708348 (paperback)
Subjects: LCSH: Graphic novels. | BISAC: JUVENILE FICTION / Comics & Graphic
  Novels / Media Tie-In.
Classification: LCC PZ7.7.M646 Min 2019 | DDC 741.5/973--dc23
LC record available at https://lccn.loc.gov/2019000776

# MINECRAFT™

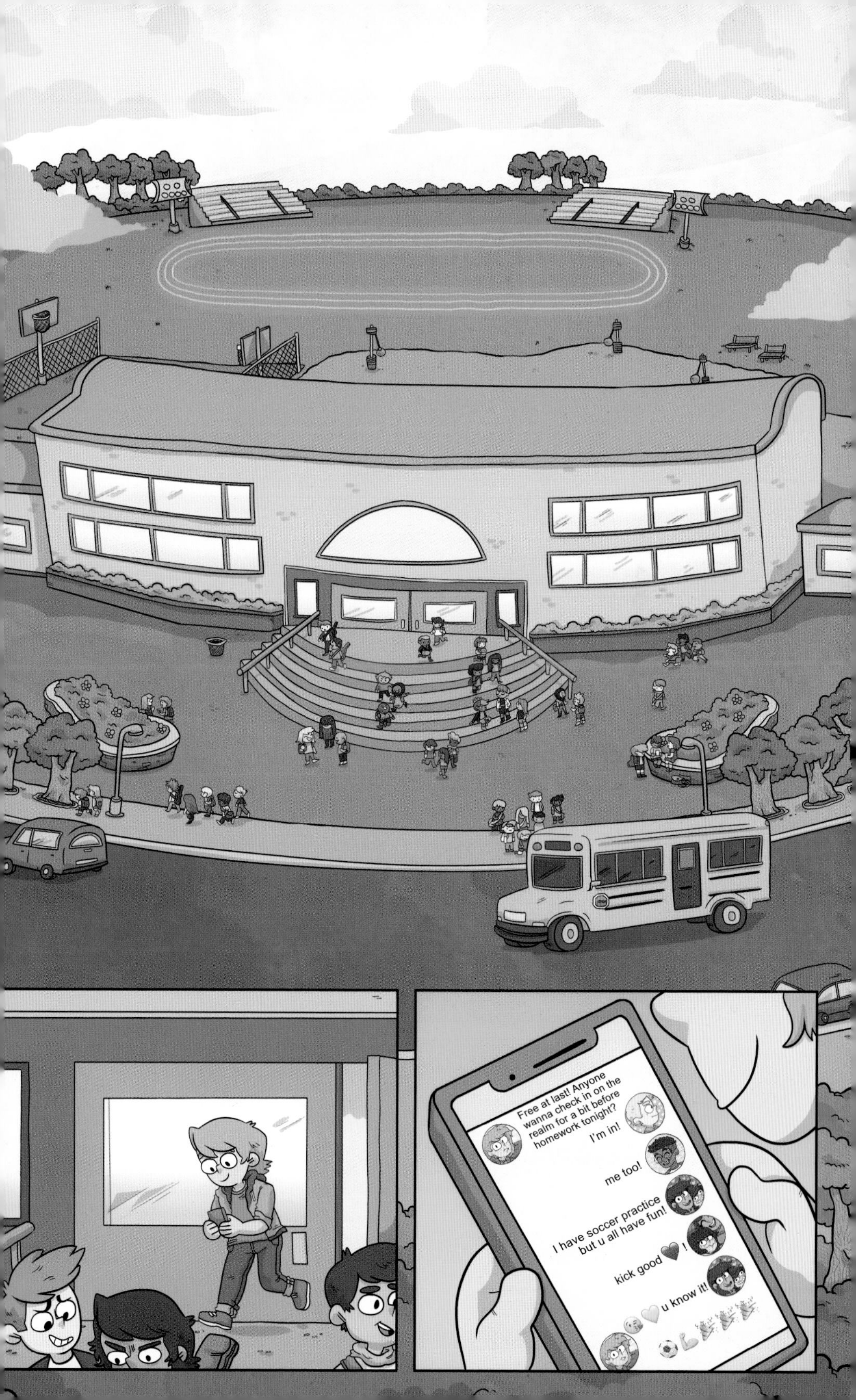

Free at last! Anyone wanna check in on the realm for a bit before homework tonight?
I'm in!
me too!
I have soccer practice but u all have fun!
kick good ❤ !
u know it!

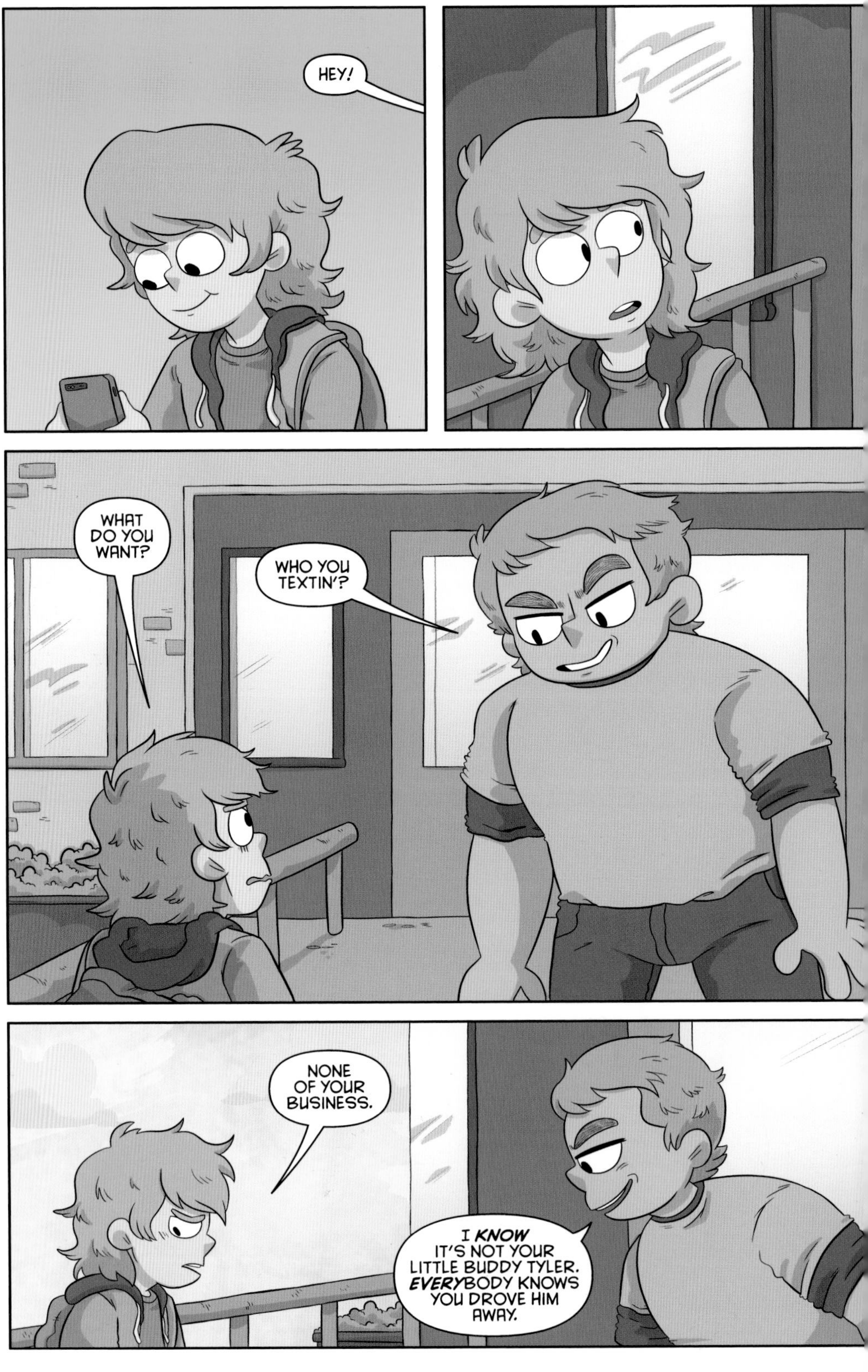
HEY!
WHAT DO YOU WANT?
WHO YOU TEXTIN'?
NONE OF YOUR BUSINESS.
I KNOW IT'S NOT YOUR LITTLE BUDDY TYLER. EVERYBODY KNOWS YOU DROVE HIM AWAY.

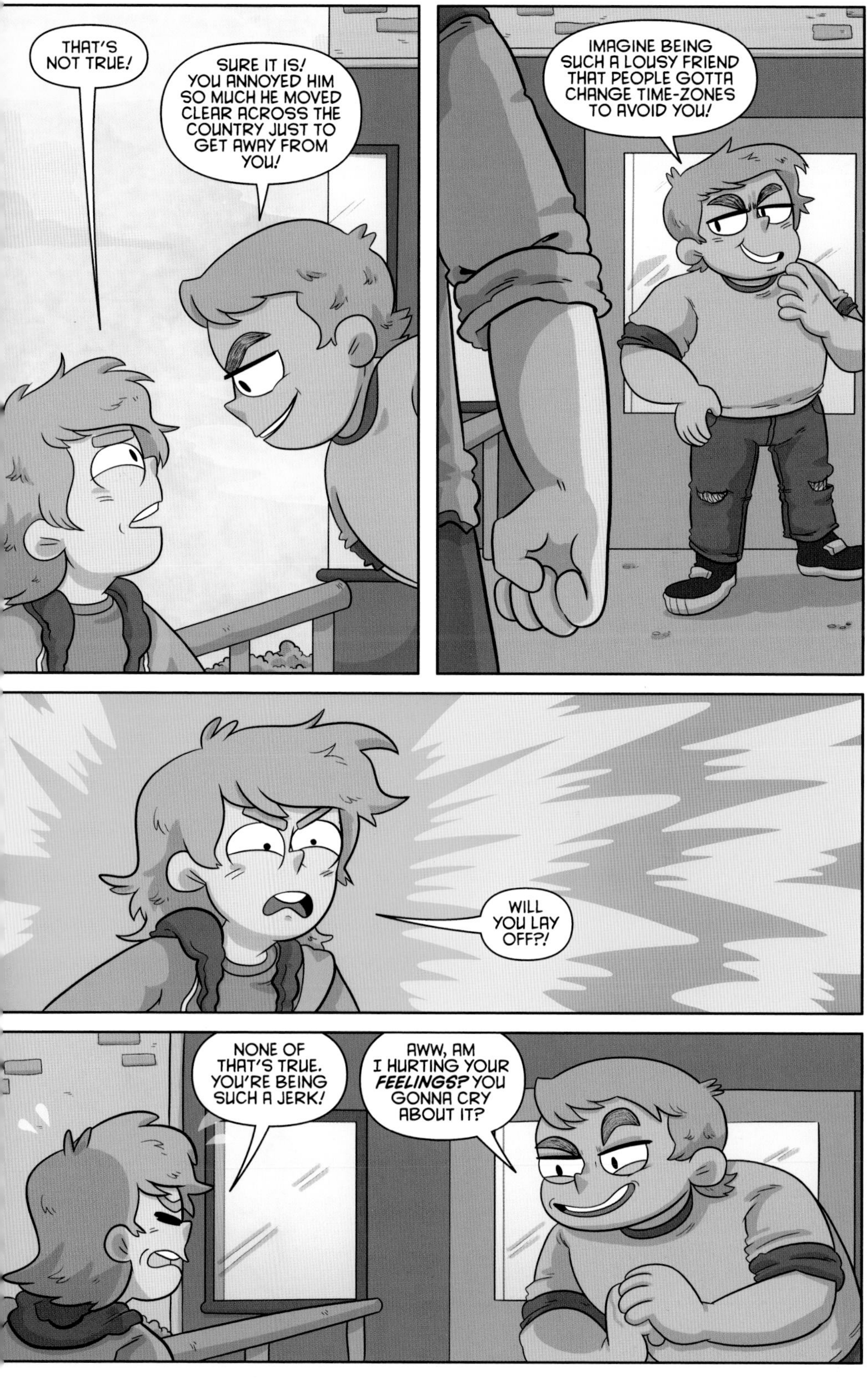
THAT'S NOT TRUE!
SURE IT IS! YOU ANNOYED HIM SO MUCH HE MOVED CLEAR ACROSS THE COUNTRY JUST TO GET AWAY FROM YOU!
IMAGINE BEING SUCH A LOUSY FRIEND THAT PEOPLE GOTTA CHANGE TIME-ZONES TO AVOID YOU!
WILL YOU LAY OFF?!
NONE OF THAT'S TRUE. YOU'RE BEING SUCH A JERK!
AWW, AM I HURTING YOUR FEELINGS? YOU GONNA CRY ABOUT IT?

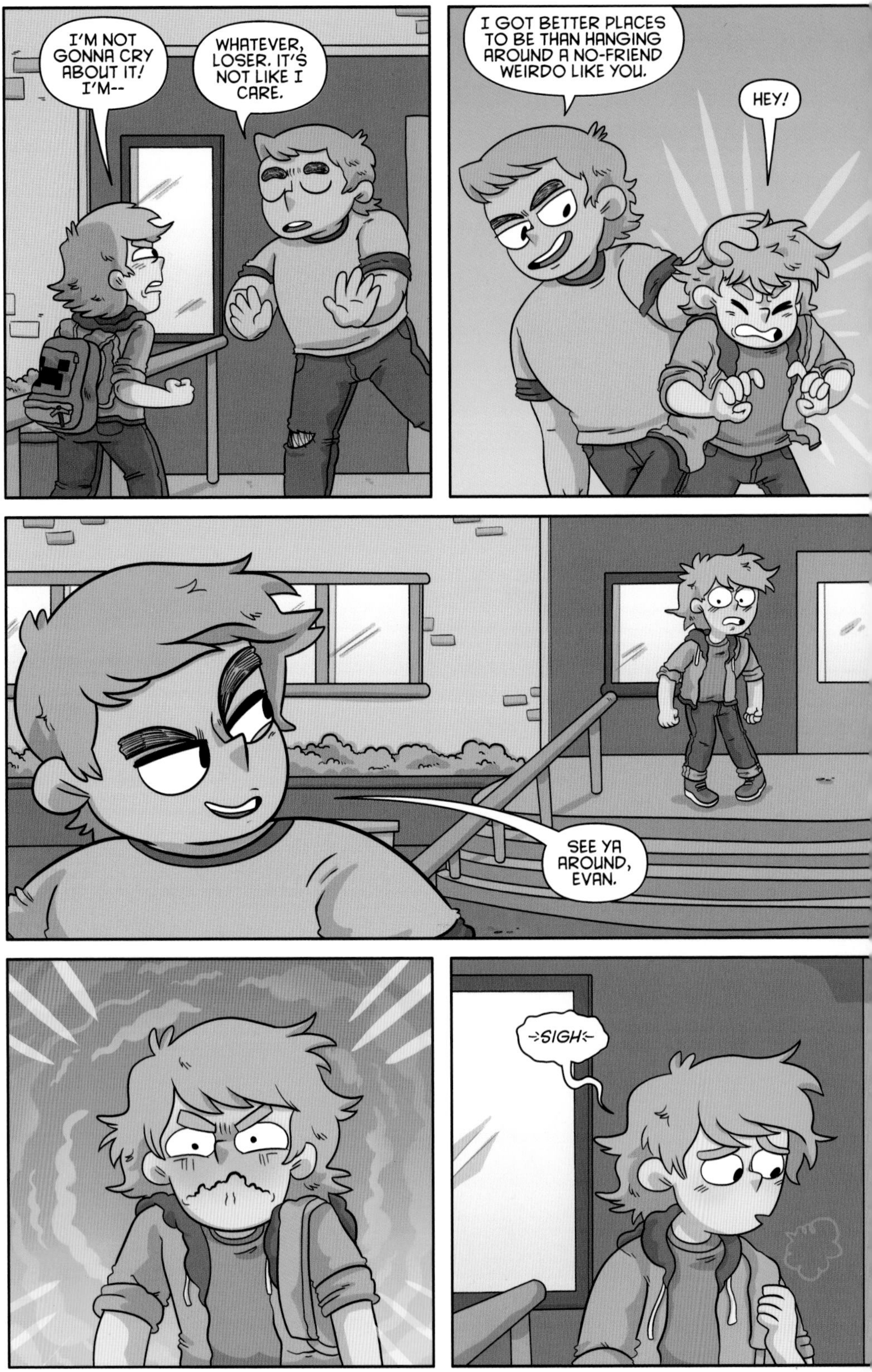
I'M NOT GONNA CRY ABOUT IT! I'M--
WHATEVER, LOSER. IT'S NOT LIKE I CARE.
I GOT BETTER PLACES TO BE THAN HANGING AROUND A NO-FRIEND WEIRDO LIKE YOU.
HEY!
SEE YA AROUND, EVAN.
SIGH

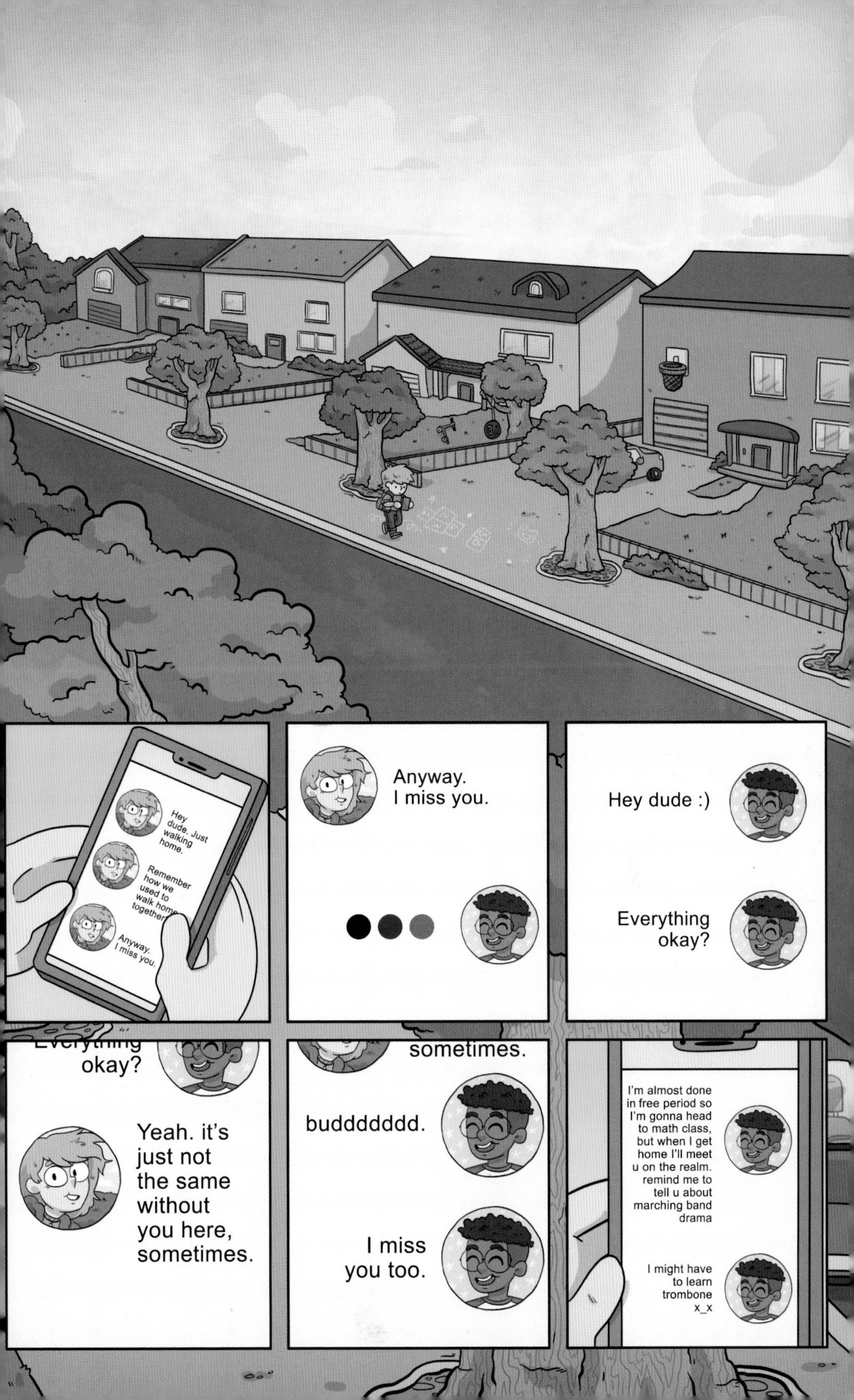
Hey dude. Just walking home.
Remember how we used to walk home together
Anyway. I miss you.
Anyway. I miss you.
Hey dude :)
Everything okay?
okay?
Yeah. it's just not the same without you here, sometimes.
sometimes.
buddddddd.
I miss you too.
I'm almost done in free period so I'm gonna head to math class, but when I get home I'll meet u on the realm. remind me to tell u about marching band drama
I might have to learn trombone x_x

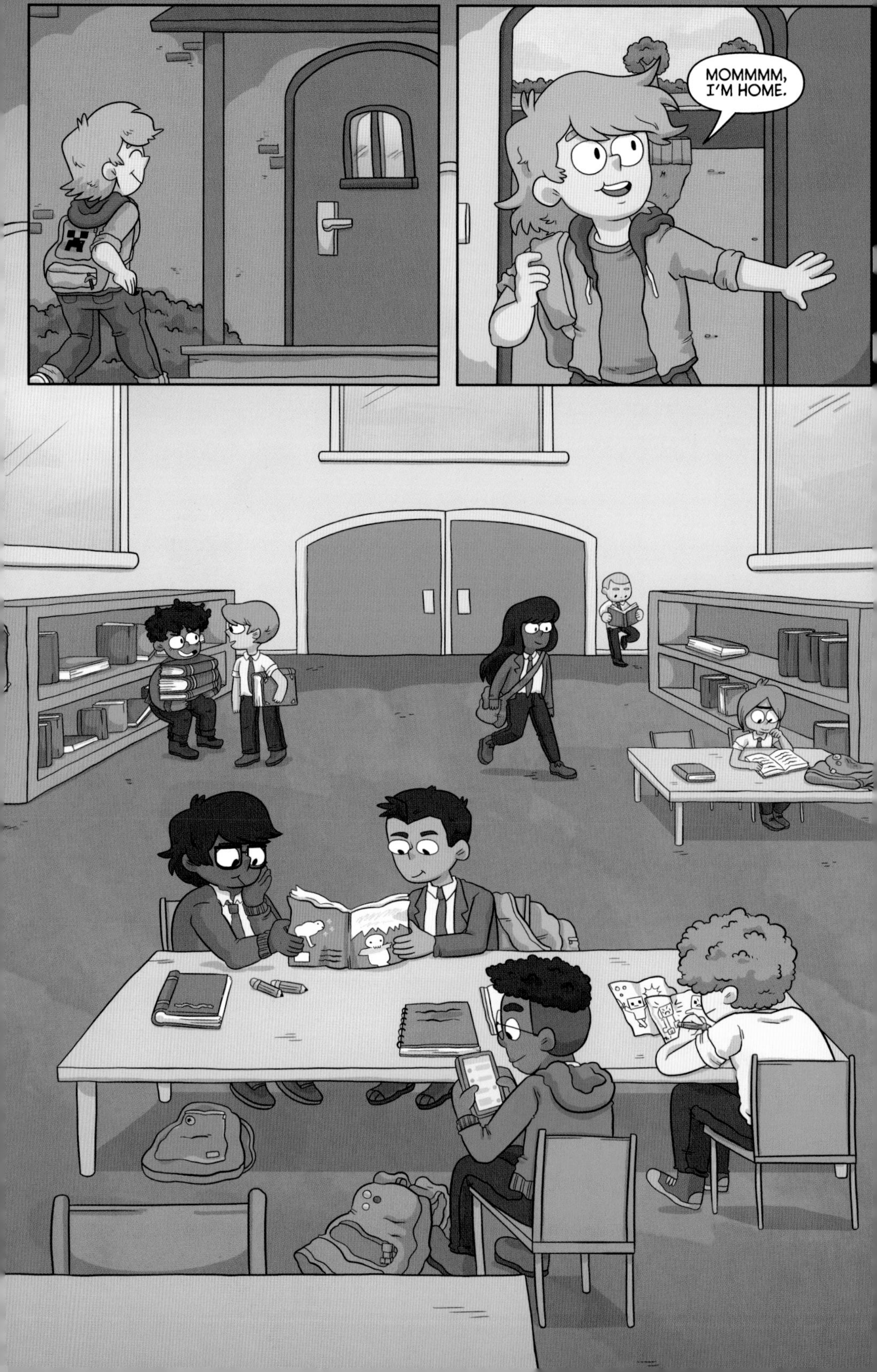
MOMMMM,
I'M HOME.

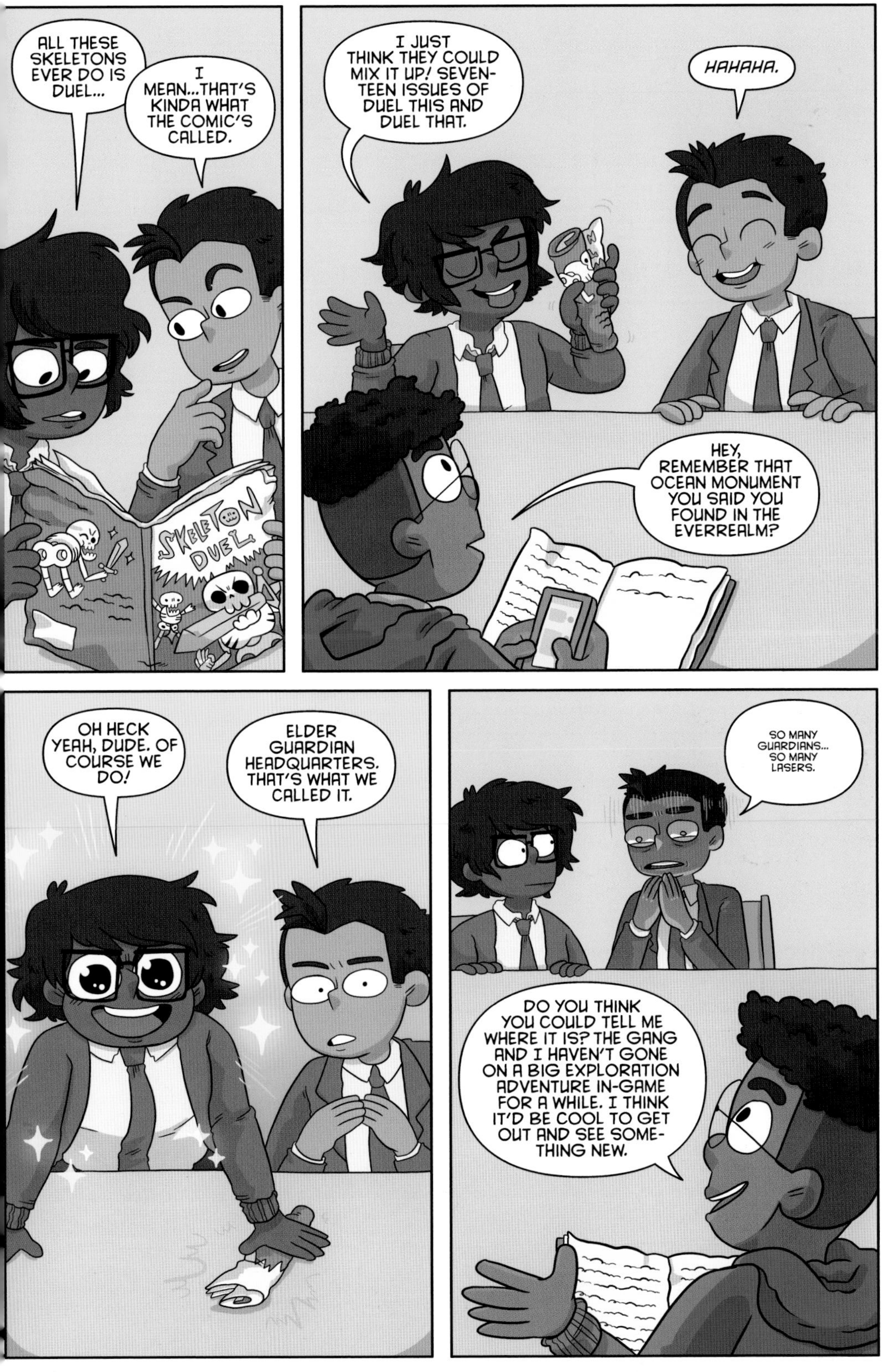
ALL THESE SKELETONS EVER DO IS DUEL...
I MEAN...THAT'S KINDA WHAT THE COMIC'S CALLED.
SKELETON DUEL
I JUST THINK THEY COULD MIX IT UP! SEVEN-TEEN ISSUES OF DUEL THIS AND DUEL THAT.
HAHAHA.
HEY, REMEMBER THAT OCEAN MONUMENT YOU SAID YOU FOUND IN THE EVERREALM?
OH HECK YEAH, DUDE. OF COURSE WE DO!
ELDER GUARDIAN HEADQUARTERS. THAT'S WHAT WE CALLED IT.
SO MANY GUARDIANS... SO MANY LASERS.
DO YOU THINK YOU COULD TELL ME WHERE IT IS? THE GANG AND I HAVEN'T GONE ON A BIG EXPLORATION ADVENTURE IN-GAME FOR A WHILE. I THINK IT'D BE COOL TO GET OUT AND SEE SOME-THING NEW.

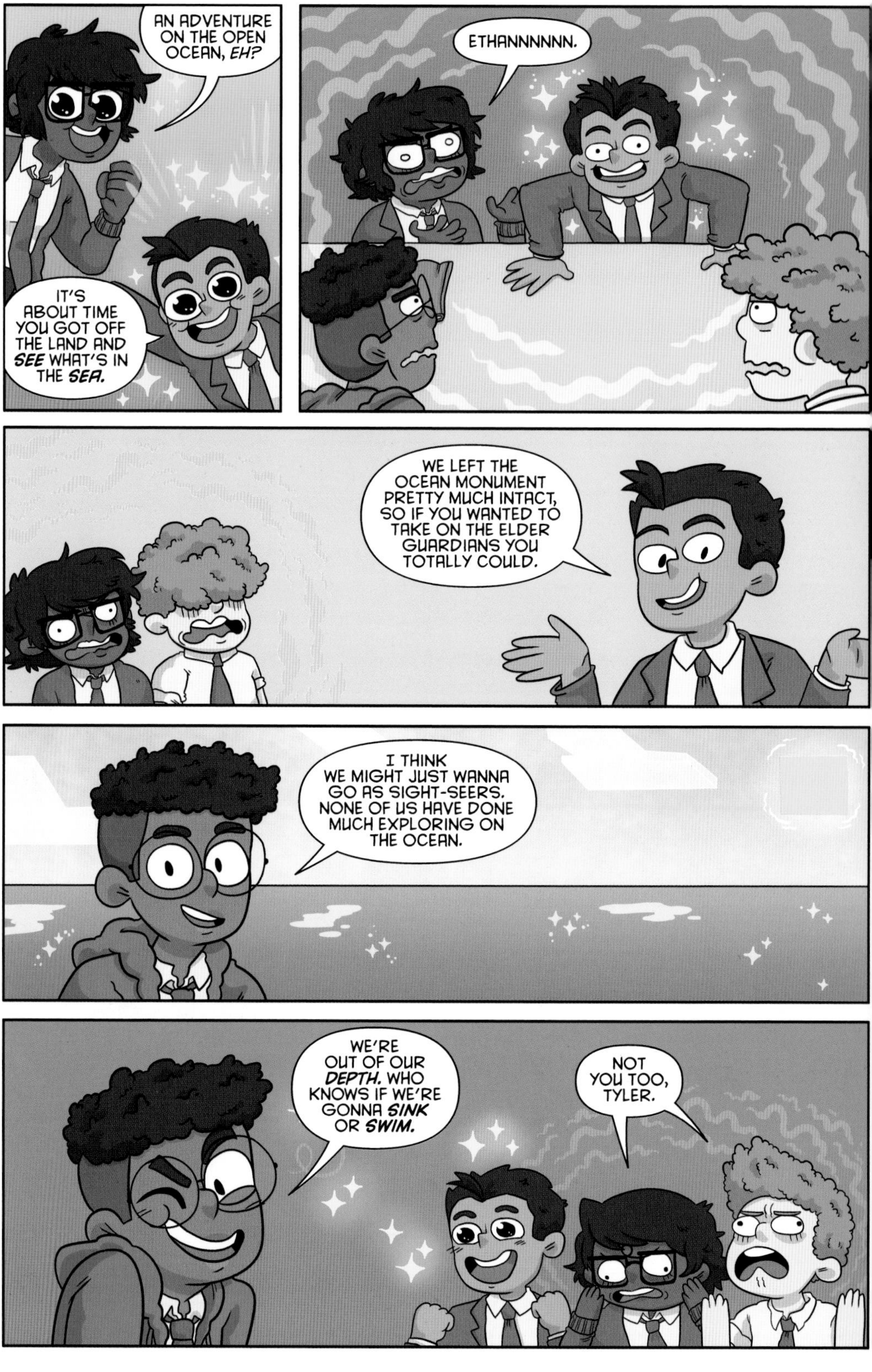
AN ADVENTURE ON THE OPEN OCEAN, *EH?*
IT'S ABOUT TIME YOU GOT OFF THE LAND AND *SEE* WHAT'S IN THE *SEA.*
ETHANNNNNN.
WE LEFT THE OCEAN MONUMENT PRETTY MUCH INTACT, SO IF YOU WANTED TO TAKE ON THE ELDER GUARDIANS YOU TOTALLY COULD.
I THINK WE MIGHT JUST WANNA GO AS SIGHT-SEERS. NONE OF US HAVE DONE MUCH EXPLORING ON THE OCEAN.
WE'RE OUT OF OUR *DEPTH.* WHO KNOWS IF WE'RE GONNA *SINK* OR *SWIM.*
NOT YOU TOO, TYLER.

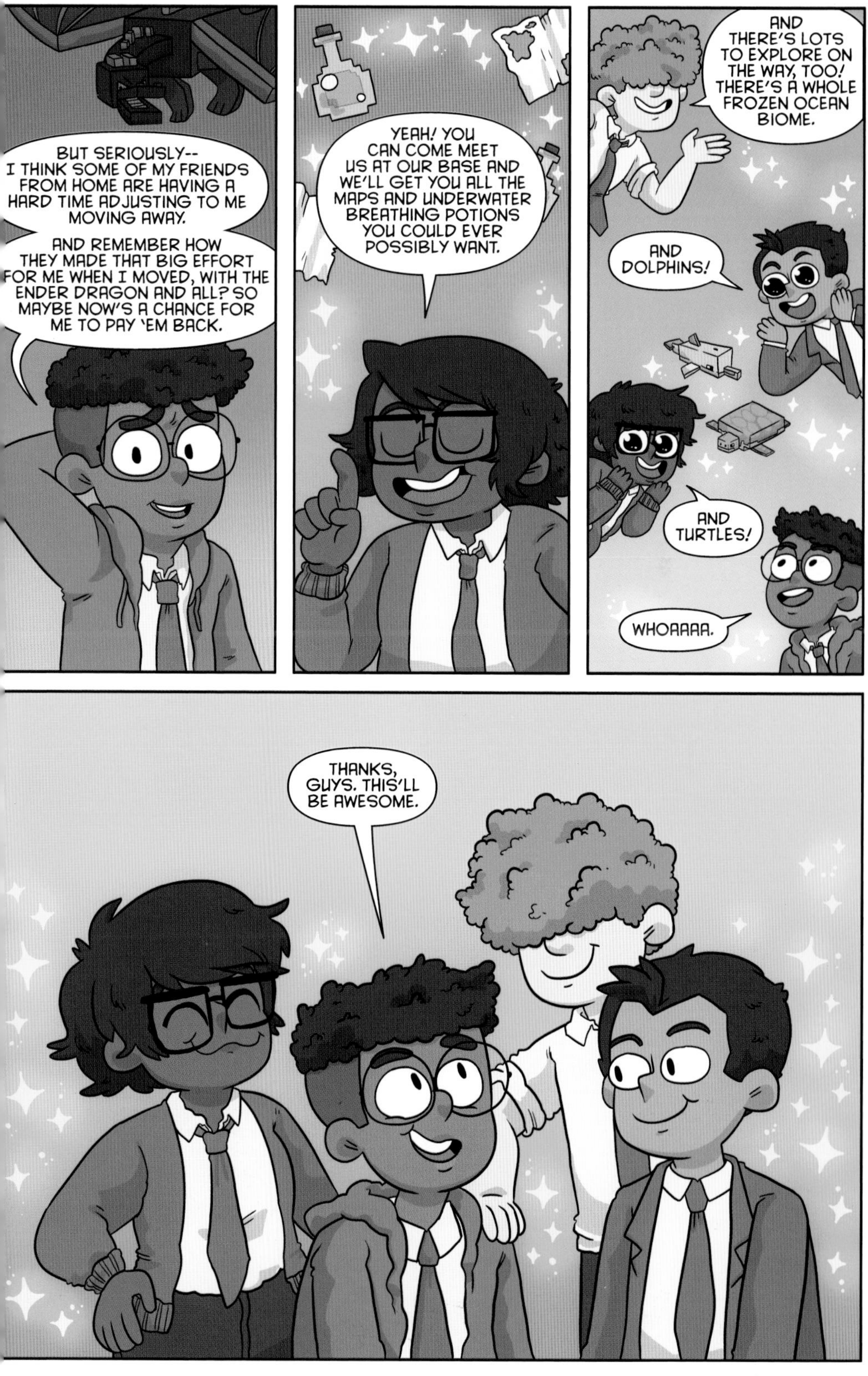
BUT SERIOUSLY-- I THINK SOME OF MY FRIENDS FROM HOME ARE HAVING A HARD TIME ADJUSTING TO ME MOVING AWAY.
AND REMEMBER HOW THEY MADE THAT BIG EFFORT FOR ME WHEN I MOVED, WITH THE ENDER DRAGON AND ALL? SO MAYBE NOW'S A CHANCE FOR ME TO PAY 'EM BACK.
YEAH! YOU CAN COME MEET US AT OUR BASE AND WE'LL GET YOU ALL THE MAPS AND UNDERWATER BREATHING POTIONS YOU COULD EVER POSSIBLY WANT.
AND THERE'S LOTS TO EXPLORE ON THE WAY, TOO! THERE'S A WHOLE FROZEN OCEAN BIOME.
AND DOLPHINS!
AND TURTLES!
WHOAAAA.
THANKS, GUYS. THIS'LL BE AWESOME.

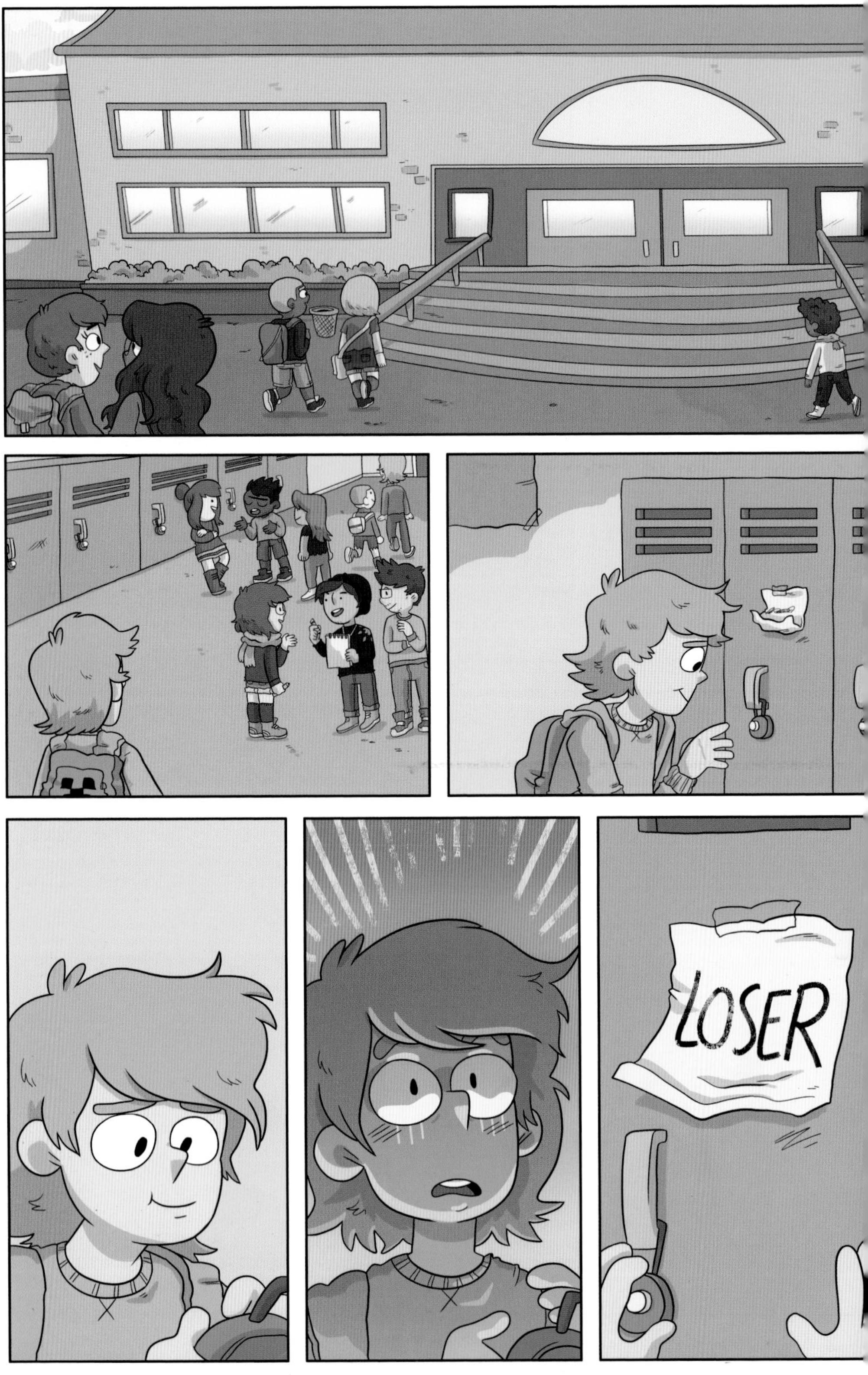

LOSER

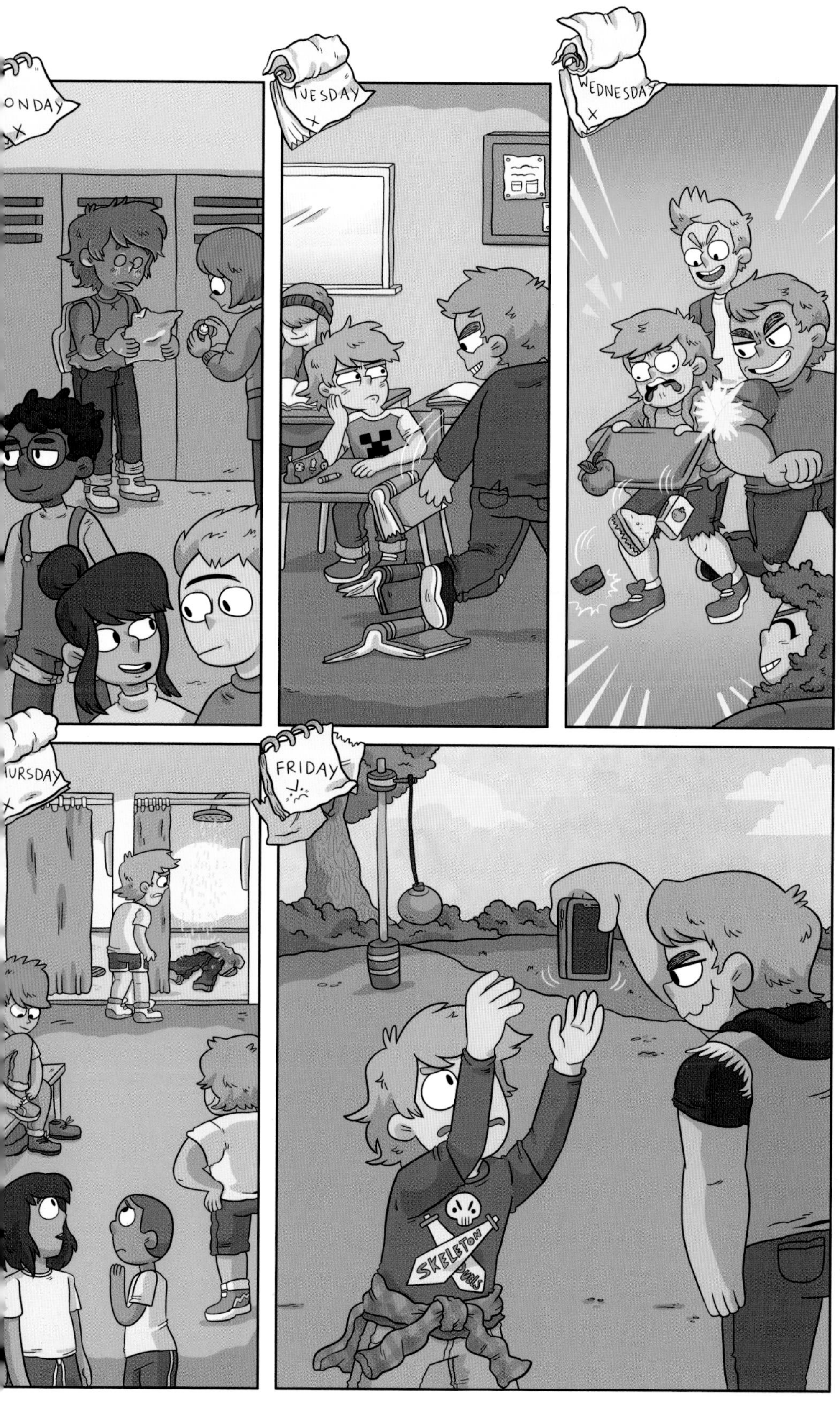
ONDAY
TUESDAY
WEDNESDAY
HURSDAY
FRIDAY
SKELETON
DUELS

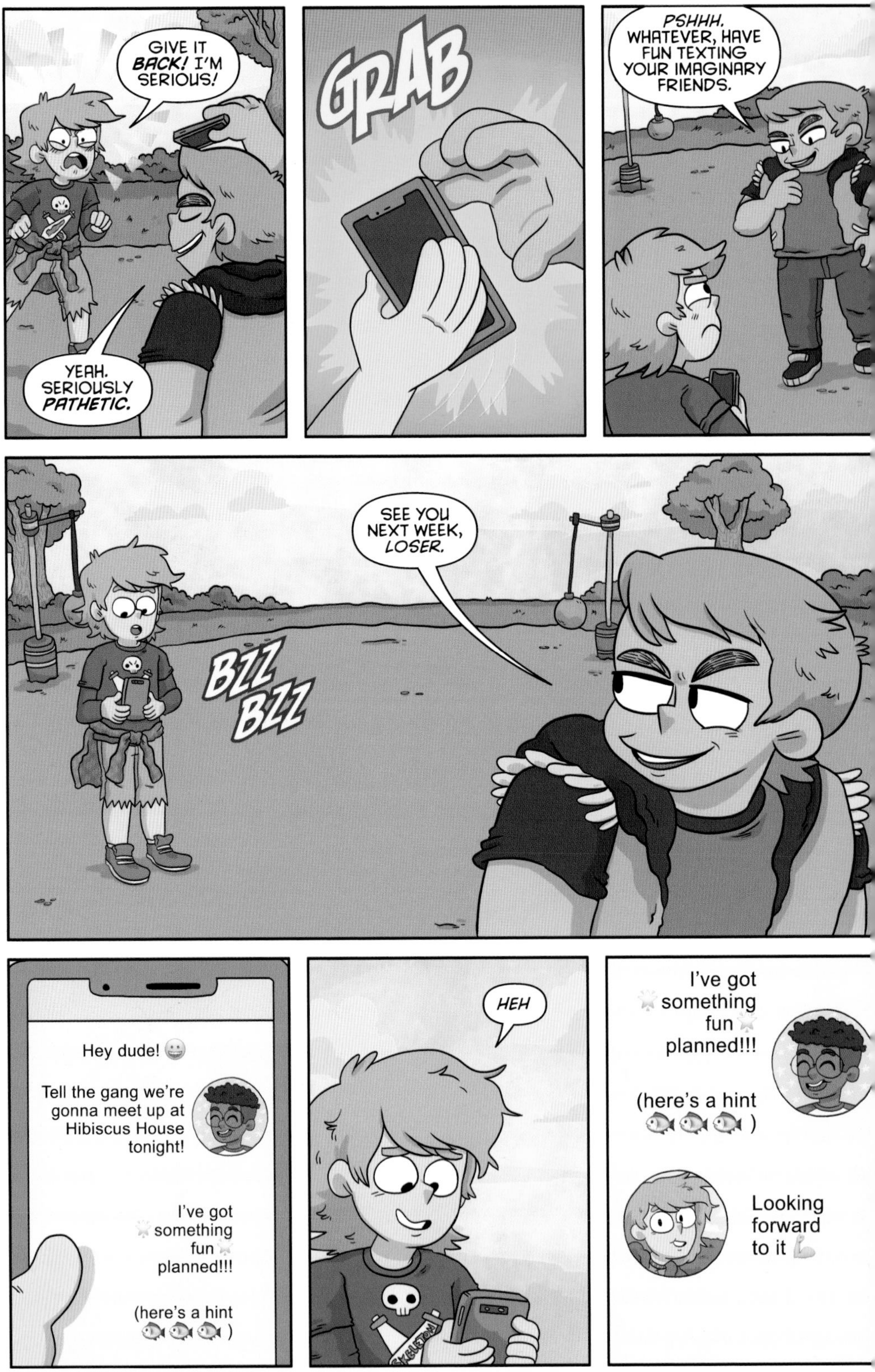
GIVE IT BACK! I'M SERIOUS!
YEAH. SERIOUSLY PATHETIC.
GRAB
PSHHH. WHATEVER, HAVE FUN TEXTING YOUR IMAGINARY FRIENDS.
SEE YOU NEXT WEEK, LOSER.
BZZ BZZ
Hey dude!
Tell the gang we're gonna meet up at Hibiscus House tonight!
I've got something fun planned!!!
(here's a hint )
HEH
I've got something fun planned!!!
(here's a hint )
Looking forward to it

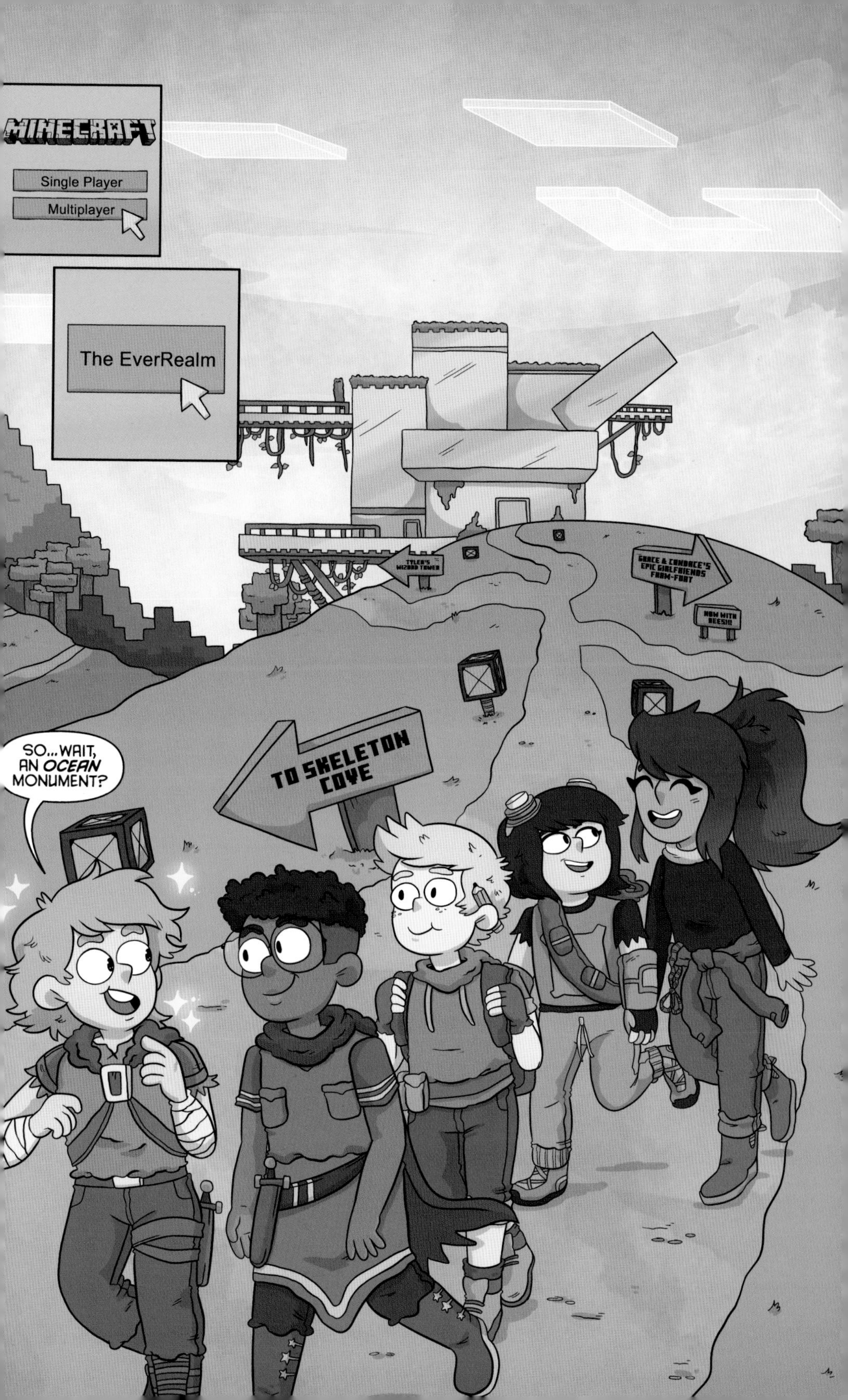
MINECRAFT
Single Player
Multiplayer
The EverRealm
TYLER'S WIZARD TOWER
GRACE & CANDACE'S EPIC GIRLFRIENDS FARM-FORT
NOW WITH BEES!!
SO...WAIT, AN *OCEAN* MONUMENT?
TO SKELETON COVE

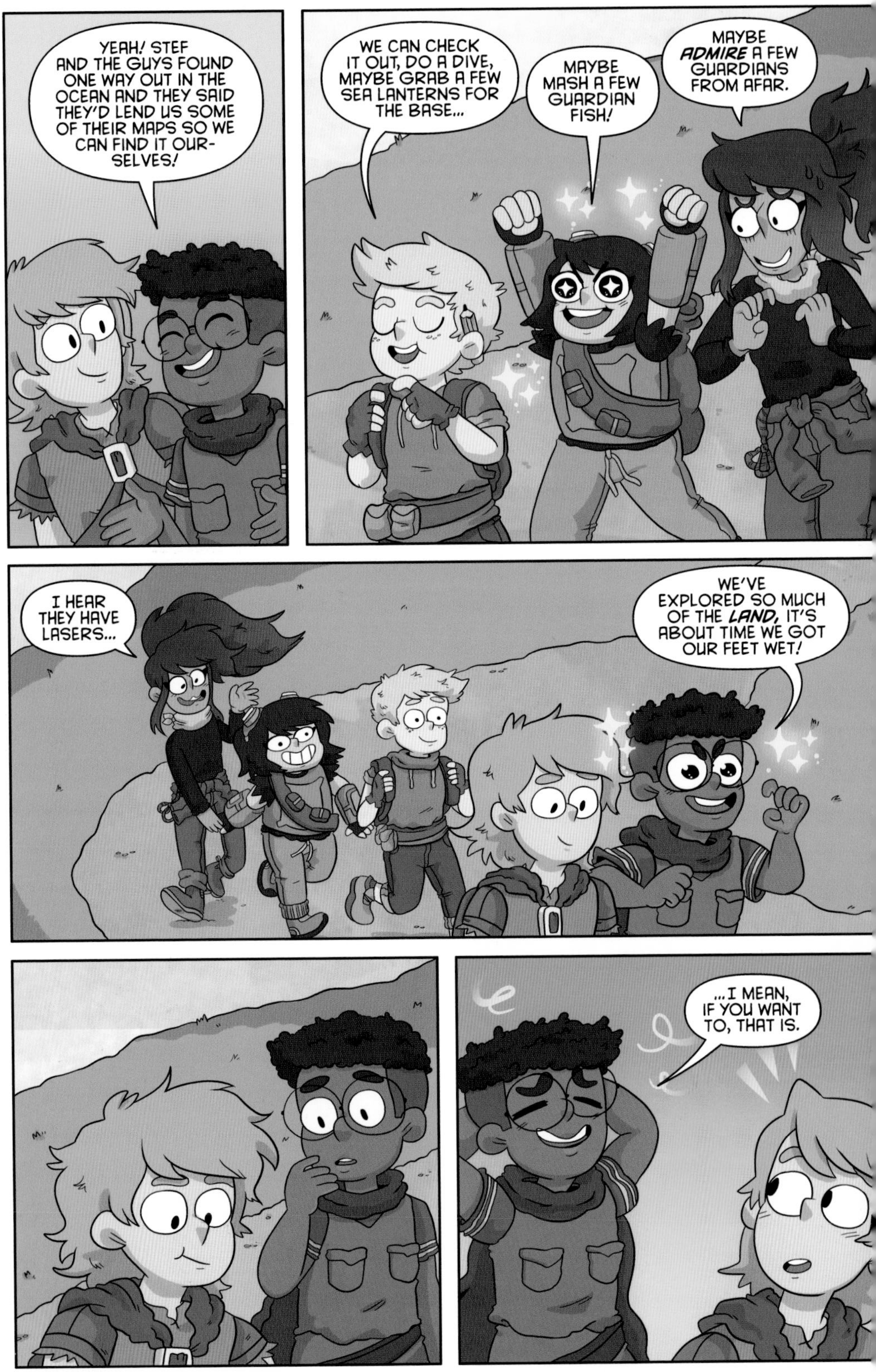
YEAH! STEF AND THE GUYS FOUND ONE WAY OUT IN THE OCEAN AND THEY SAID THEY'D LEND US SOME OF THEIR MAPS SO WE CAN FIND IT OUR-SELVES!
WE CAN CHECK IT OUT, DO A DIVE, MAYBE GRAB A FEW SEA LANTERNS FOR THE BASE...
MAYBE MASH A FEW GUARDIAN FISH!
MAYBE *ADMIRE* A FEW GUARDIANS FROM AFAR.
I HEAR THEY HAVE LASERS...
WE'VE EXPLORED SO MUCH OF THE *LAND,* IT'S ABOUT TIME WE GOT OUR FEET WET!
...I MEAN, IF YOU WANT TO, THAT IS.

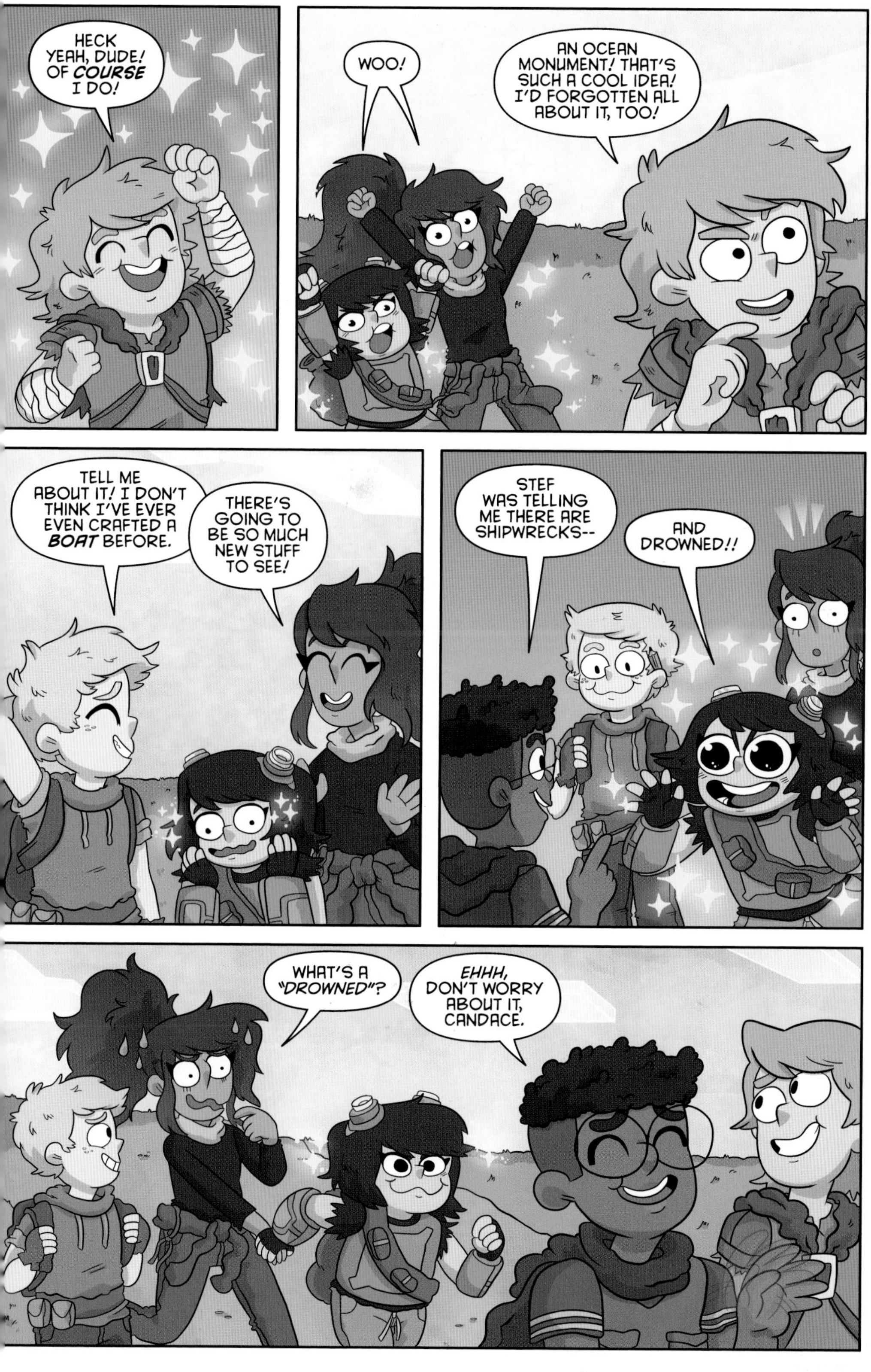
HECK YEAH, DUDE! OF *COURSE* I DO!
WOO!
AN OCEAN MONUMENT! THAT'S SUCH A COOL IDEA! I'D FORGOTTEN ALL ABOUT IT, TOO!
TELL ME ABOUT IT! I DON'T THINK I'VE EVER EVEN CRAFTED A *BOAT* BEFORE.
THERE'S GOING TO BE SO MUCH NEW STUFF TO SEE!
STEF WAS TELLING ME THERE ARE SHIPWRECKS--
AND DROWNED!!
WHAT'S A *"DROWNED"*?
*EHHH*, DON'T WORRY ABOUT IT, CANDACE.

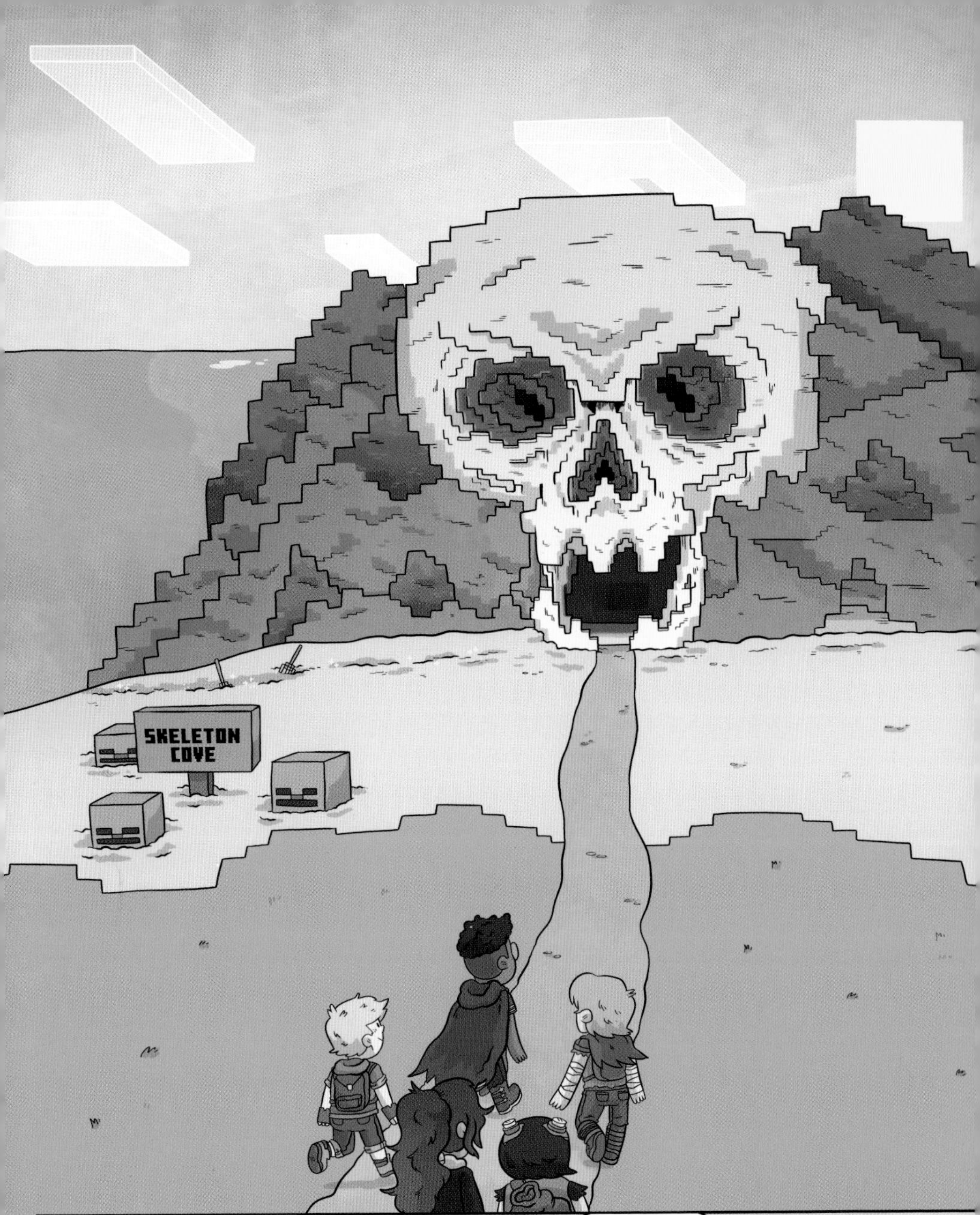
SKELETON
COVE

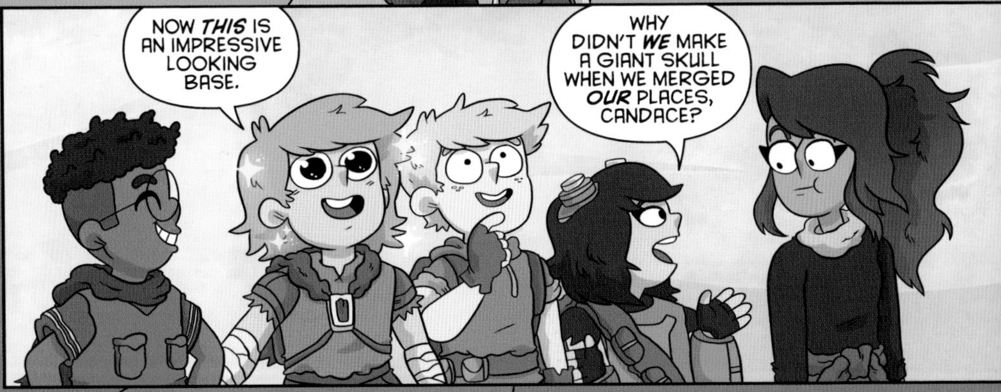
NOW *THIS* IS AN IMPRESSIVE LOOKING BASE.
WHY DIDN'T *WE* MAKE A GIANT SKULL WHEN WE MERGED *OUR* PLACES, CANDACE?

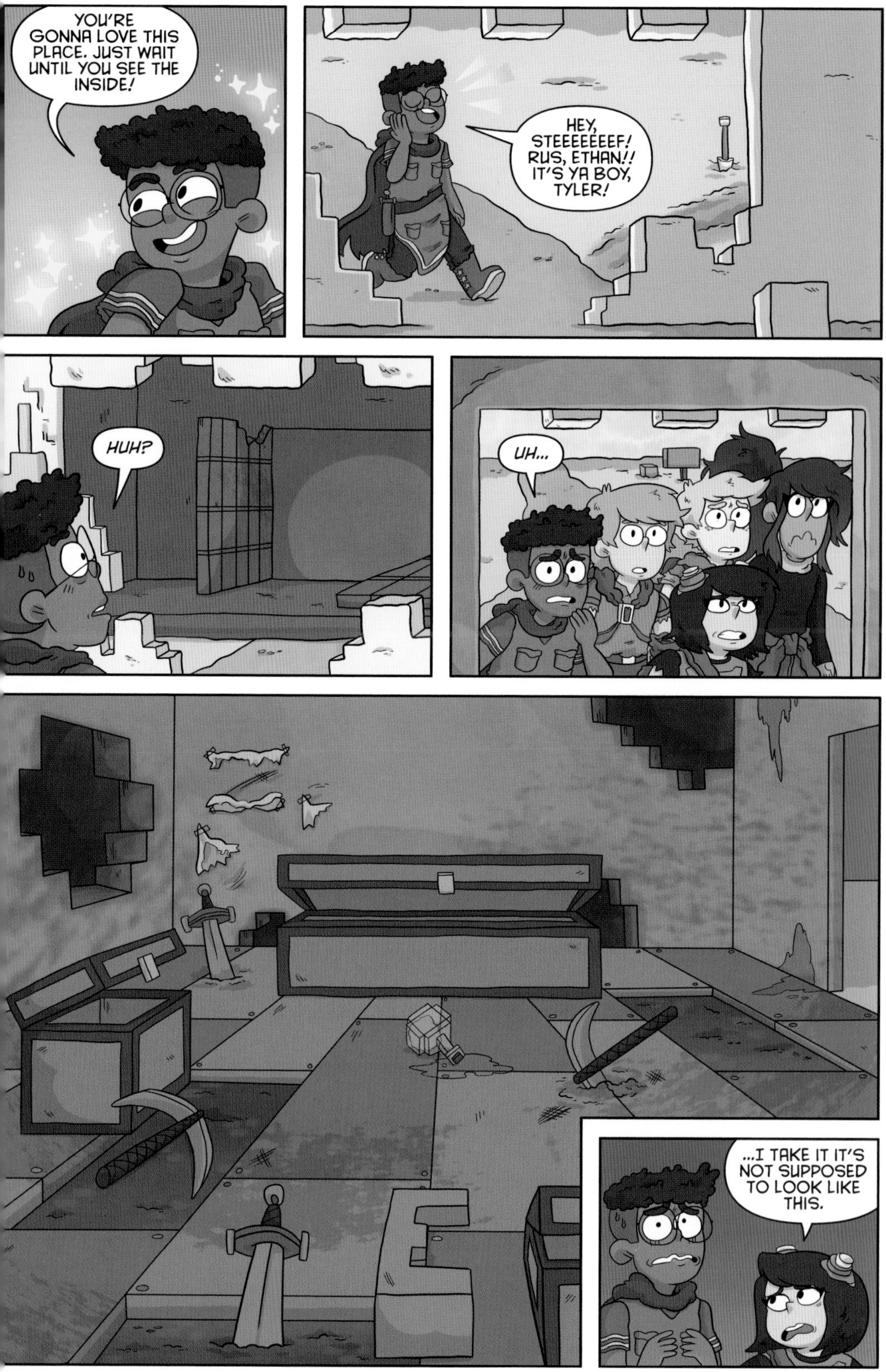
YOU'RE GONNA LOVE THIS PLACE. JUST WAIT UNTIL YOU SEE THE INSIDE!
HEY, STEEEEEEEF! RUS, ETHAN!! IT'S YA BOY, TYLER!
HUH?
UH...
...I TAKE IT IT'S NOT SUPPOSED TO LOOK LIKE THIS.

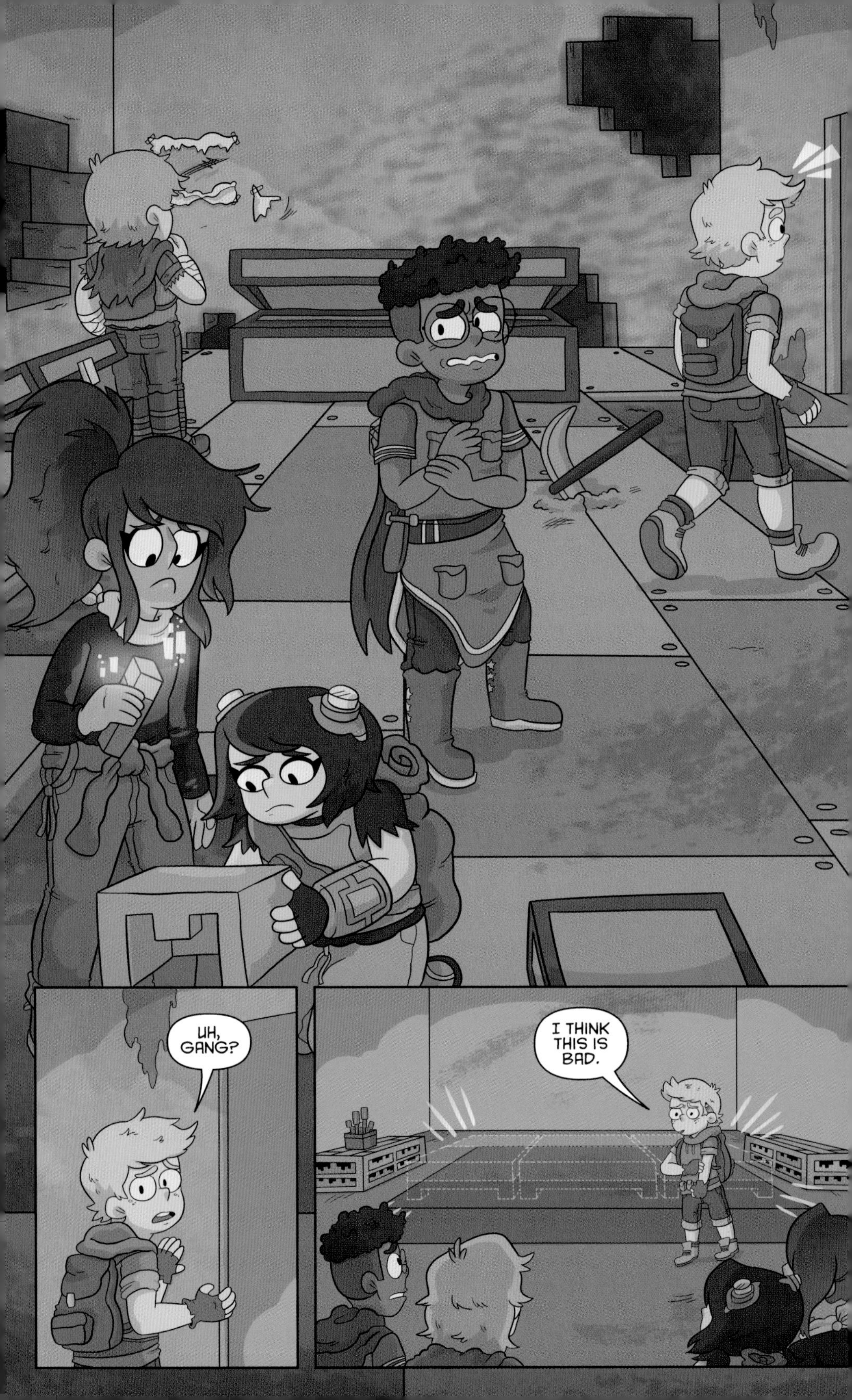
UH, GANG?
I THINK THIS IS BAD.

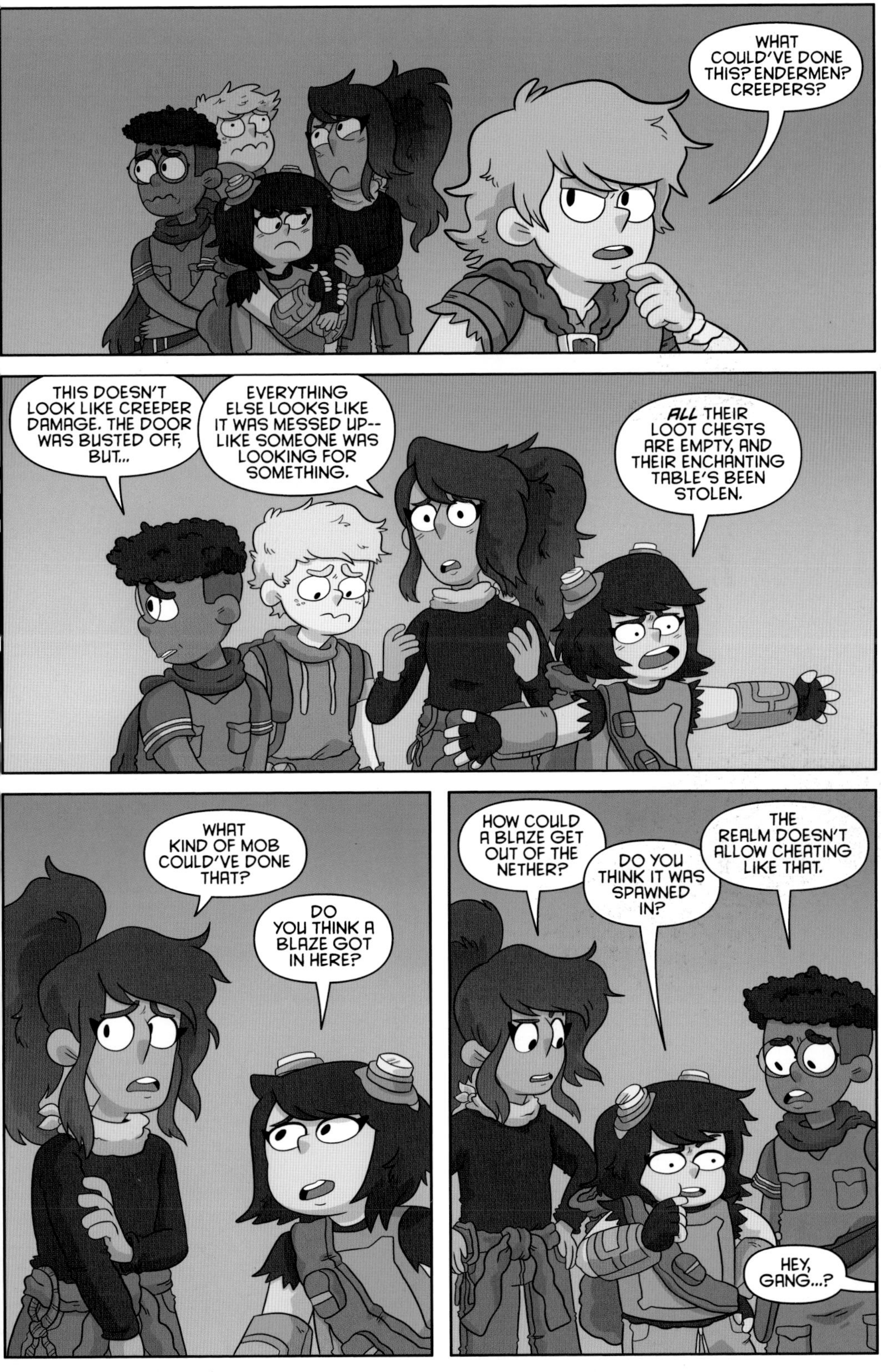
WHAT COULD'VE DONE THIS? ENDERMEN? CREEPERS?
THIS DOESN'T LOOK LIKE CREEPER DAMAGE. THE DOOR WAS BUSTED OFF, BUT...
EVERYTHING ELSE LOOKS LIKE IT WAS MESSED UP-- LIKE SOMEONE WAS LOOKING FOR SOMETHING.
ALL THEIR LOOT CHESTS ARE EMPTY, AND THEIR ENCHANTING TABLE'S BEEN STOLEN.
WHAT KIND OF MOB COULD'VE DONE THAT?
DO YOU THINK A BLAZE GOT IN HERE?
HOW COULD A BLAZE GET OUT OF THE NETHER?
DO YOU THINK IT WAS SPAWNED IN?
THE REALM DOESN'T ALLOW CHEATING LIKE THAT.
HEY, GANG...?

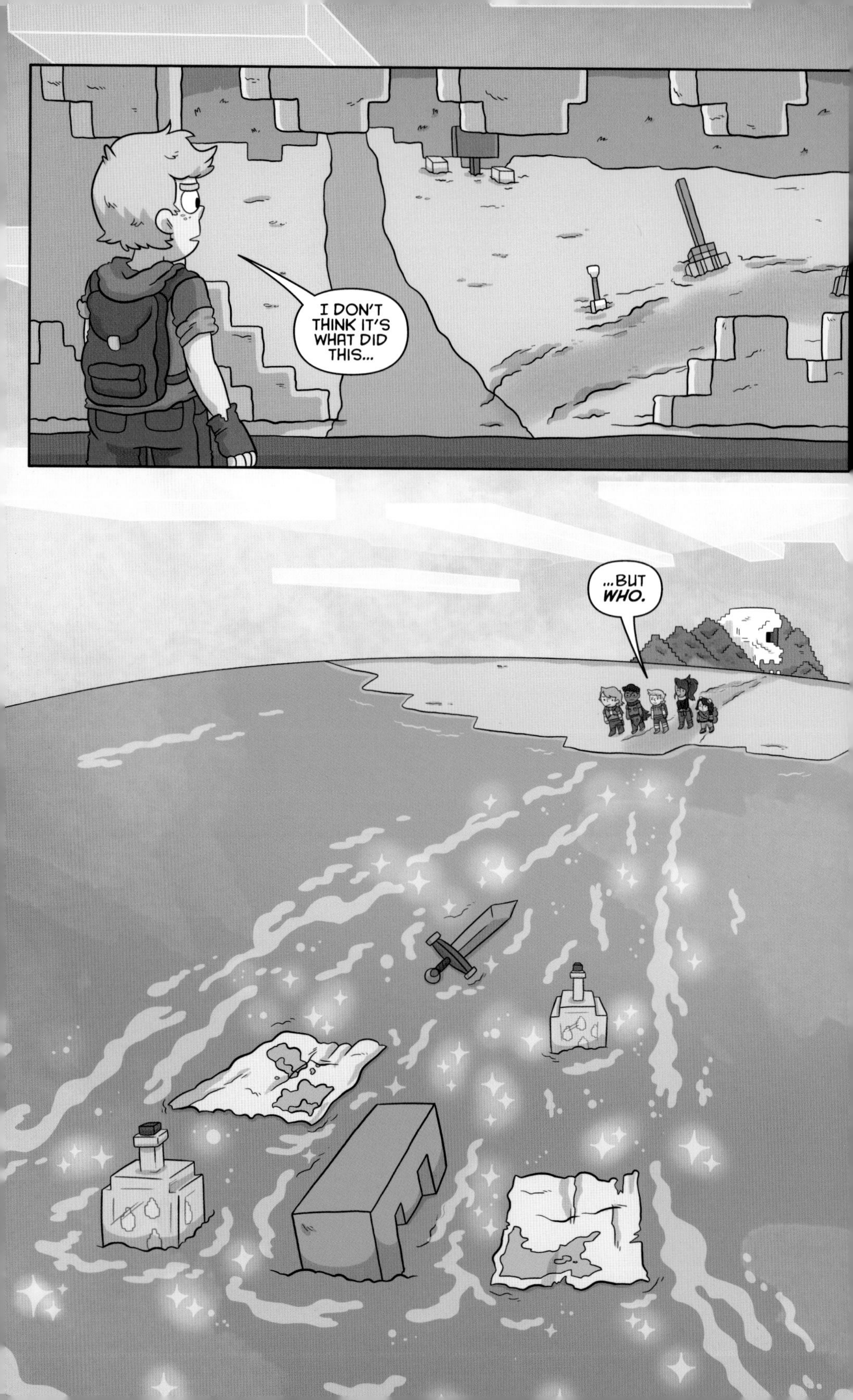
I DON'T THINK IT'S WHAT DID THIS...
...BUT *WHO.*

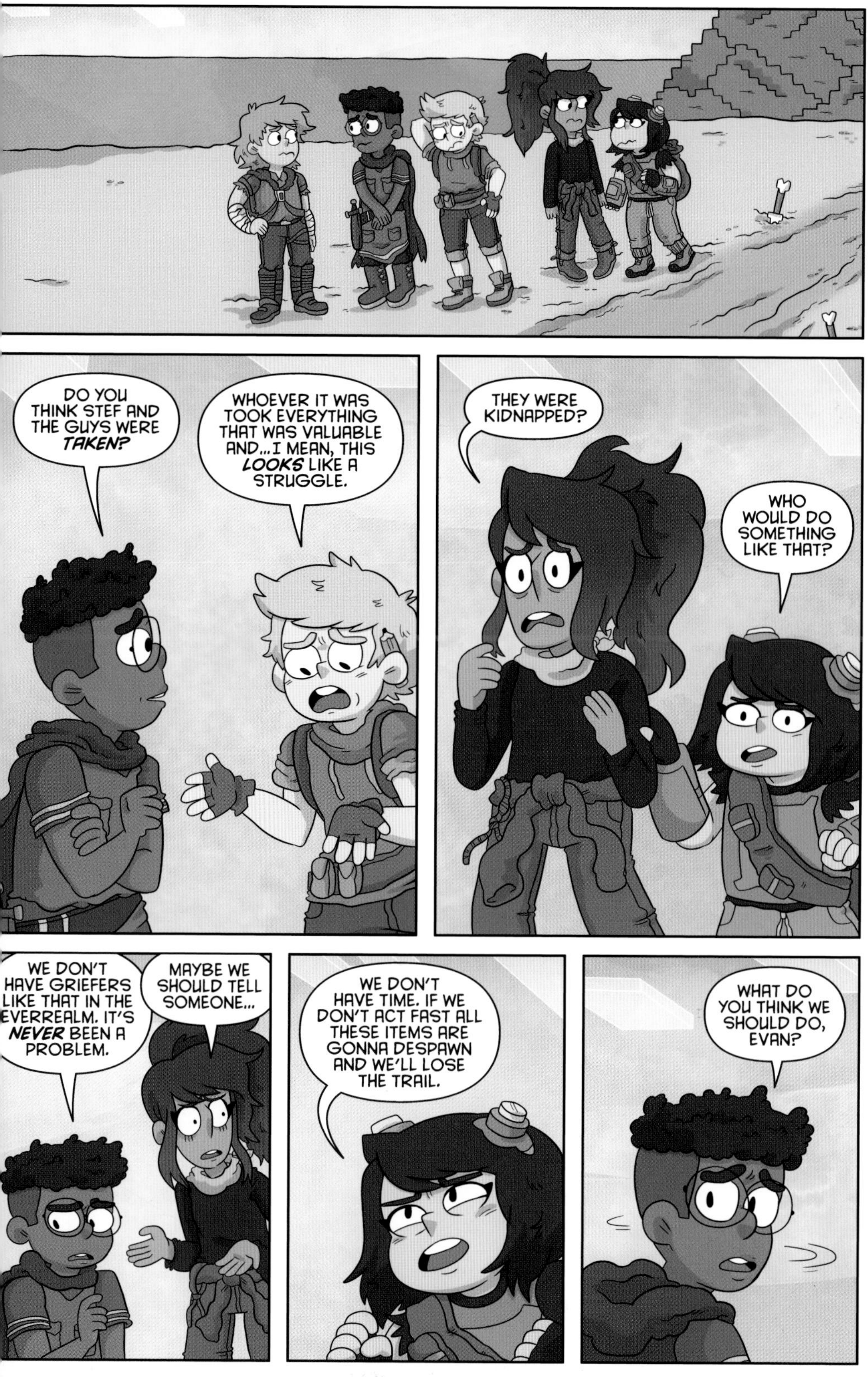
DO YOU THINK STEF AND THE GUYS WERE *TAKEN?*
WHOEVER IT WAS TOOK EVERYTHING THAT WAS VALUABLE AND...I MEAN, THIS *LOOKS* LIKE A STRUGGLE.
THEY WERE KIDNAPPED?
WHO WOULD DO SOMETHING LIKE THAT?
WE DON'T HAVE GRIEFERS LIKE THAT IN THE EVERREALM. IT'S *NEVER* BEEN A PROBLEM.
MAYBE WE SHOULD TELL SOMEONE...
WE DON'T HAVE TIME. IF WE DON'T ACT FAST ALL THESE ITEMS ARE GONNA DESPAWN AND WE'LL LOSE THE TRAIL.
WHAT DO YOU THINK WE SHOULD DO, EVAN?

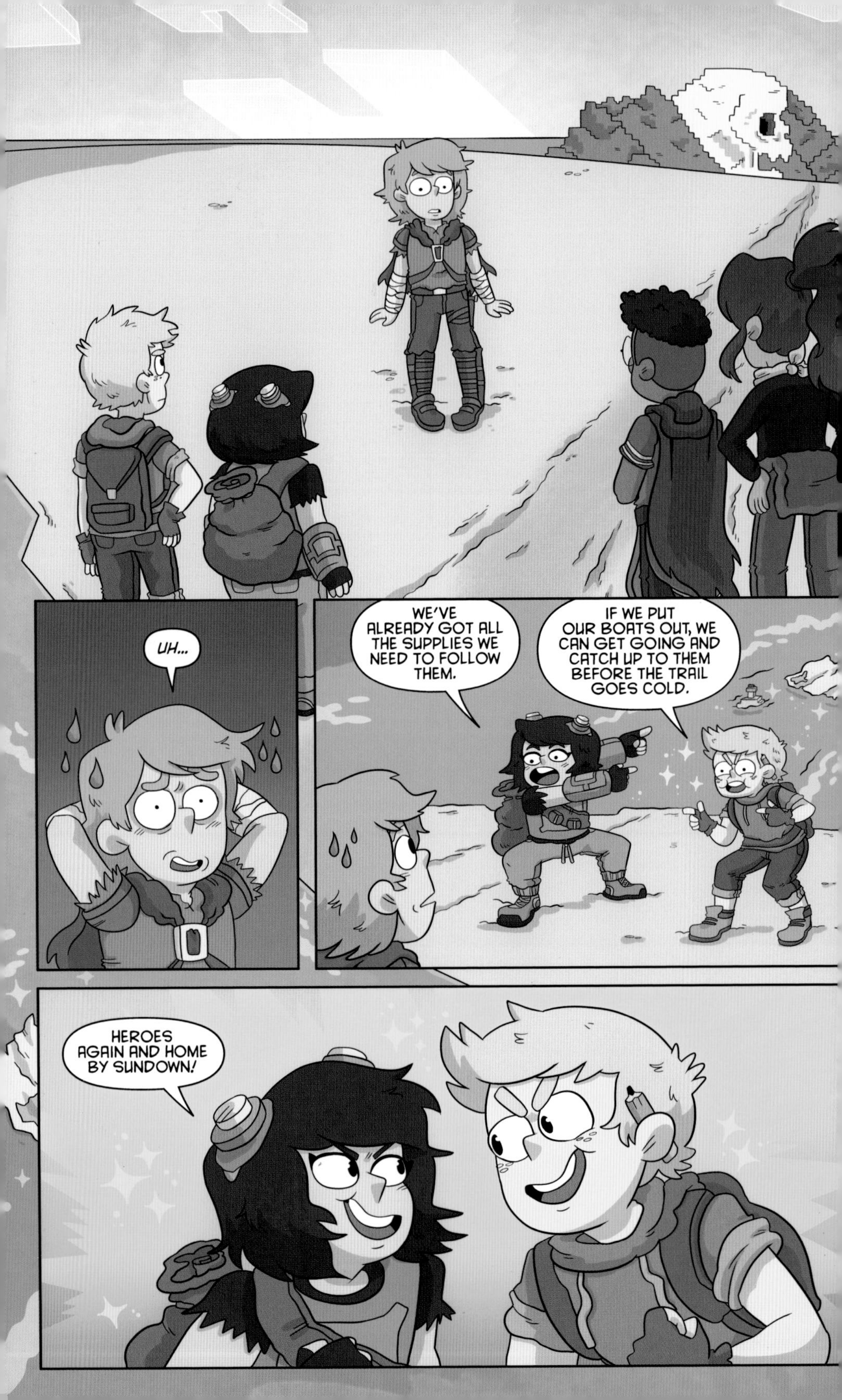
UH...
WE'VE ALREADY GOT ALL THE SUPPLIES WE NEED TO FOLLOW THEM.
IF WE PUT OUR BOATS OUT, WE CAN GET GOING AND CATCH UP TO THEM BEFORE THE TRAIL GOES COLD.
HEROES AGAIN AND HOME BY SUNDOWN!

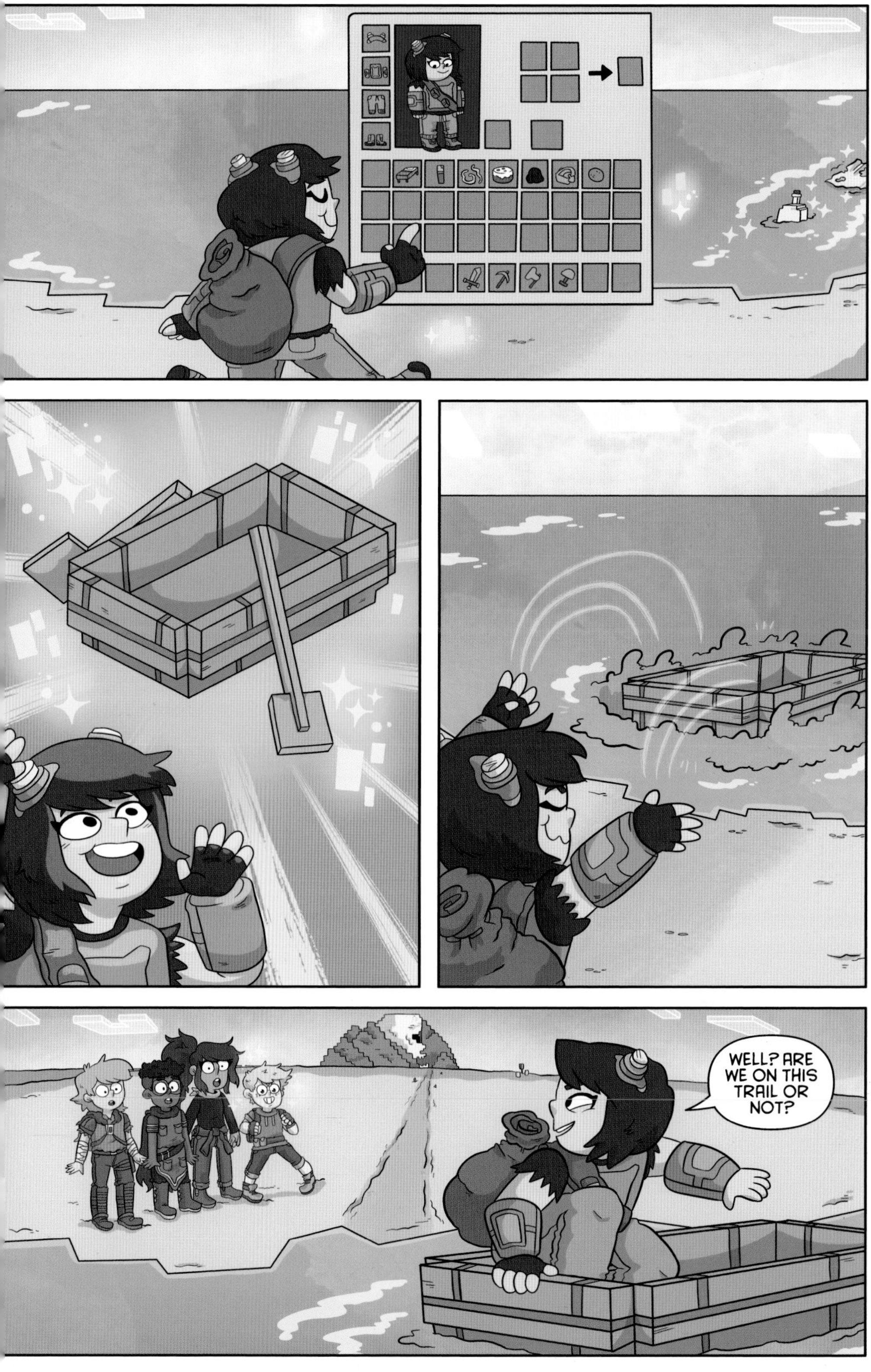
WELL? ARE WE ON THIS TRAIL OR NOT?

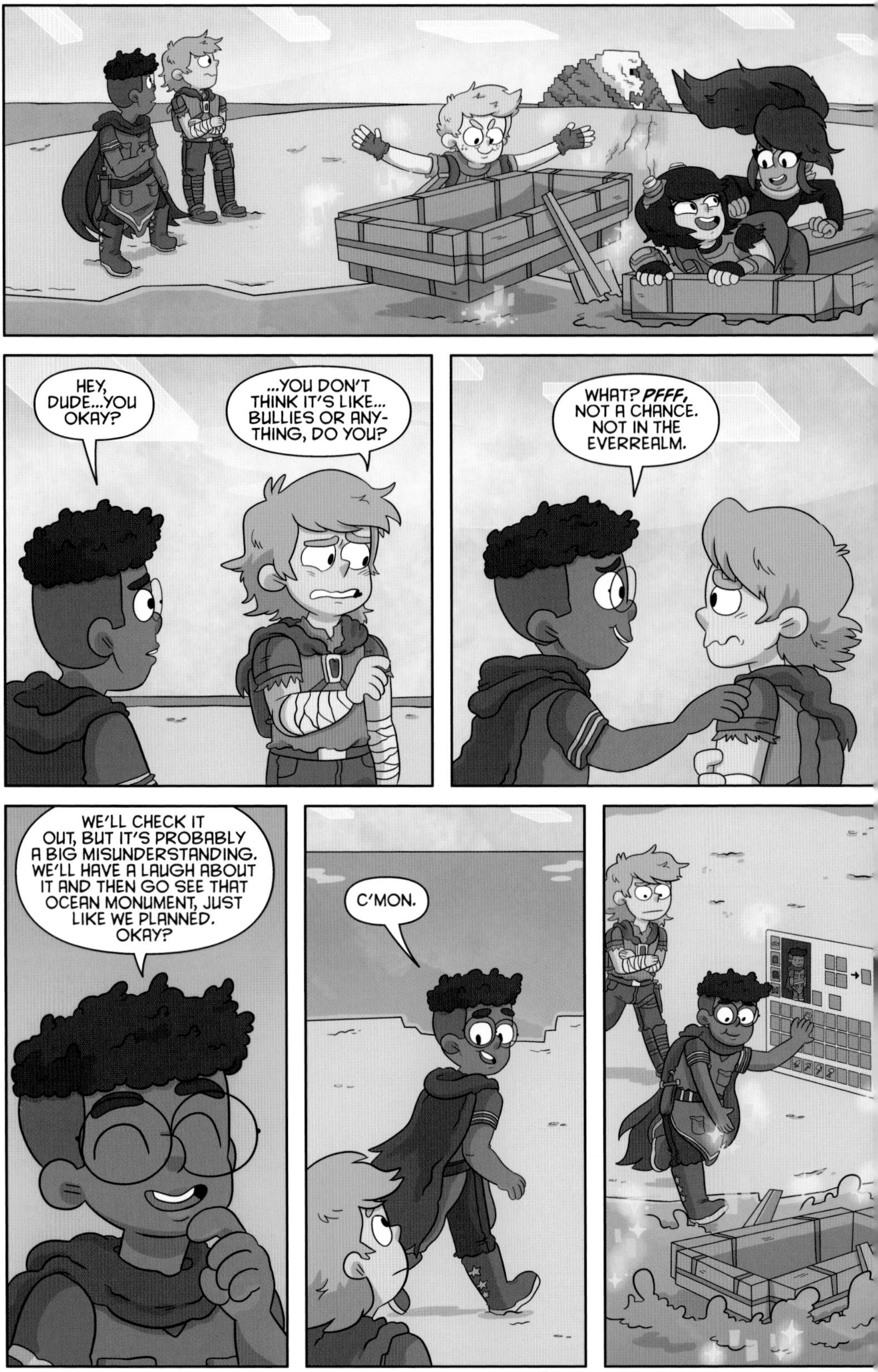
HEY, DUDE...YOU OKAY?
...YOU DON'T THINK IT'S LIKE... BULLIES OR ANY-THING, DO YOU?
WHAT? PFFF, NOT A CHANCE. NOT IN THE EVERREALM.
WE'LL CHECK IT OUT, BUT IT'S PROBABLY A BIG MISUNDERSTANDING. WE'LL HAVE A LAUGH ABOUT IT AND THEN GO SEE THAT OCEAN MONUMENT, JUST LIKE WE PLANNED. OKAY?
C'MON.

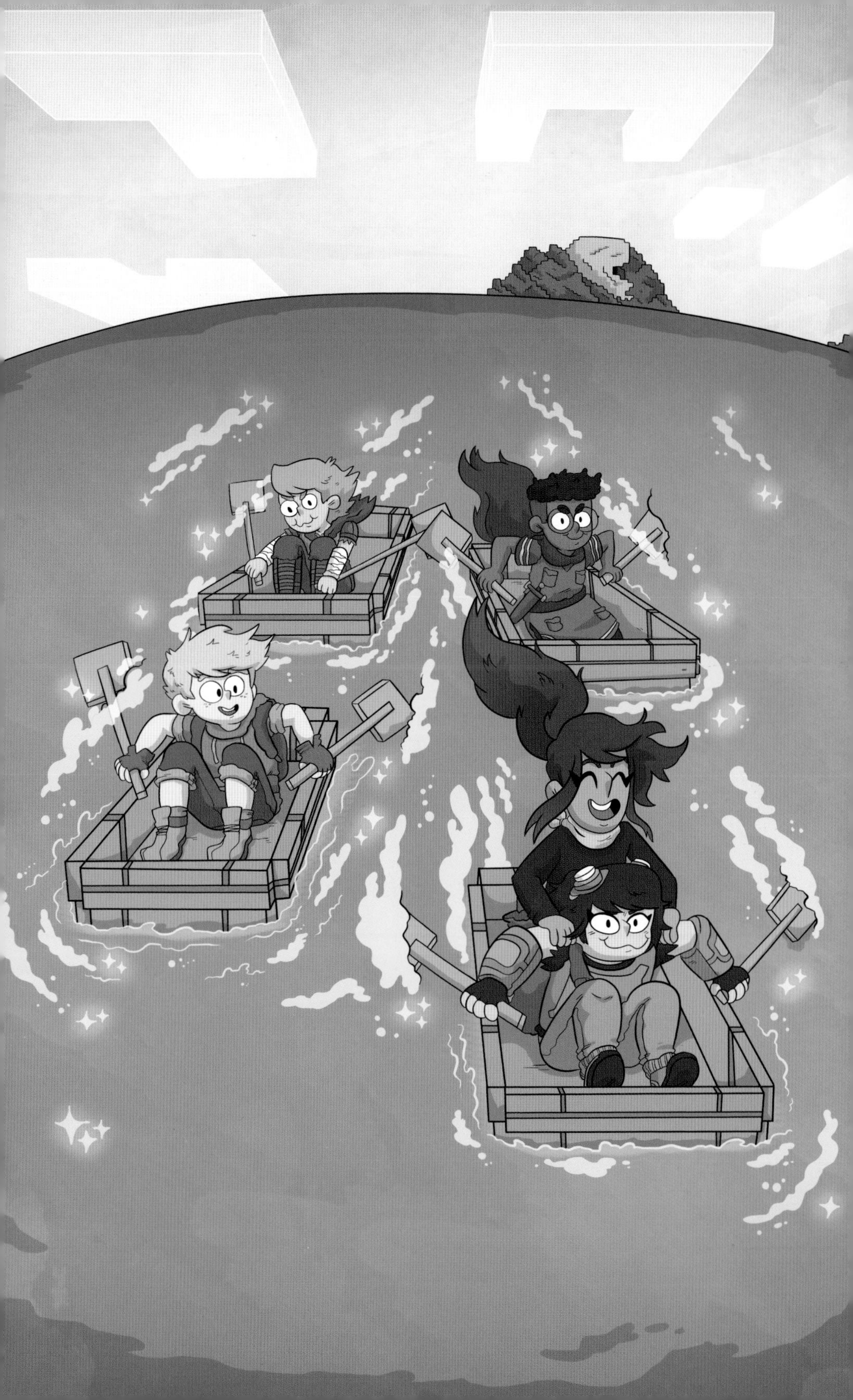

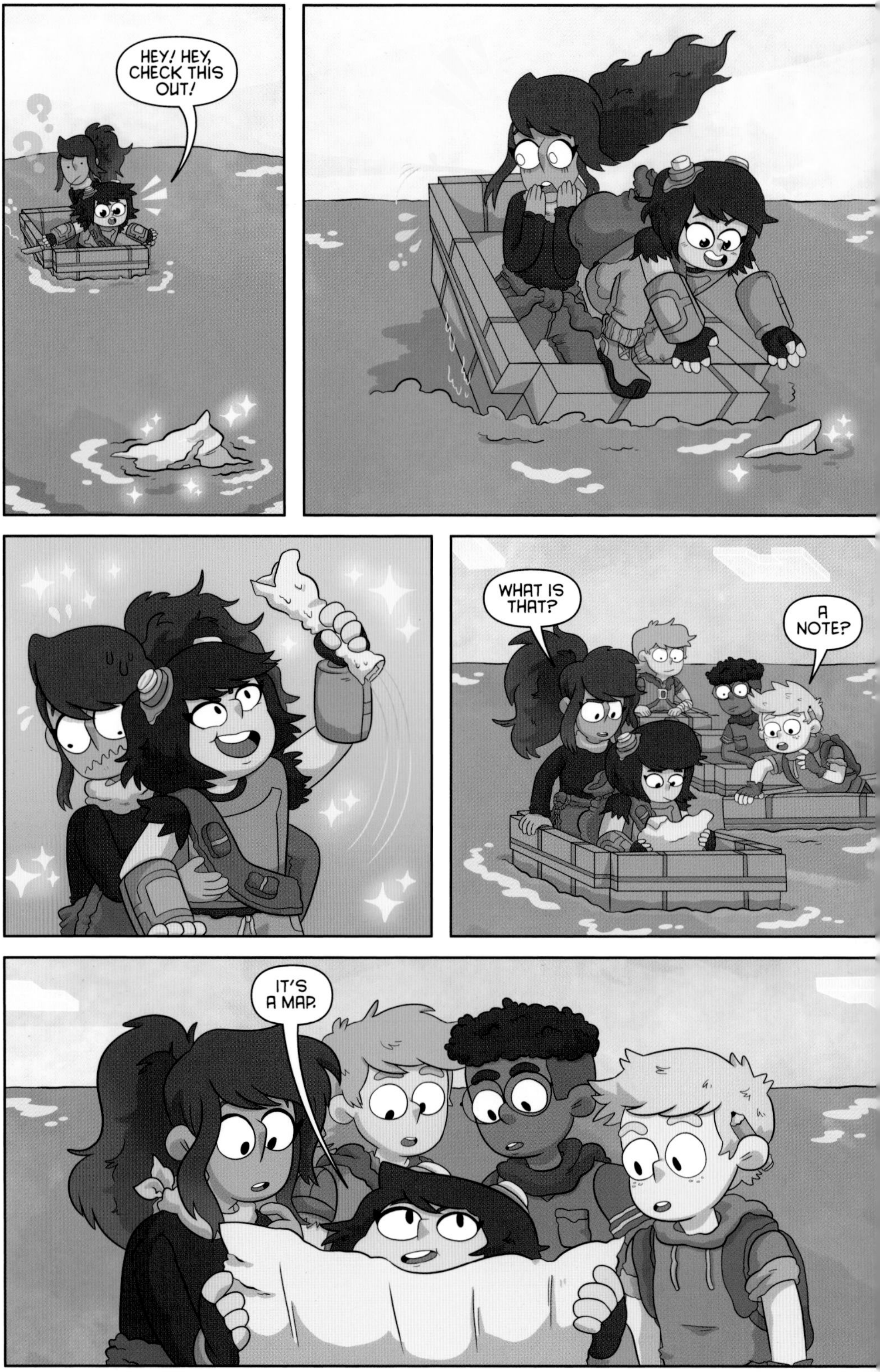
HEY! HEY, CHECK THIS OUT!
WHAT IS THAT?
A NOTE?
IT'S A MAP.

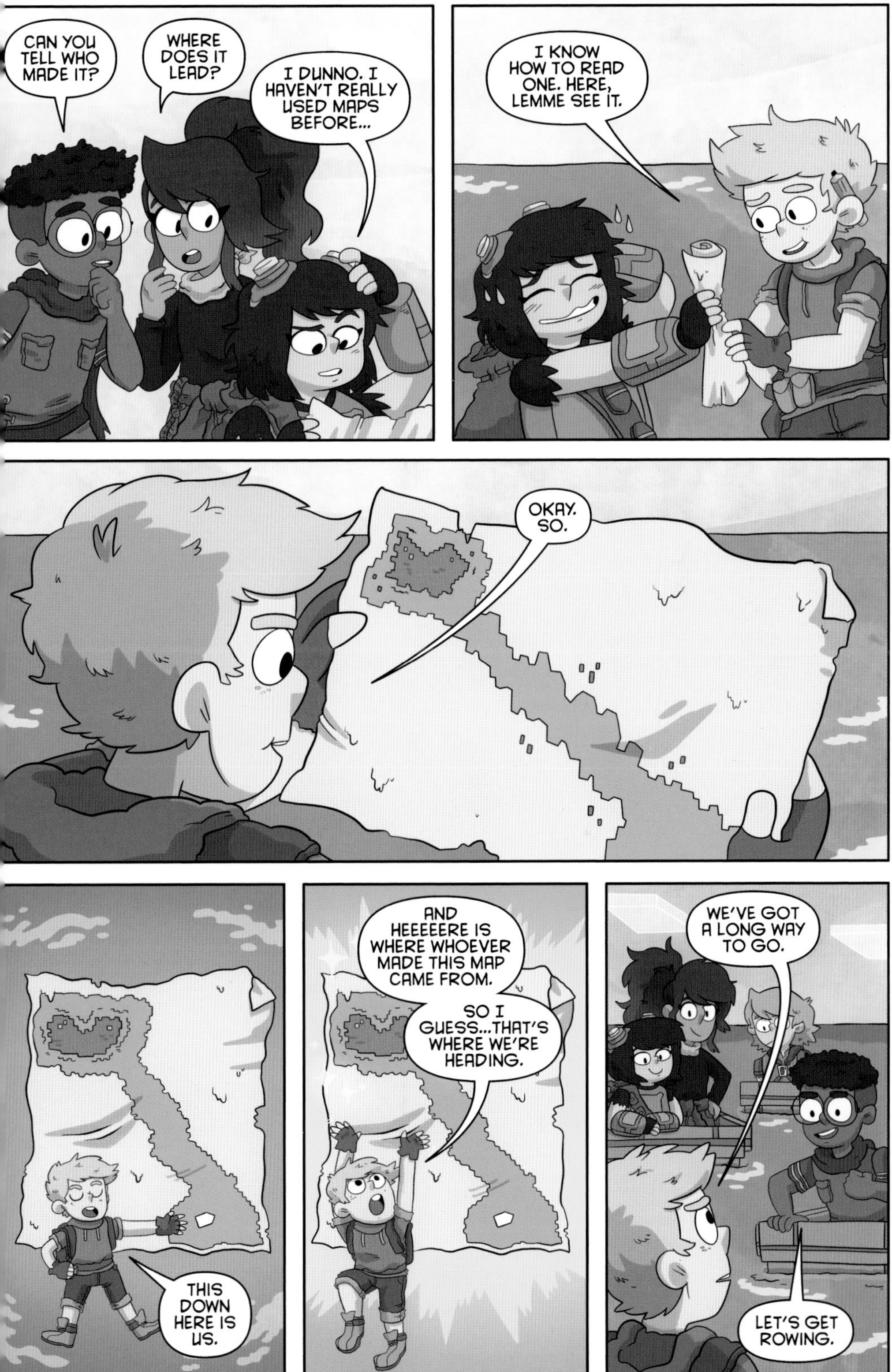

CAN YOU TELL WHO MADE IT?
WHERE DOES IT LEAD?
I DUNNO. I HAVEN'T REALLY USED MAPS BEFORE...
I KNOW HOW TO READ ONE. HERE, LEMME SEE IT.
OKAY. SO.
THIS DOWN HERE IS US.
AND HEEEEERE IS WHERE WHOEVER MADE THIS MAP CAME FROM.
SO I GUESS...THAT'S WHERE WE'RE HEADING.
WE'VE GOT A LONG WAY TO GO.
LET'S GET ROWING.

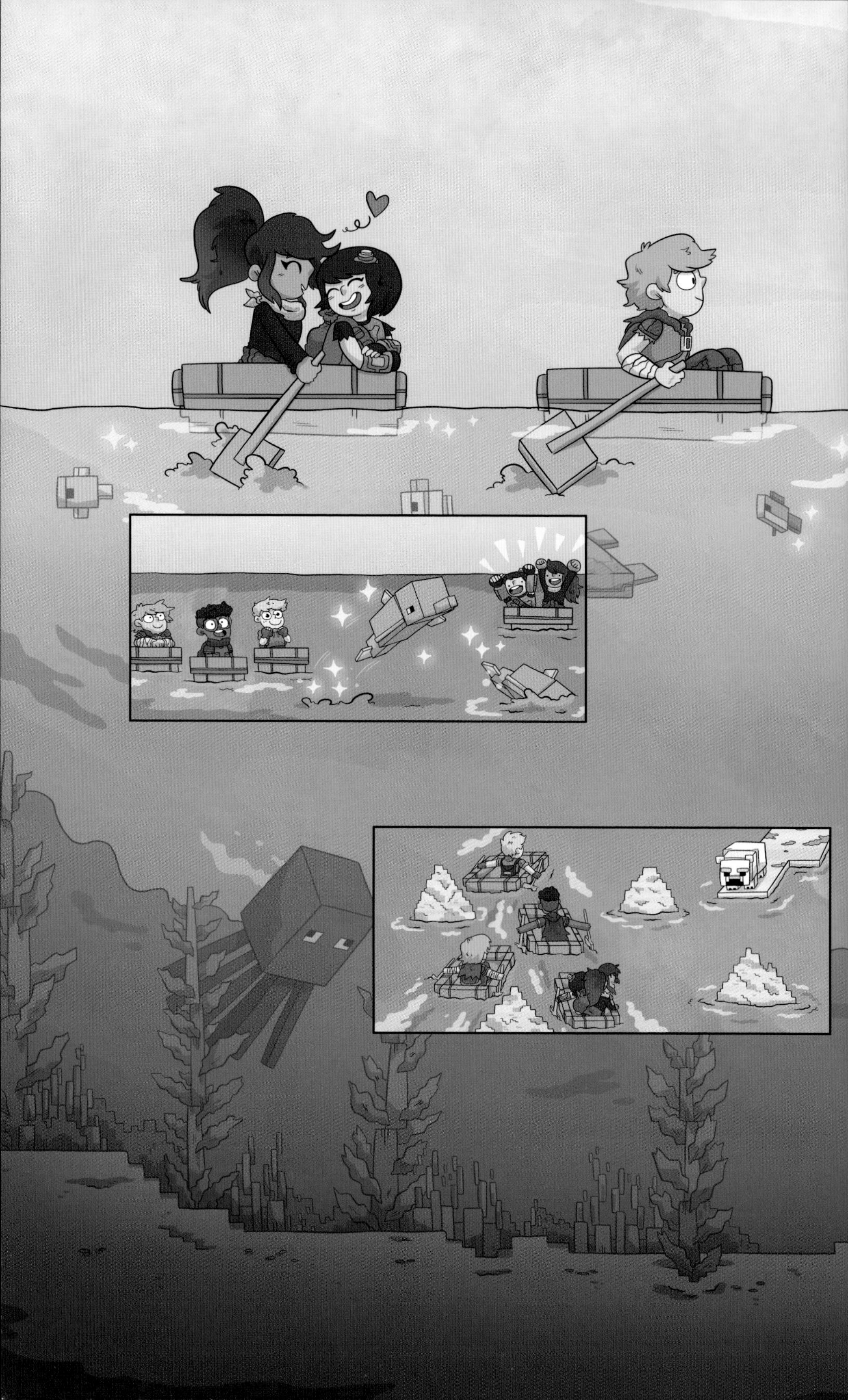

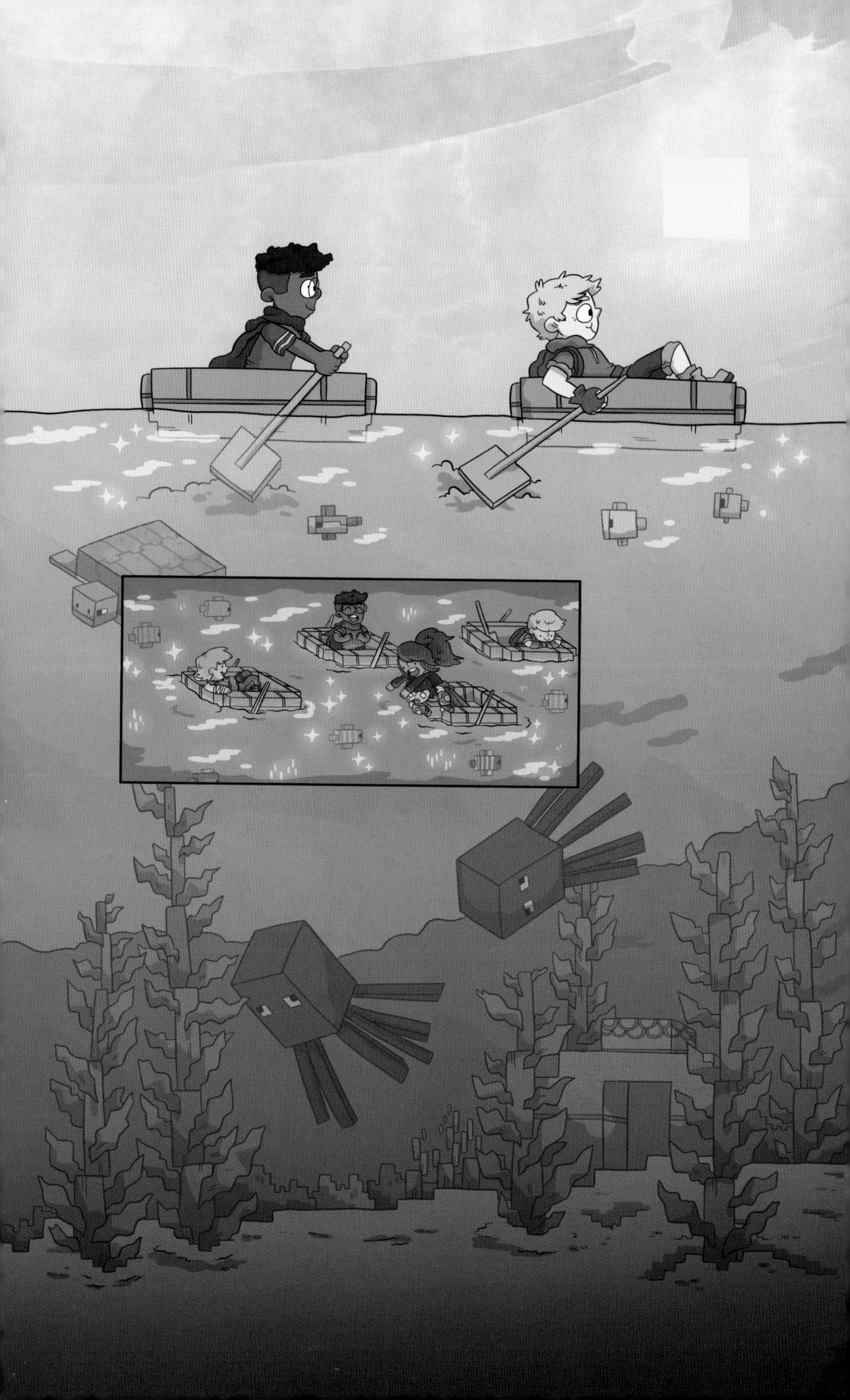

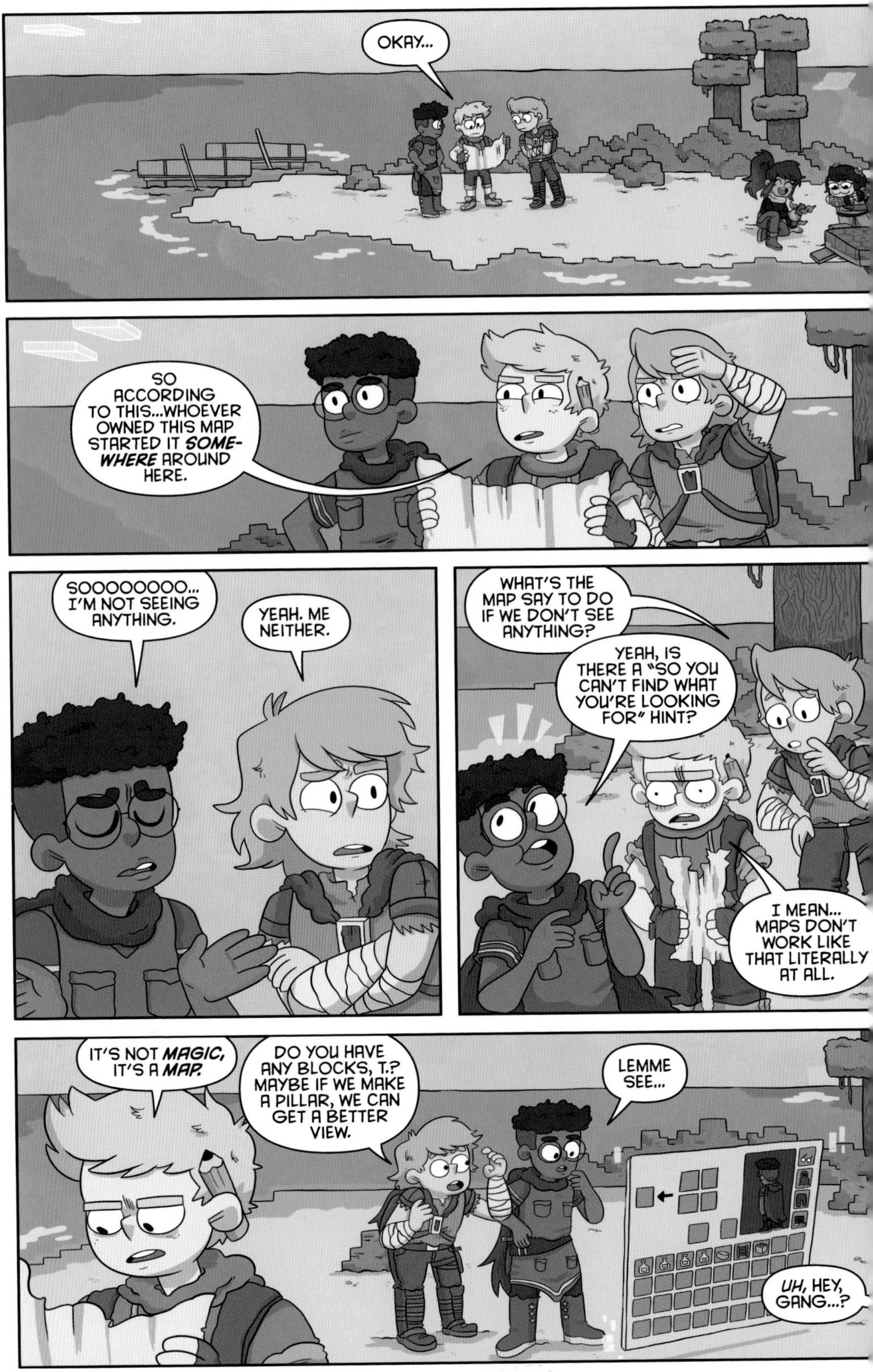
OKAY...
SO ACCORDING TO THIS...WHOEVER OWNED THIS MAP STARTED IT *SOME-WHERE* AROUND HERE.
SOOOOOOOO... I'M NOT SEEING ANYTHING.
YEAH. ME NEITHER.
WHAT'S THE MAP SAY TO DO IF WE DON'T SEE ANYTHING?
YEAH, IS THERE A "SO YOU CAN'T FIND WHAT YOU'RE LOOKING FOR" HINT?
I MEAN... MAPS DON'T WORK LIKE THAT LITERALLY AT ALL.
IT'S NOT *MAGIC*, IT'S A *MAP*.
DO YOU HAVE ANY BLOCKS, T.? MAYBE IF WE MAKE A PILLAR, WE CAN GET A BETTER VIEW.
LEMME SEE...
*UH*, HEY, GANG...?

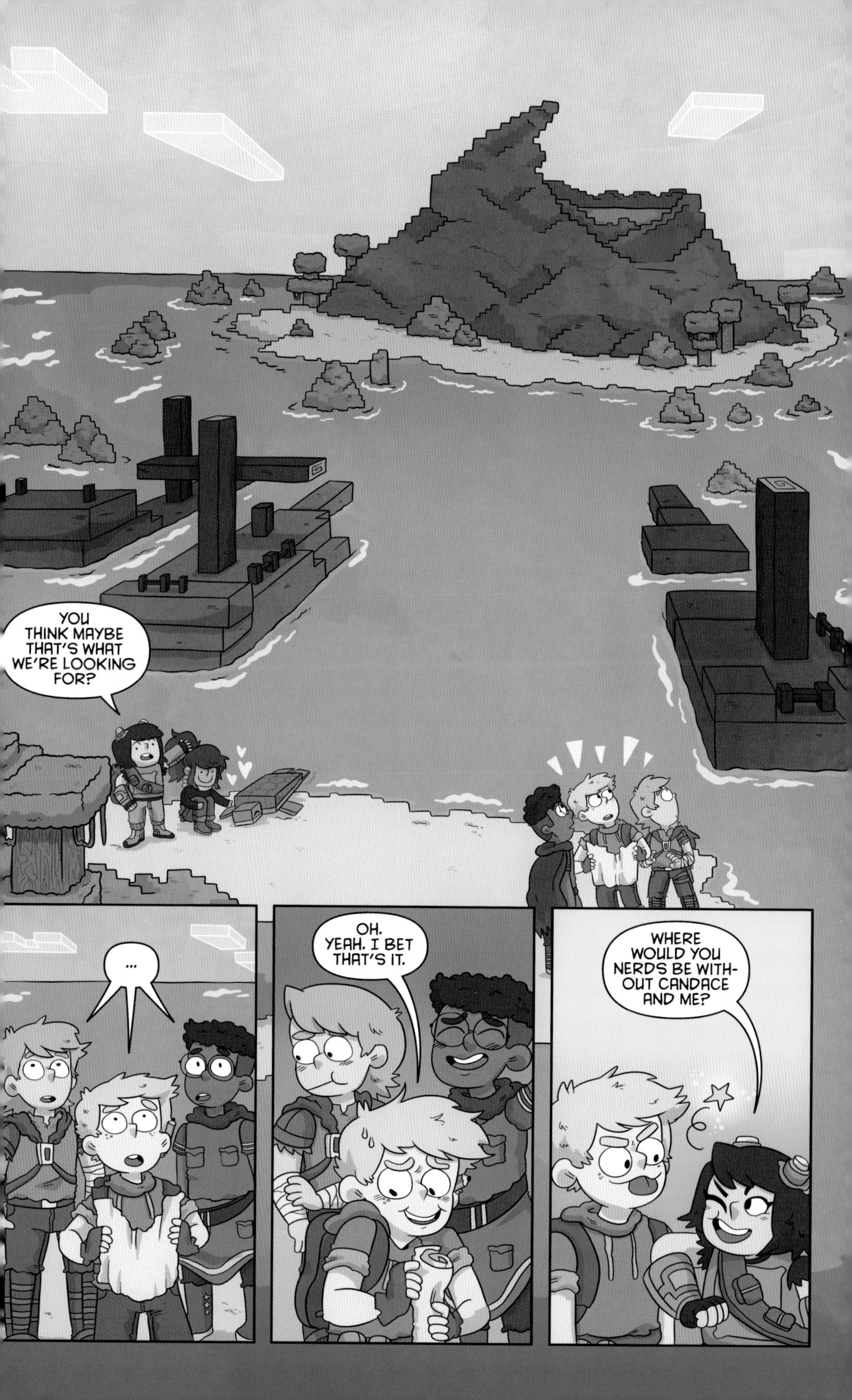
YOU THINK MAYBE THAT'S WHAT WE'RE LOOKING FOR?
...
OH. YEAH. I BET THAT'S IT.
WHERE WOULD YOU NERDS BE WITH-OUT CANDACE AND ME?

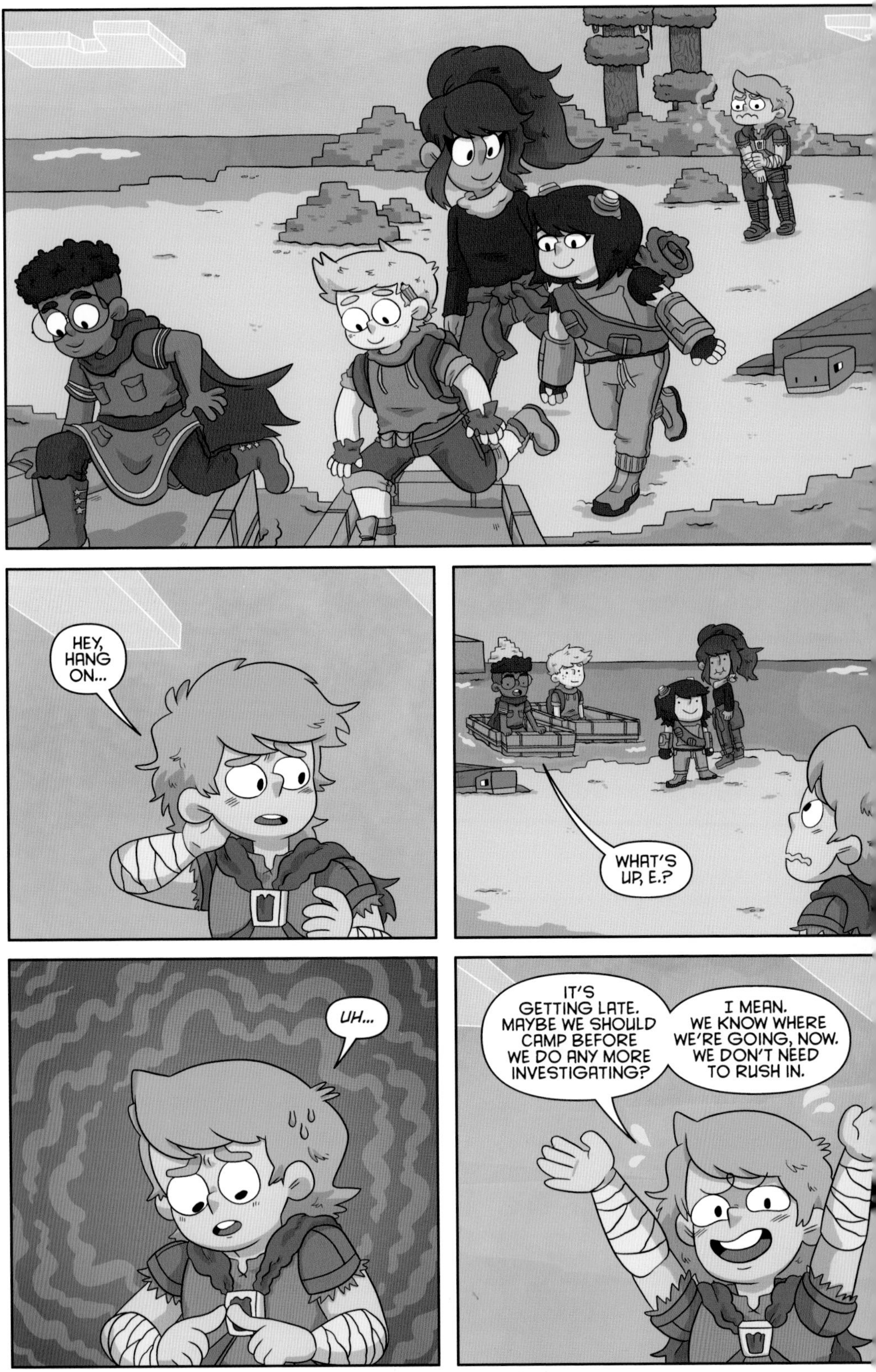
HEY, HANG ON...
WHAT'S UP, E.?
UH...
IT'S GETTING LATE. MAYBE WE SHOULD CAMP BEFORE WE DO ANY MORE INVESTIGATING?
I MEAN. WE KNOW WHERE WE'RE GOING, NOW. WE DON'T NEED TO RUSH IN.

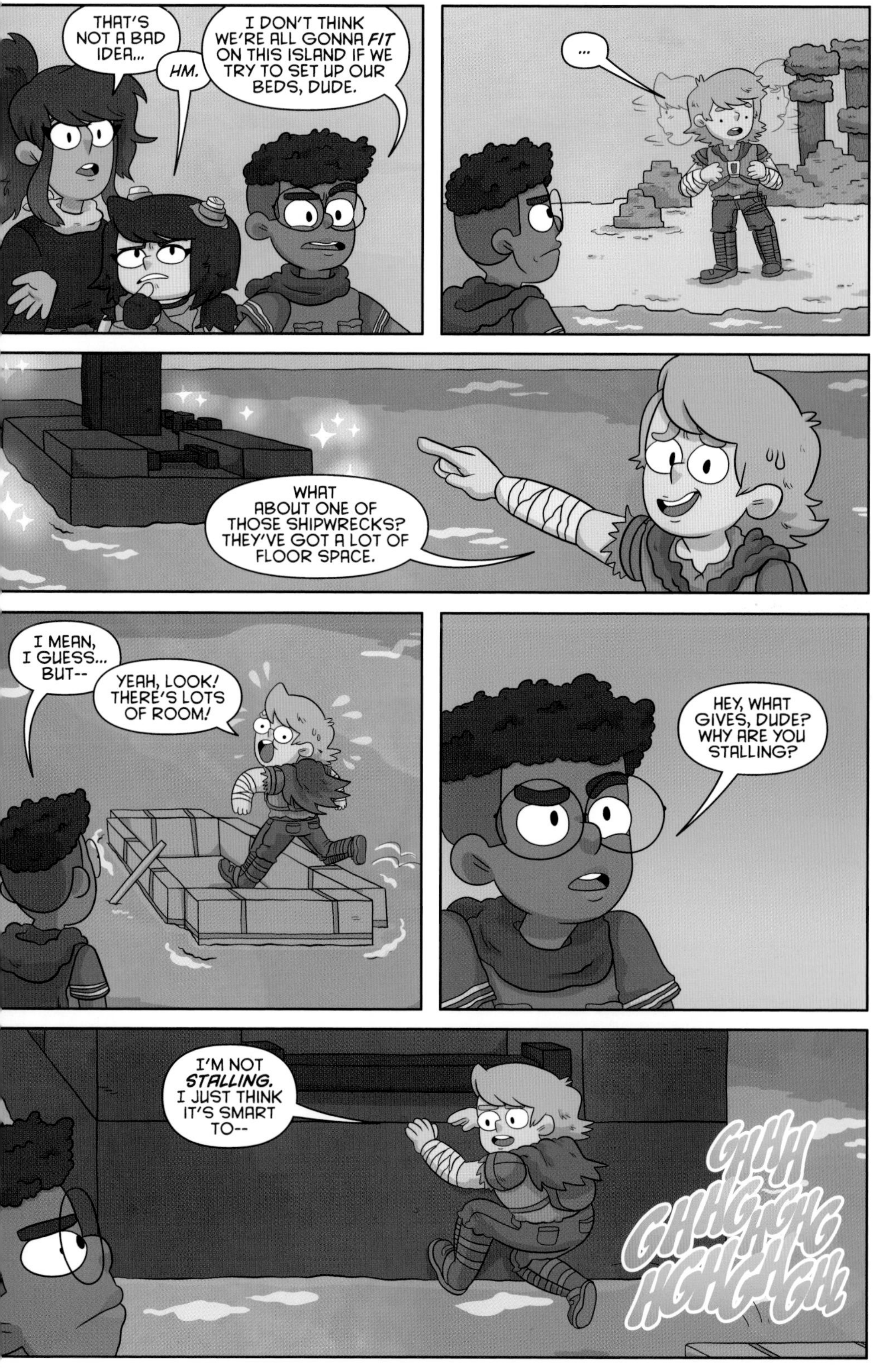
THAT'S NOT A BAD IDEA...
HM.
I DON'T THINK WE'RE ALL GONNA FIT ON THIS ISLAND IF WE TRY TO SET UP OUR BEDS, DUDE.
...
WHAT ABOUT ONE OF THOSE SHIPWRECKS? THEY'VE GOT A LOT OF FLOOR SPACE.
I MEAN, I GUESS... BUT--
YEAH, LOOK! THERE'S LOTS OF ROOM!
HEY, WHAT GIVES, DUDE? WHY ARE YOU STALLING?
I'M NOT STALLING. I JUST THINK IT'S SMART TO--
GHHH GHHGHGHG HGHGHGHGHL

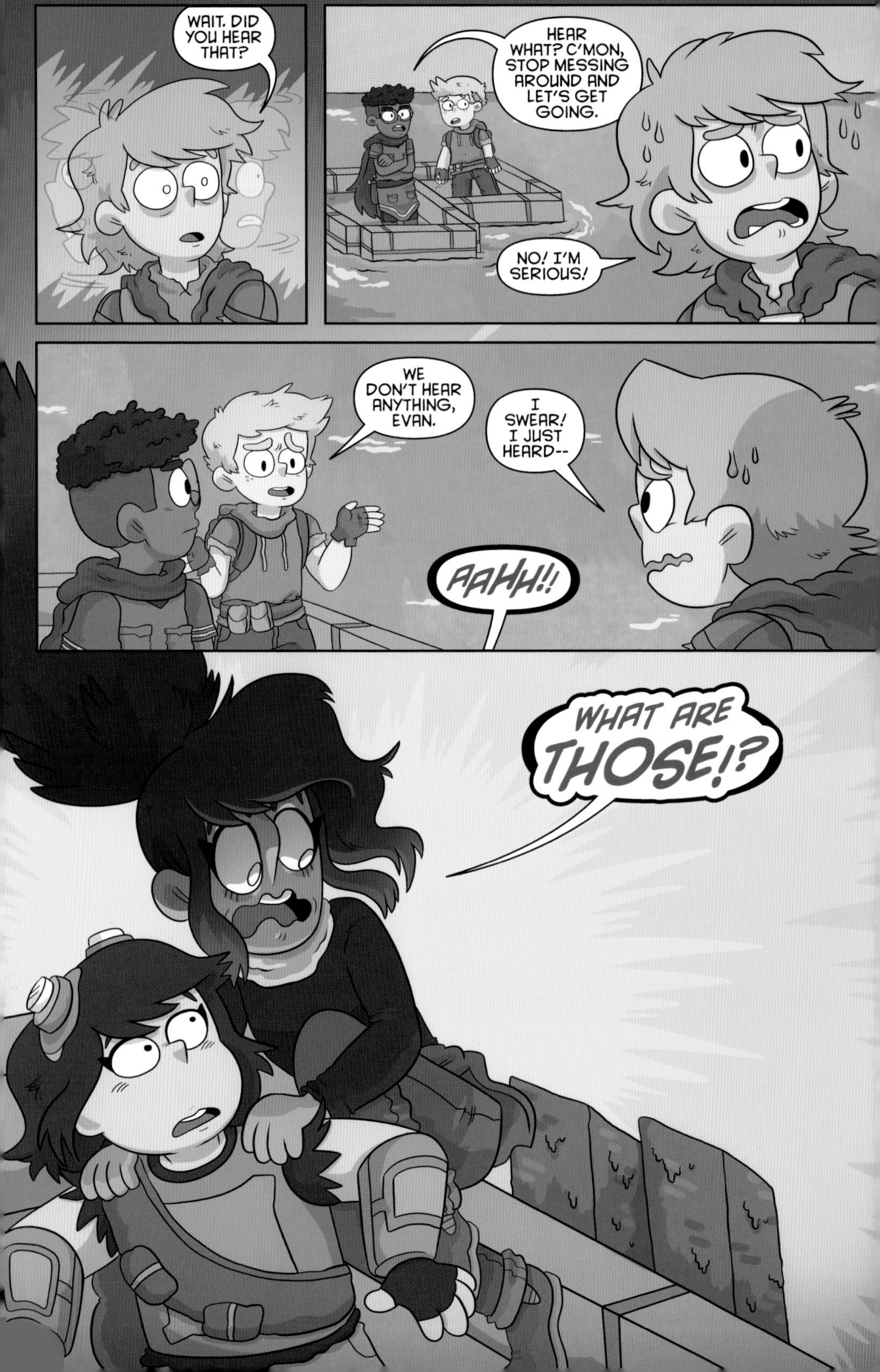
WAIT. DID YOU HEAR THAT?
HEAR WHAT? C'MON, STOP MESSING AROUND AND LET'S GET GOING.
NO! I'M SERIOUS!
WE DON'T HEAR ANYTHING, EVAN.
I SWEAR! I JUST HEARD--
AAHH!!
WHAT ARE THOSE!?

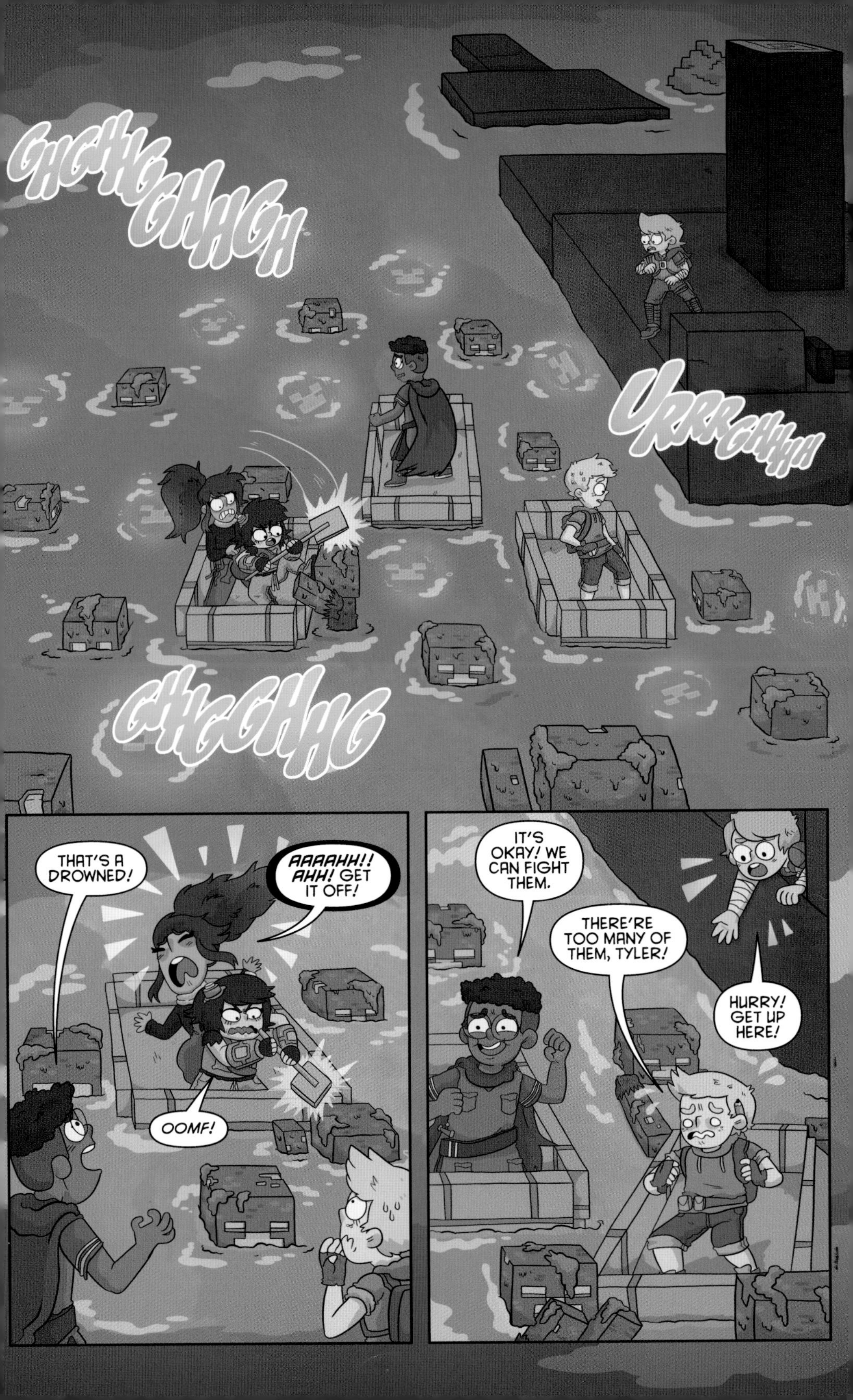
GHGHGGHHGH
URRRGHHHH
GHGGHHG
THAT'S A DROWNED!
AAAAHH!! AHH! GET IT OFF!
OOMF!
IT'S OKAY! WE CAN FIGHT THEM.
THERE'RE TOO MANY OF THEM, TYLER!
HURRY! GET UP HERE!

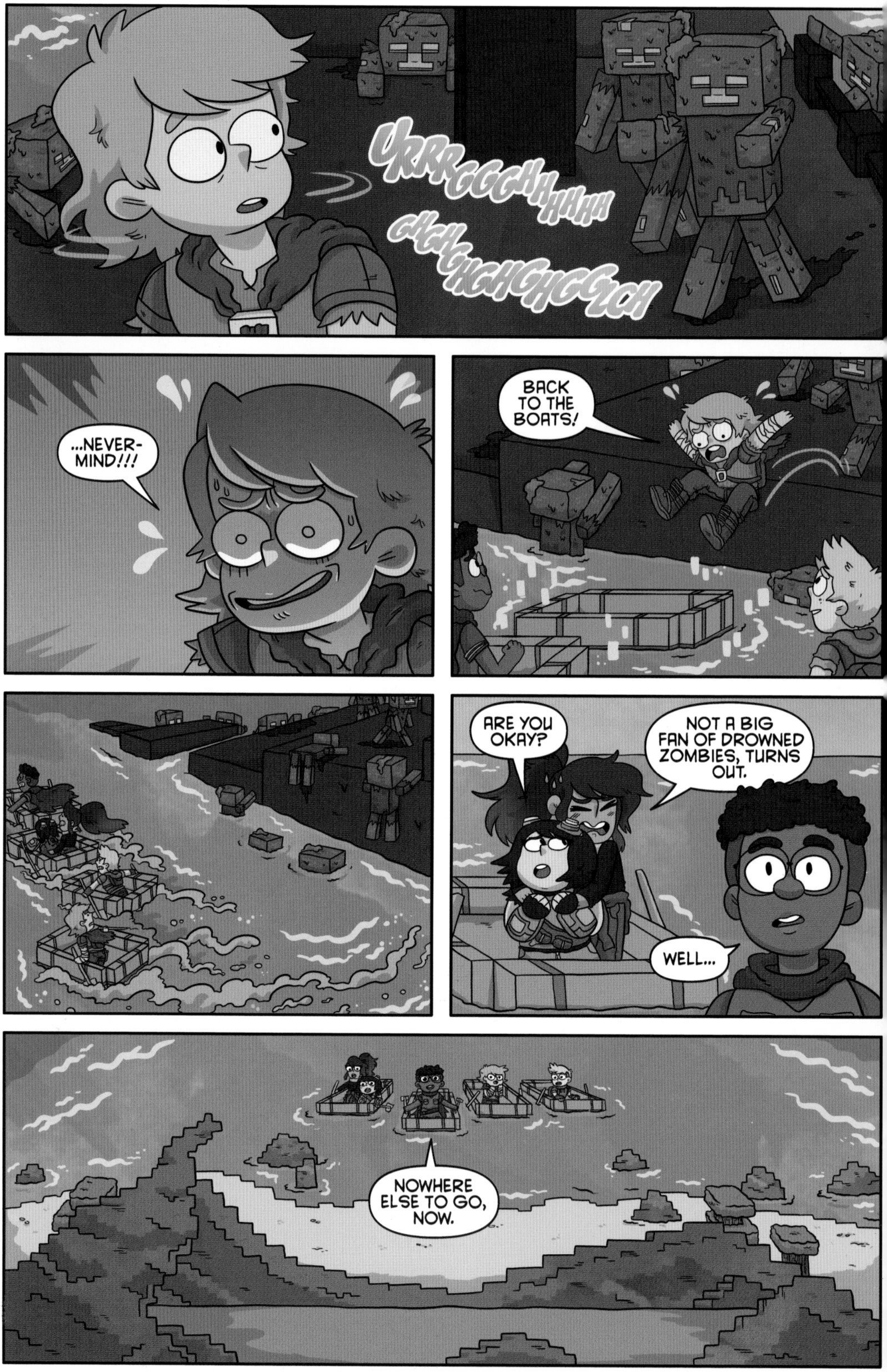
URRRGGGHHHHHH
GHGHGHGHGHGGLCH
...NEVER-MIND!!!
BACK TO THE BOATS!
ARE YOU OKAY?
NOT A BIG FAN OF DROWNED ZOMBIES, TURNS OUT.
WELL...
NOWHERE ELSE TO GO, NOW.

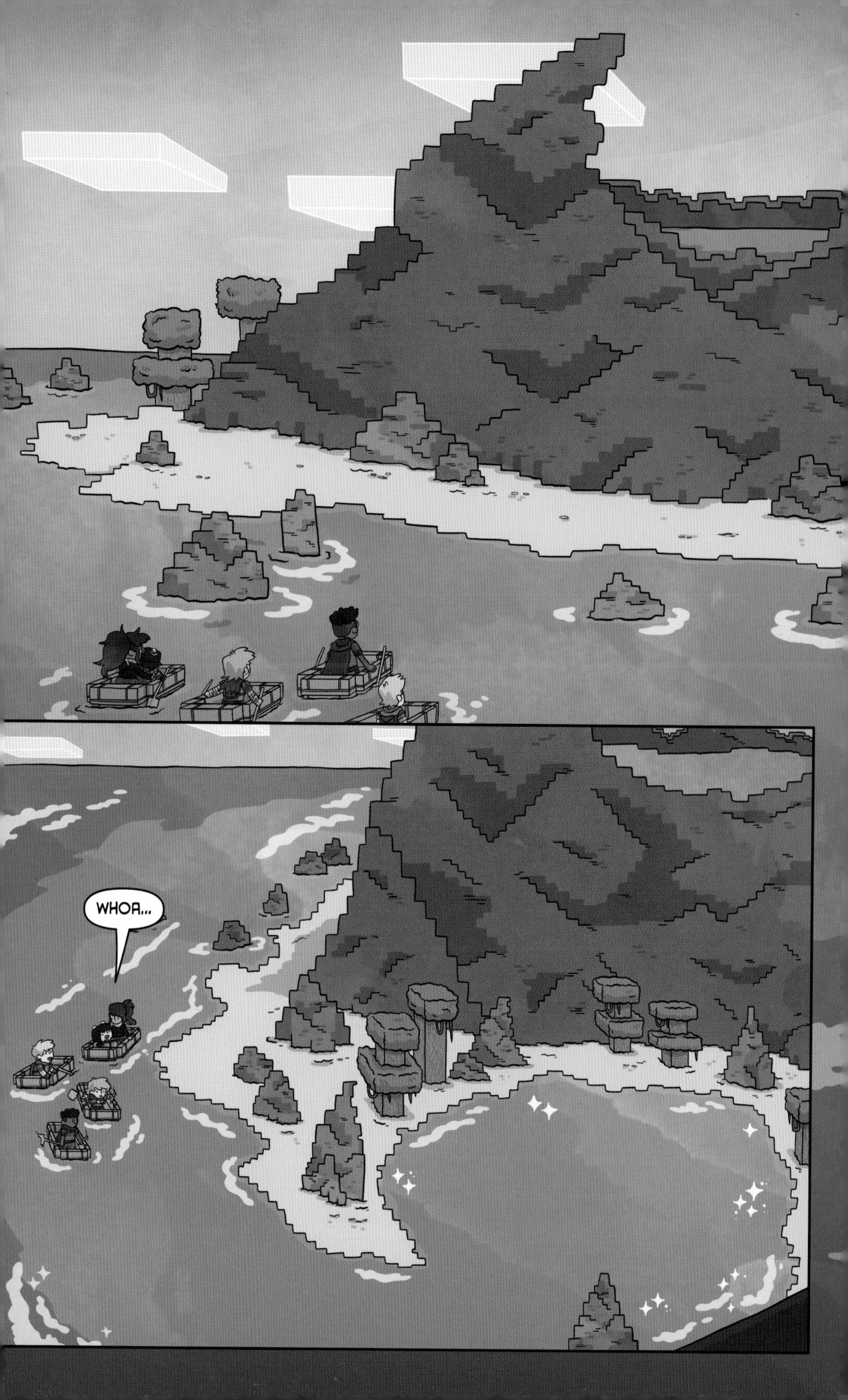
WHOA...

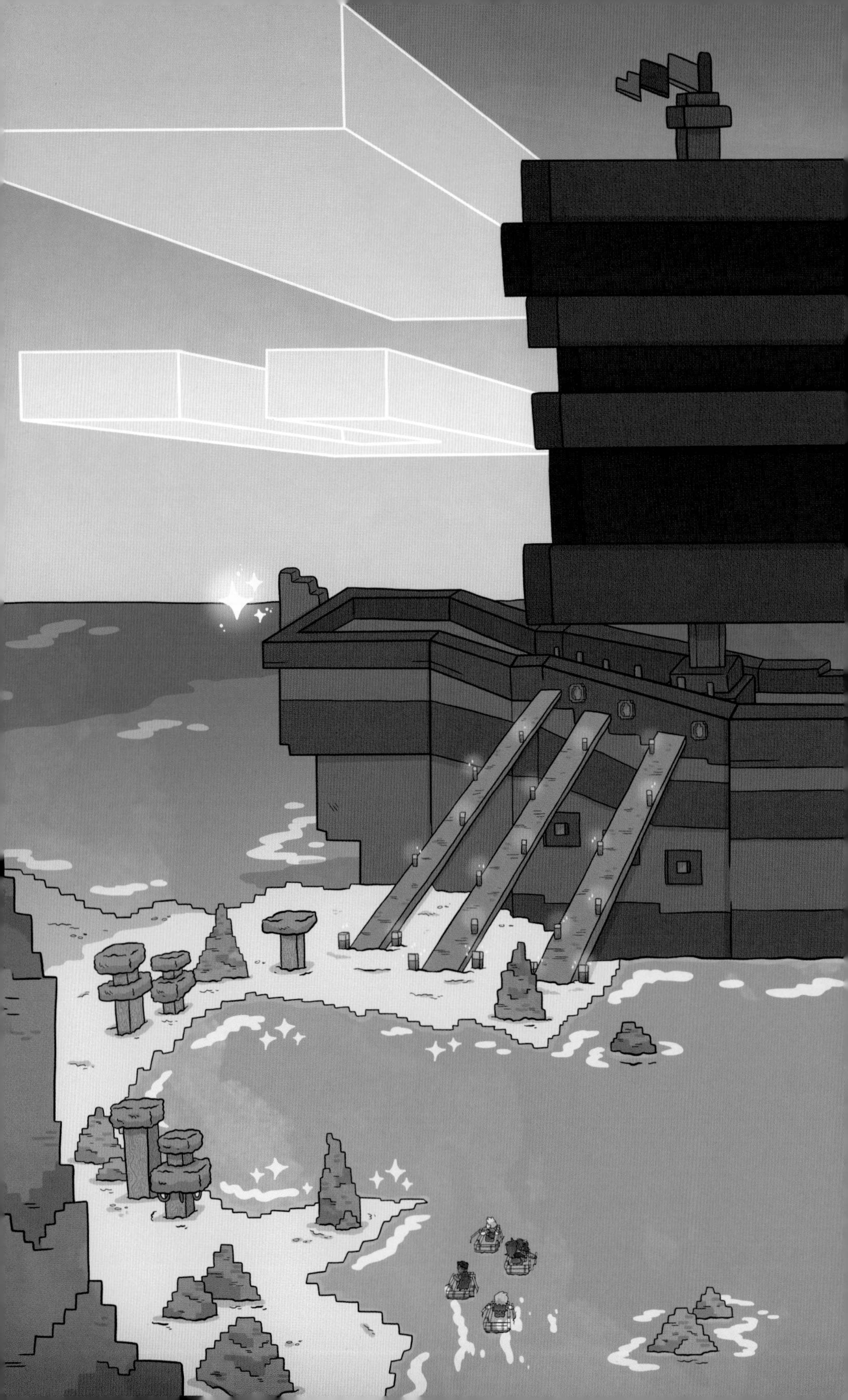

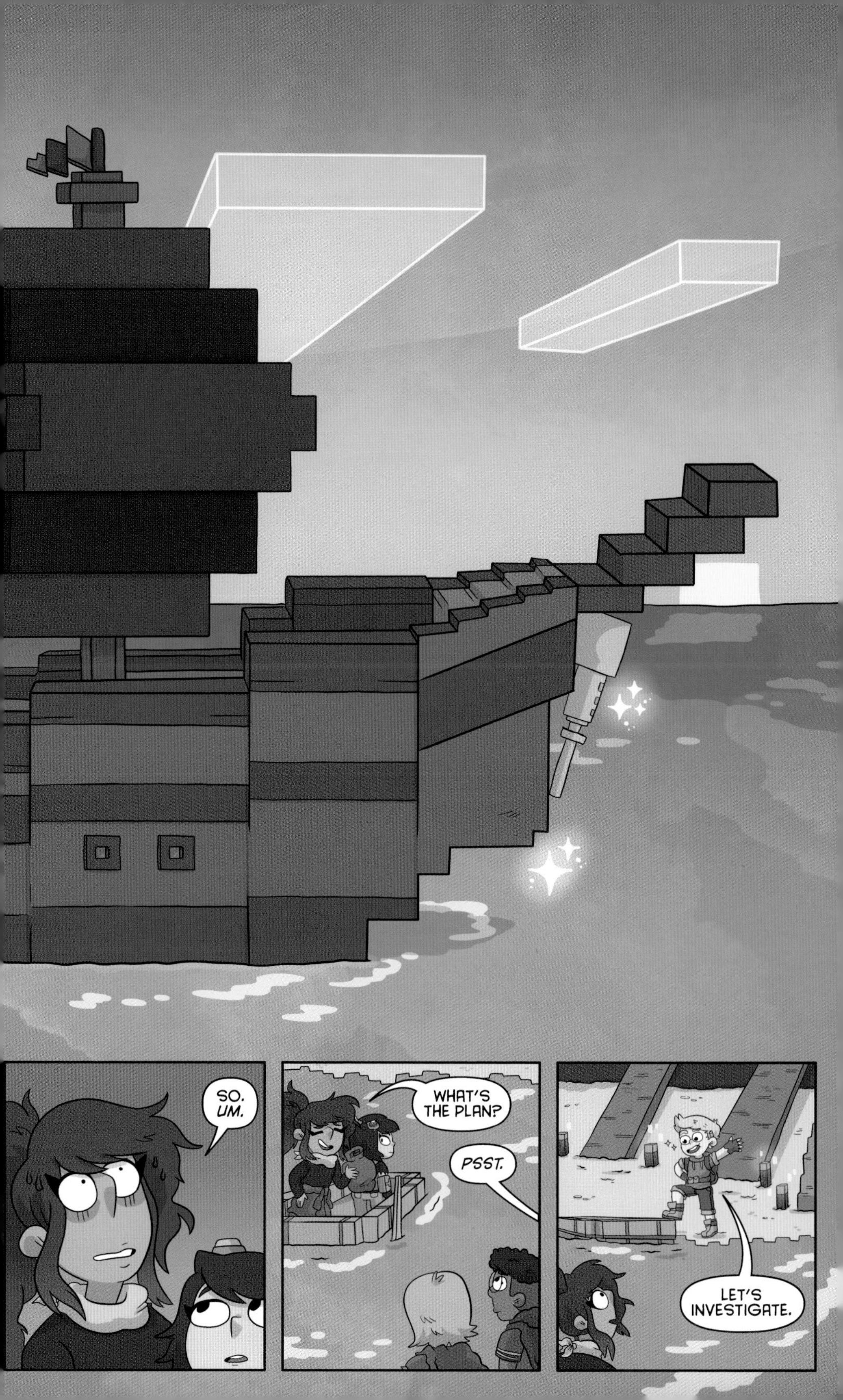
SO.
UM.
WHAT'S THE PLAN?
PSST.
LET'S INVESTIGATE.

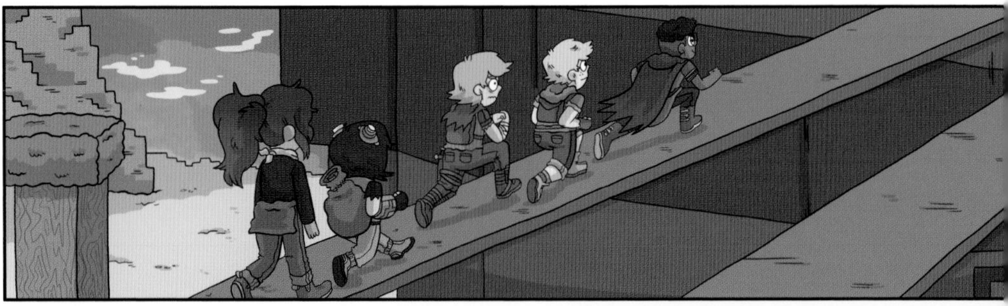

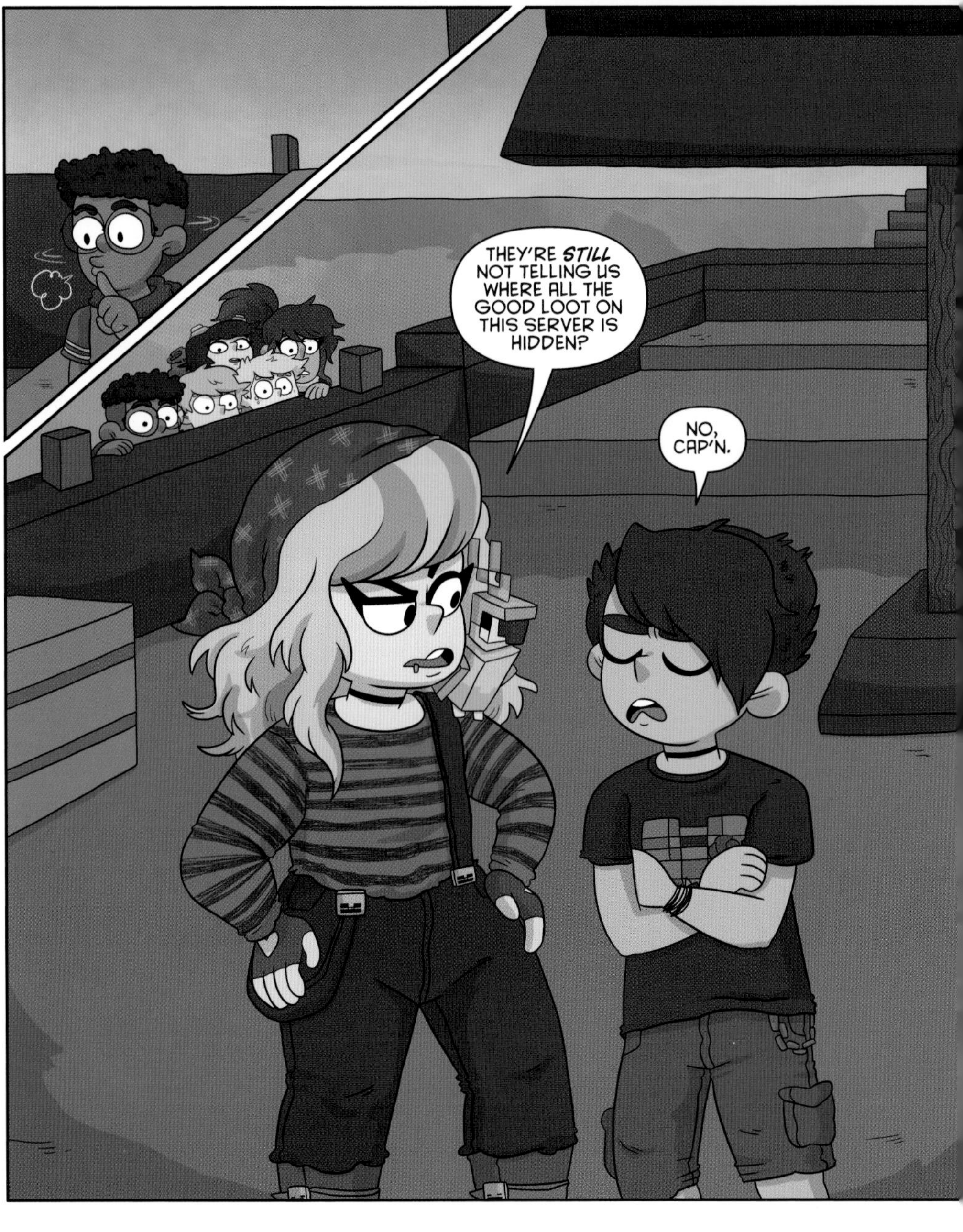
THEY'RE *STILL* NOT TELLING US WHERE ALL THE GOOD LOOT ON THIS SERVER IS HIDDEN?
NO, CAP'N.

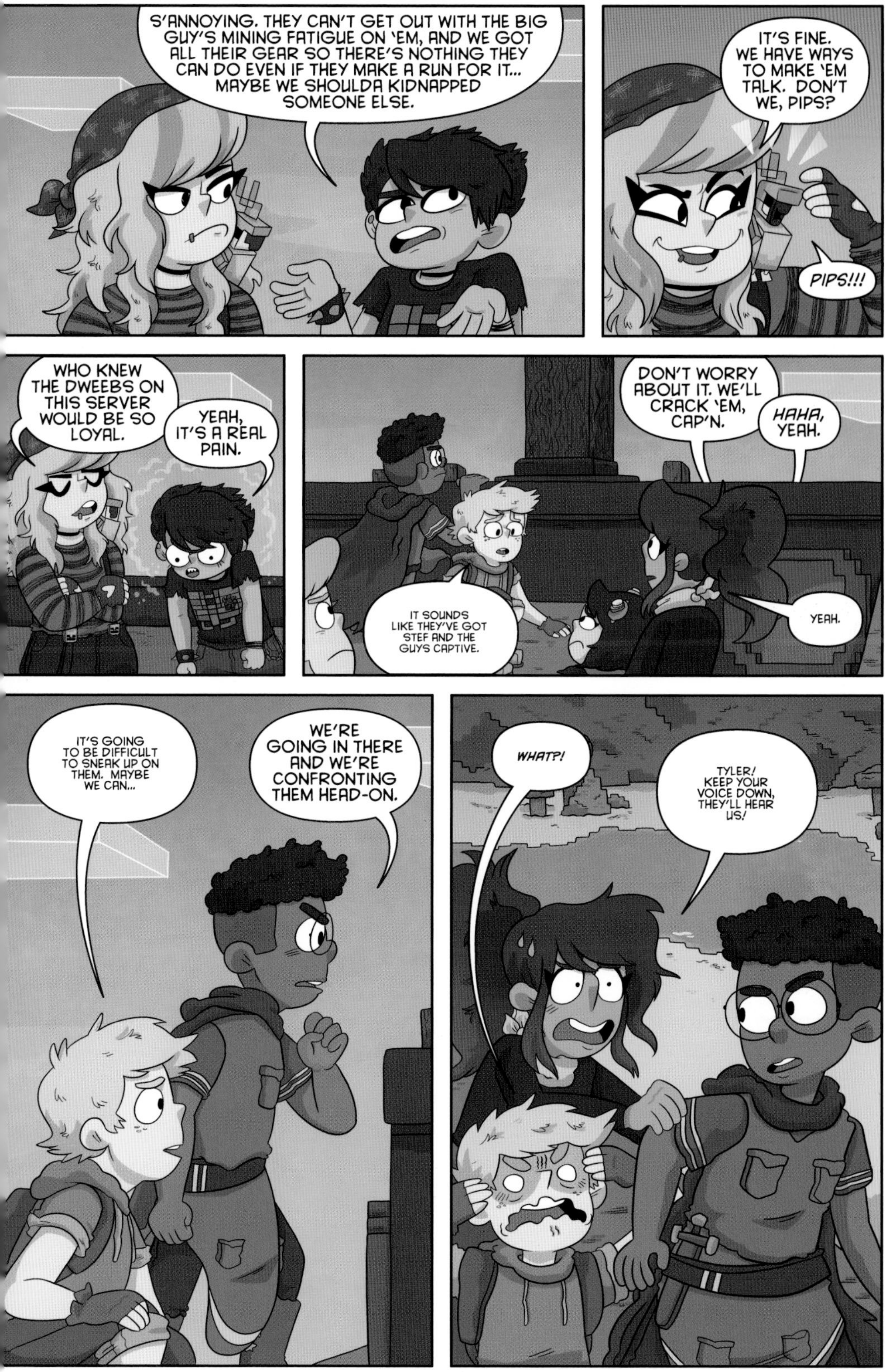
S'ANNOYING. THEY CAN'T GET OUT WITH THE BIG GUY'S MINING FATIGUE ON 'EM, AND WE GOT ALL THEIR GEAR SO THERE'S NOTHING THEY CAN DO EVEN IF THEY MAKE A RUN FOR IT... MAYBE WE SHOULDA KIDNAPPED SOMEONE ELSE.
IT'S FINE. WE HAVE WAYS TO MAKE 'EM TALK. DON'T WE, PIPS?
PIPS!!!
WHO KNEW THE DWEEBS ON THIS SERVER WOULD BE SO LOYAL.
YEAH, IT'S A REAL PAIN.
DON'T WORRY ABOUT IT. WE'LL CRACK 'EM, CAP'N.
HAHA, YEAH.
IT SOUNDS LIKE THEY'VE GOT STEF AND THE GUYS CAPTIVE.
YEAH.
IT'S GOING TO BE DIFFICULT TO SNEAK UP ON THEM. MAYBE WE CAN...
WE'RE GOING IN THERE AND WE'RE CONFRONTING THEM HEAD-ON.
WHAT?!
TYLER! KEEP YOUR VOICE DOWN, THEY'LL HEAR US!

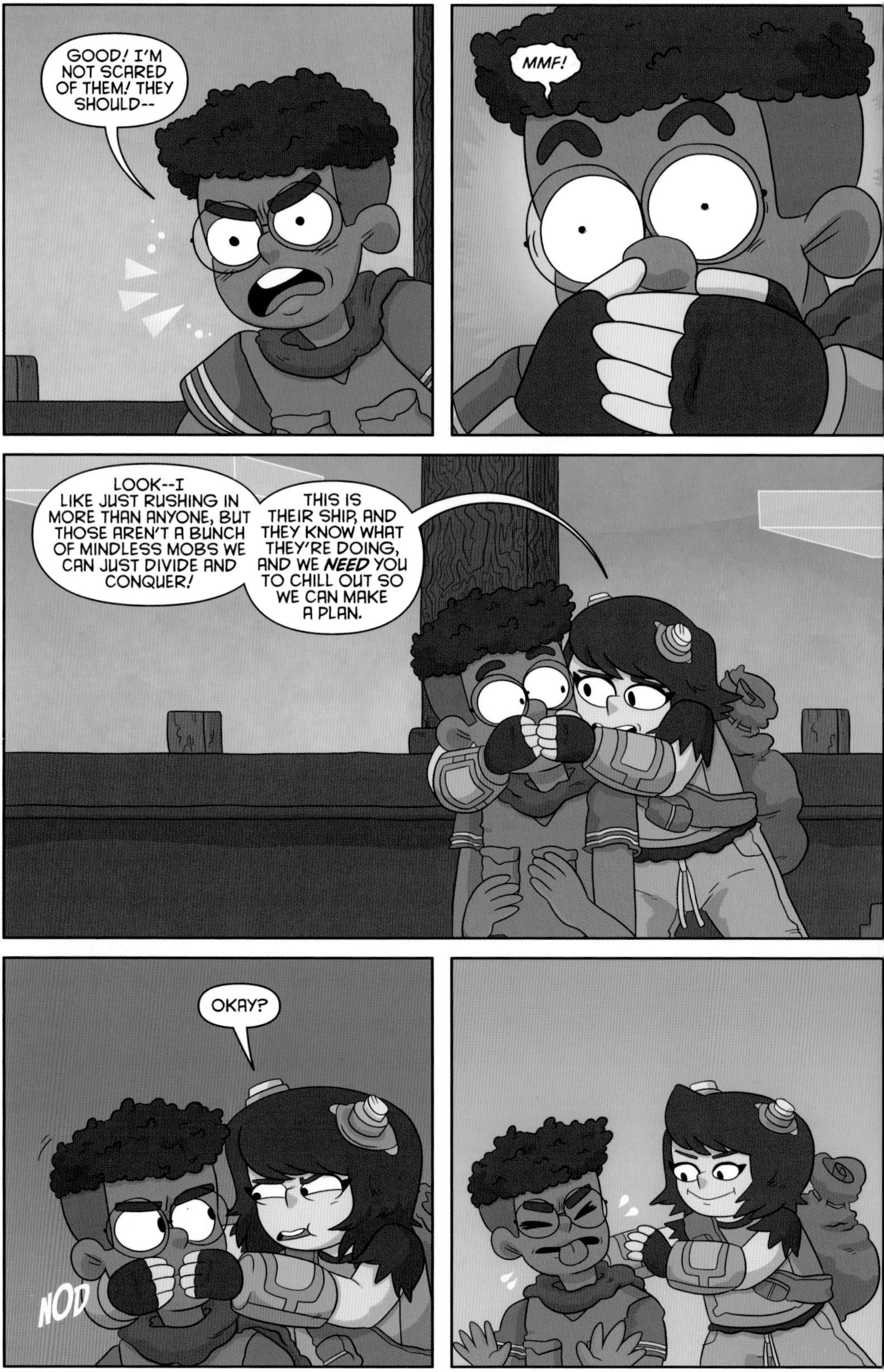
GOOD! I'M NOT SCARED OF THEM! THEY SHOULD--
MMF!
LOOK--I LIKE JUST RUSHING IN MORE THAN ANYONE, BUT THOSE AREN'T A BUNCH OF MINDLESS MOBS WE CAN JUST DIVIDE AND CONQUER!
THIS IS THEIR SHIP, AND THEY KNOW WHAT THEY'RE DOING, AND WE NEED YOU TO CHILL OUT SO WE CAN MAKE A PLAN.
OKAY?
NOD

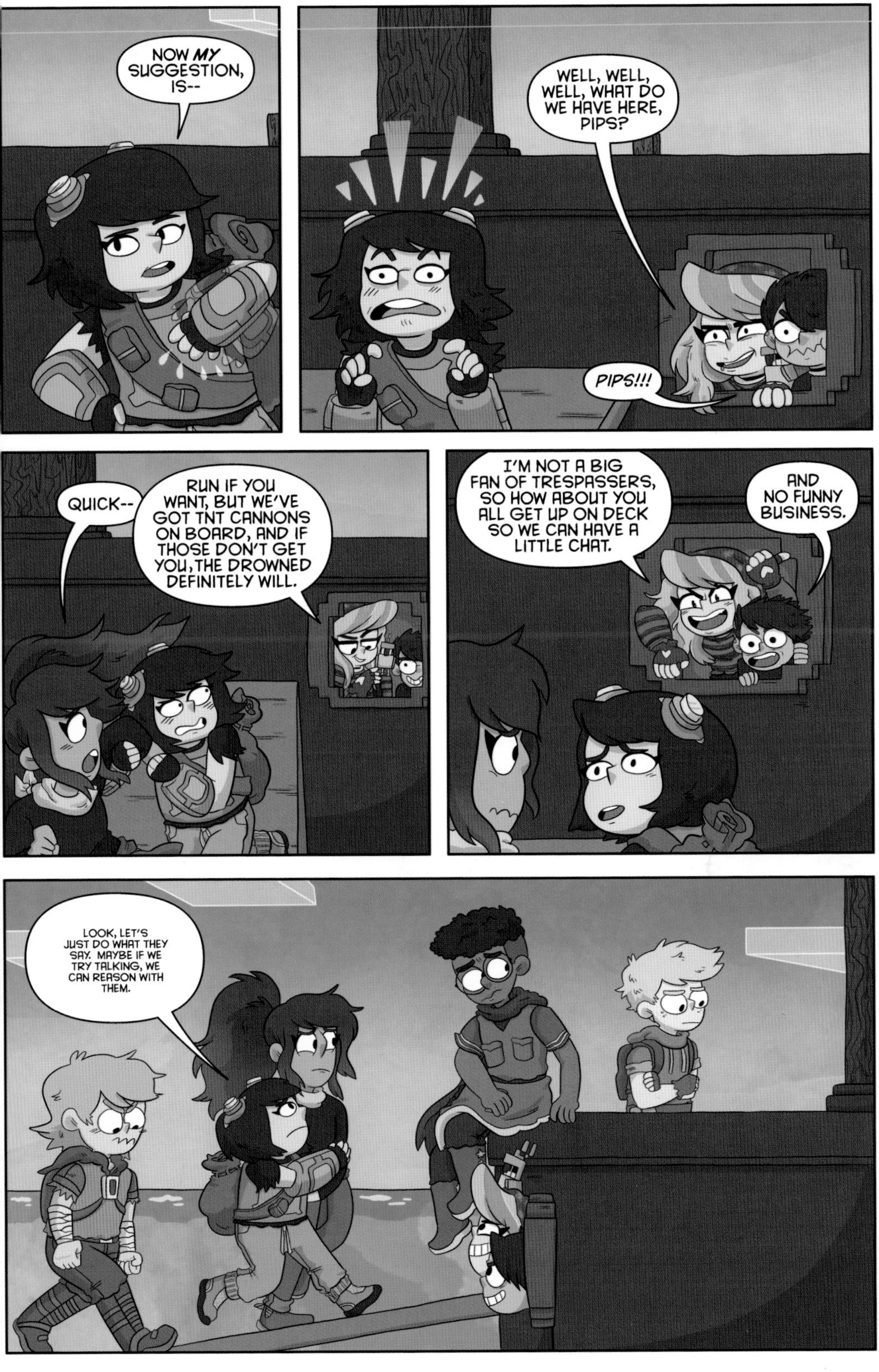
NOW MY SUGGESTION, IS--
WELL, WELL, WELL, WHAT DO WE HAVE HERE, PIPS?
PIPS!!!
QUICK--
RUN IF YOU WANT, BUT WE'VE GOT TNT CANNONS ON BOARD, AND IF THOSE DON'T GET YOU, THE DROWNED DEFINITELY WILL.
I'M NOT A BIG FAN OF TRESPASSERS, SO HOW ABOUT YOU ALL GET UP ON DECK SO WE CAN HAVE A LITTLE CHAT.
AND NO FUNNY BUSINESS.
LOOK, LET'S JUST DO WHAT THEY SAY. MAYBE IF WE TRY TALKING, WE CAN REASON WITH THEM.

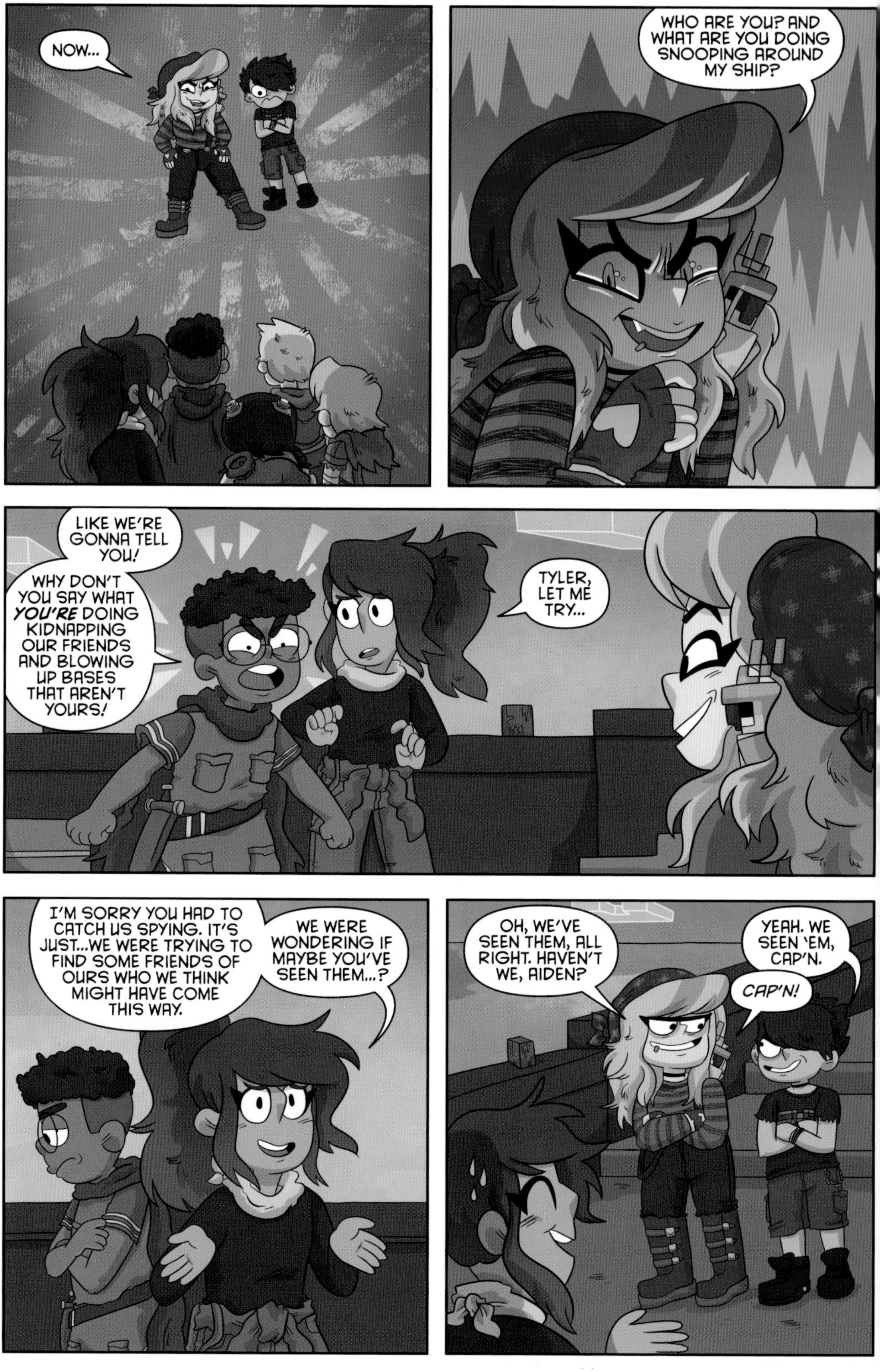
NOW...
WHO ARE YOU? AND WHAT ARE YOU DOING SNOOPING AROUND MY SHIP?
LIKE WE'RE GONNA TELL YOU!
WHY DON'T YOU SAY WHAT YOU'RE DOING KIDNAPPING OUR FRIENDS AND BLOWING UP BASES THAT AREN'T YOURS!
TYLER, LET ME TRY...
I'M SORRY YOU HAD TO CATCH US SPYING. IT'S JUST...WE WERE TRYING TO FIND SOME FRIENDS OF OURS WHO WE THINK MIGHT HAVE COME THIS WAY.
WE WERE WONDERING IF MAYBE YOU'VE SEEN THEM...?
OH, WE'VE SEEN THEM, ALL RIGHT. HAVEN'T WE, AIDEN?
YEAH. WE SEEN 'EM, CAP'N.
CAP'N!

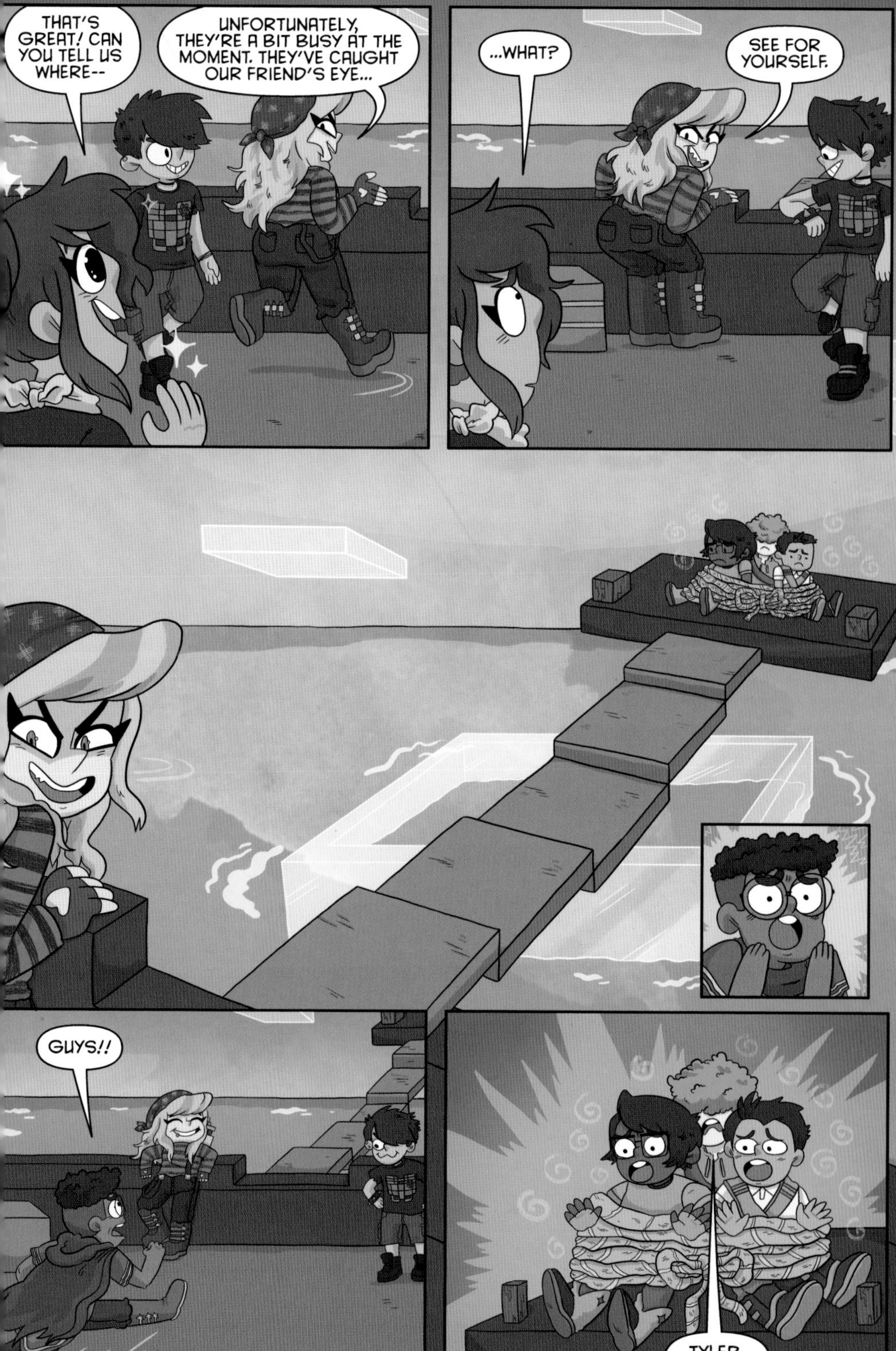
THAT'S GREAT! CAN YOU TELL US WHERE--
UNFORTUNATELY, THEY'RE A BIT BUSY AT THE MOMENT. THEY'VE CAUGHT OUR FRIEND'S EYE...
...WHAT?
SEE FOR YOURSELF.
GUYS!!
TYLER, DON'T!!!

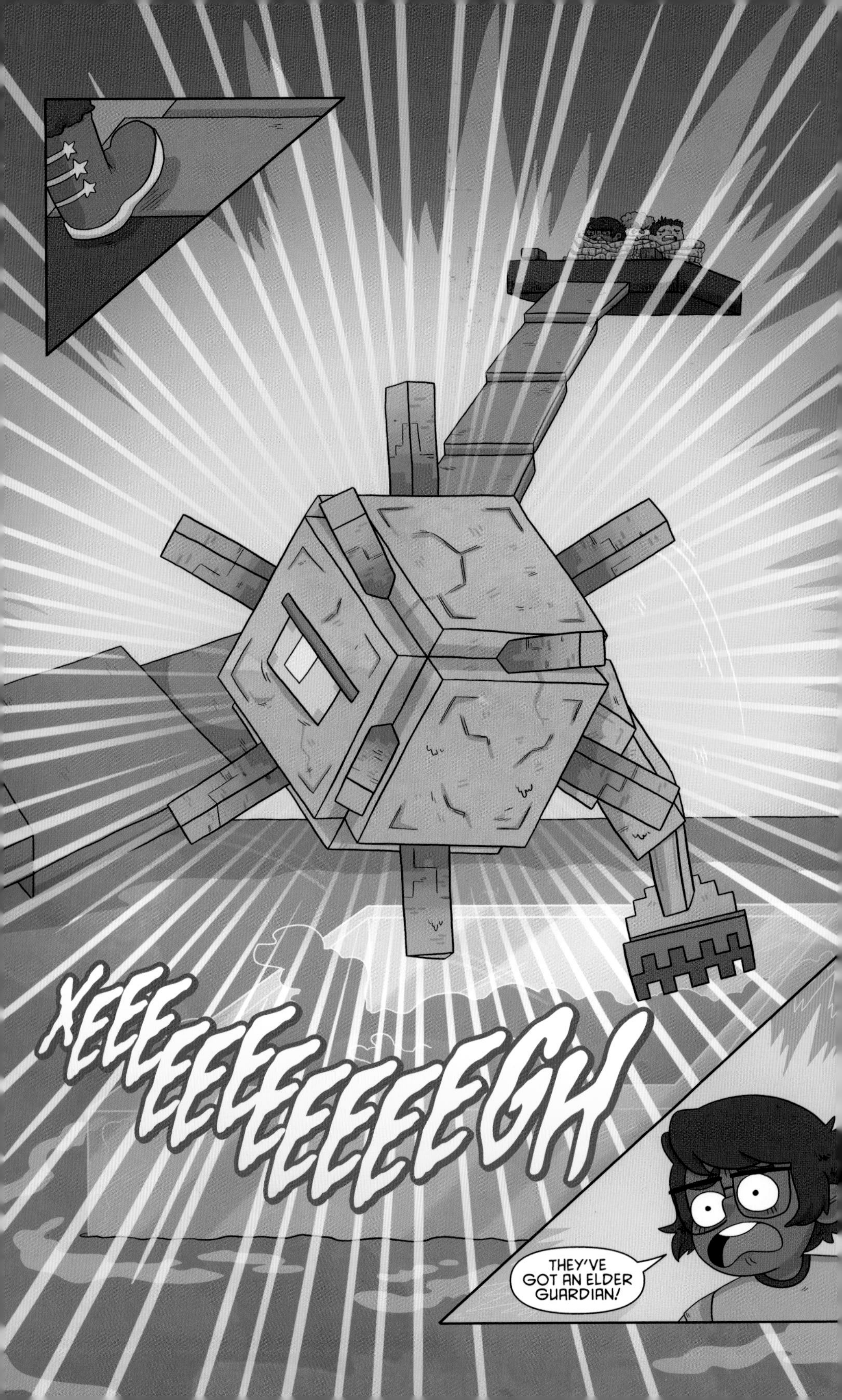
XEEEEEEEEEEEEEEGH
THEY'VE GOT AN ELDER GUARDIAN!

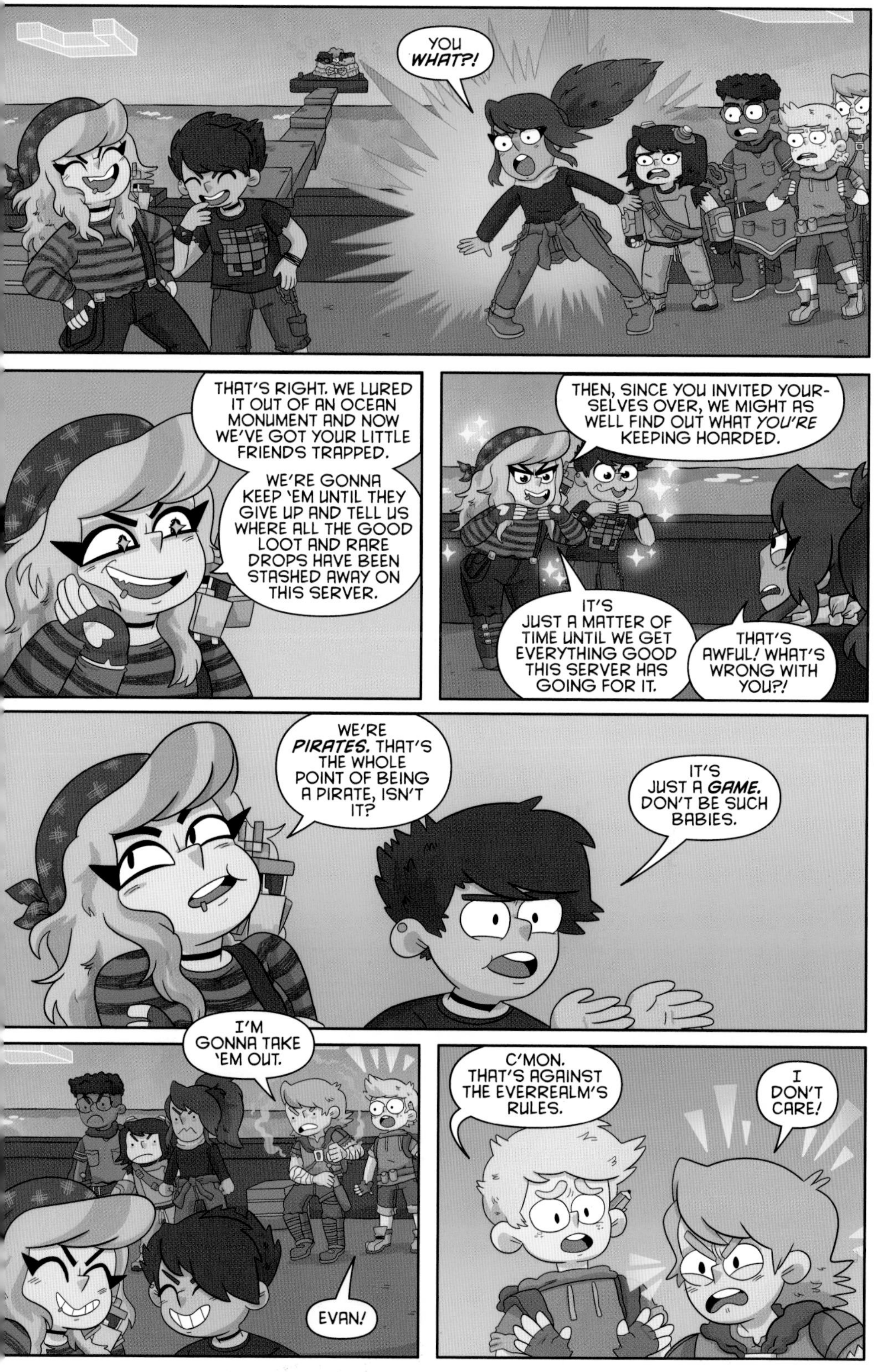
YOU *WHAT?!*
THAT'S RIGHT. WE LURED IT OUT OF AN OCEAN MONUMENT AND NOW WE'VE GOT YOUR LITTLE FRIENDS TRAPPED.
WE'RE GONNA KEEP 'EM UNTIL THEY GIVE UP AND TELL US WHERE ALL THE GOOD LOOT AND RARE DROPS HAVE BEEN STASHED AWAY ON THIS SERVER.
THEN, SINCE YOU INVITED YOURSELVES OVER, WE MIGHT AS WELL FIND OUT WHAT *YOU'RE* KEEPING HOARDED.
IT'S JUST A MATTER OF TIME UNTIL WE GET EVERYTHING GOOD THIS SERVER HAS GOING FOR IT.
THAT'S AWFUL! WHAT'S WRONG WITH YOU?!
WE'RE *PIRATES.* THAT'S THE WHOLE POINT OF BEING A PIRATE, ISN'T IT?
IT'S JUST A *GAME.* DON'T BE SUCH BABIES.
I'M GONNA TAKE 'EM OUT.
EVAN!
C'MON. THAT'S AGAINST THE EVERREALM'S RULES.
I DON'T CARE!

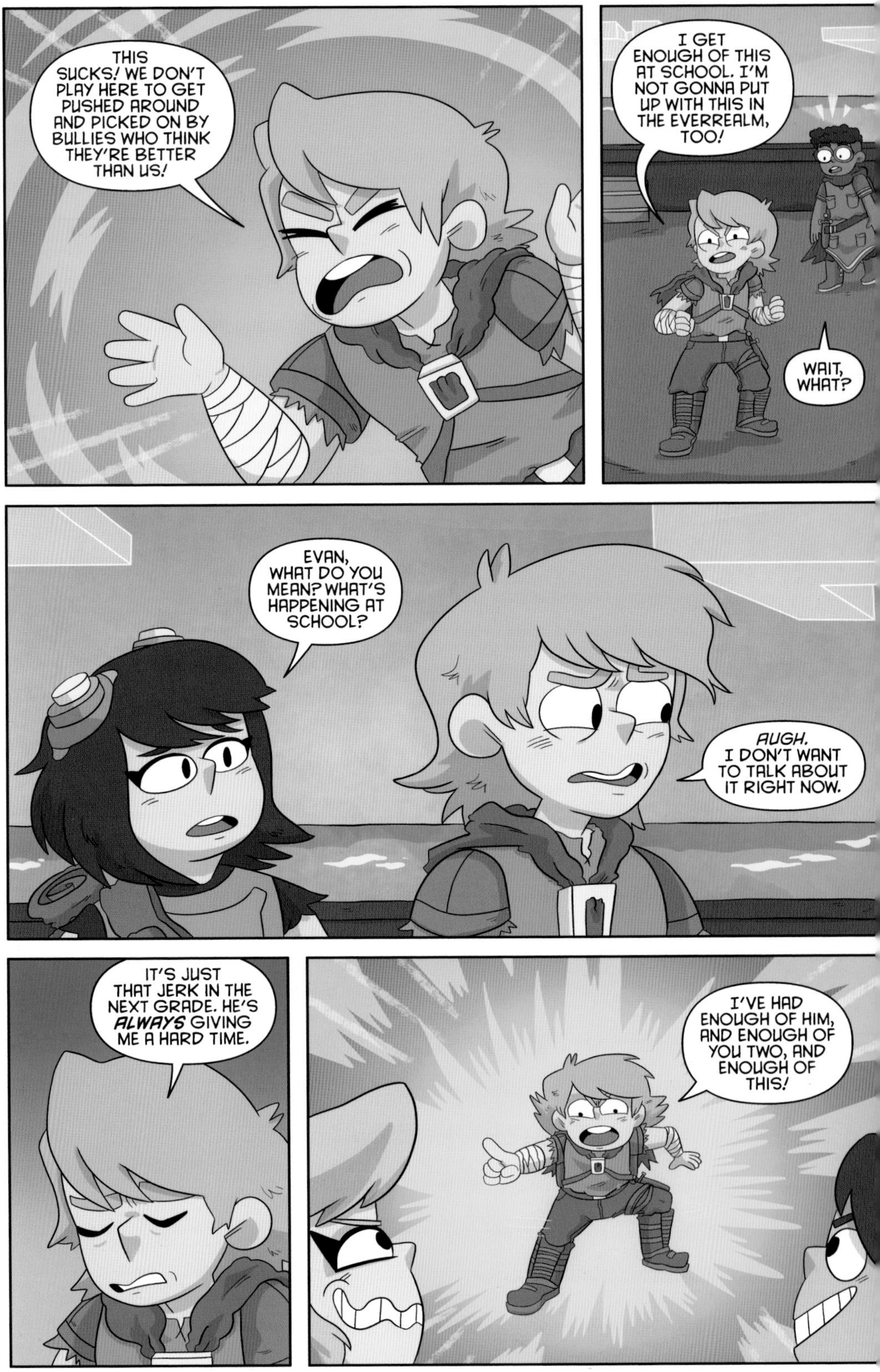
THIS SUCKS! WE DON'T PLAY HERE TO GET PUSHED AROUND AND PICKED ON BY BULLIES WHO THINK THEY'RE BETTER THAN US!
I GET ENOUGH OF THIS AT SCHOOL. I'M NOT GONNA PUT UP WITH THIS IN THE EVERREALM, TOO!
WAIT, WHAT?
EVAN, WHAT DO YOU MEAN? WHAT'S HAPPENING AT SCHOOL?
*AUGH.* I DON'T WANT TO TALK ABOUT IT RIGHT NOW.
IT'S JUST THAT JERK IN THE NEXT GRADE. HE'S ***ALWAYS*** GIVING ME A HARD TIME.
I'VE HAD ENOUGH OF HIM, AND ENOUGH OF YOU TWO, AND ENOUGH OF THIS!

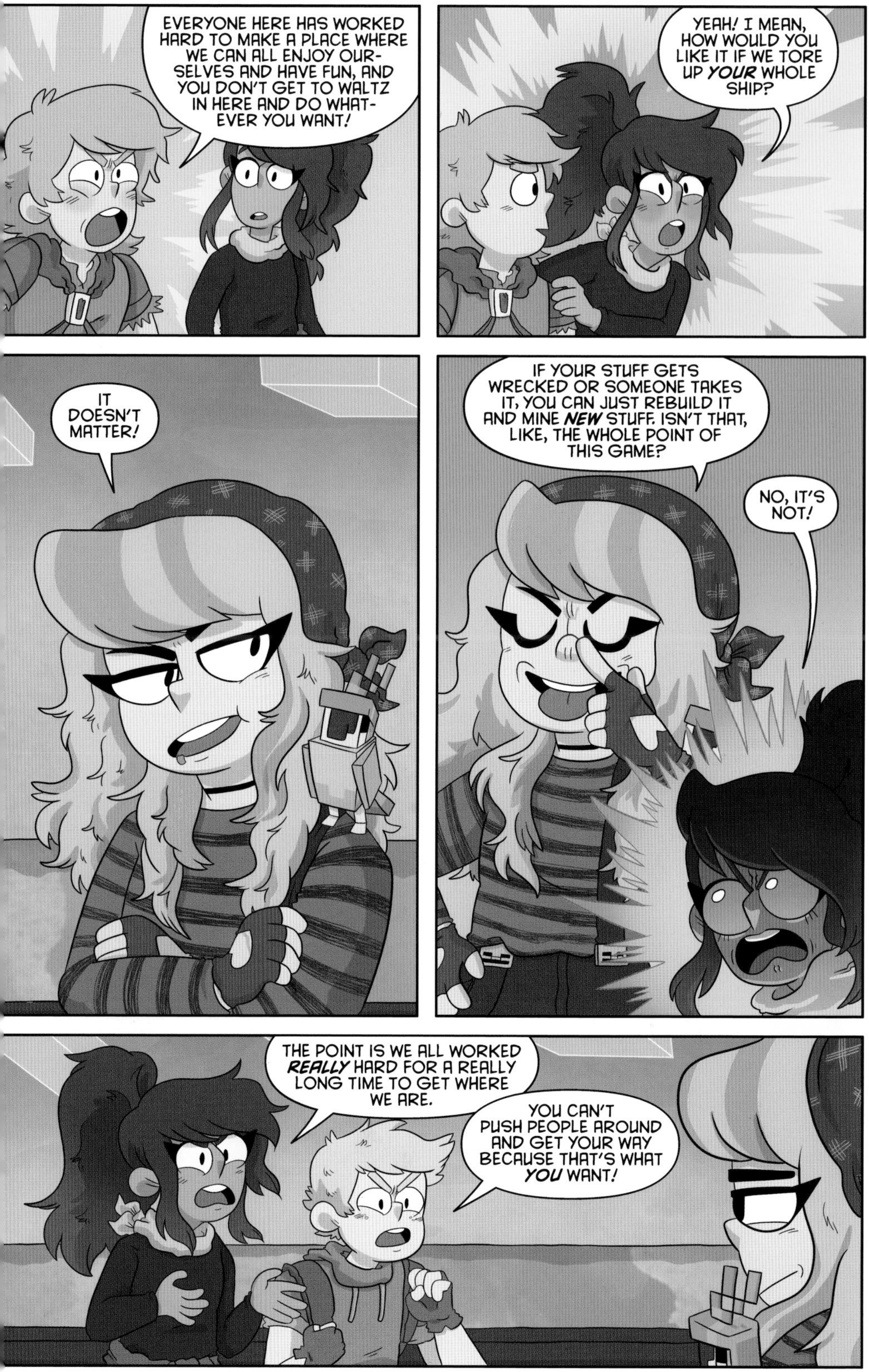

EVERYONE HERE HAS WORKED HARD TO MAKE A PLACE WHERE WE CAN ALL ENJOY OURSELVES AND HAVE FUN, AND YOU DON'T GET TO WALTZ IN HERE AND DO WHATEVER YOU WANT!
YEAH! I MEAN, HOW WOULD YOU LIKE IT IF WE TORE UP *YOUR* WHOLE SHIP?
IT DOESN'T MATTER!
IF YOUR STUFF GETS WRECKED OR SOMEONE TAKES IT, YOU CAN JUST REBUILD IT AND MINE *NEW* STUFF. ISN'T THAT, LIKE, THE WHOLE POINT OF THIS GAME?
NO, IT'S NOT!
THE POINT IS WE ALL WORKED *REALLY* HARD FOR A REALLY LONG TIME TO GET WHERE WE ARE.
YOU CAN'T PUSH PEOPLE AROUND AND GET YOUR WAY BECAUSE THAT'S WHAT *YOU* WANT!

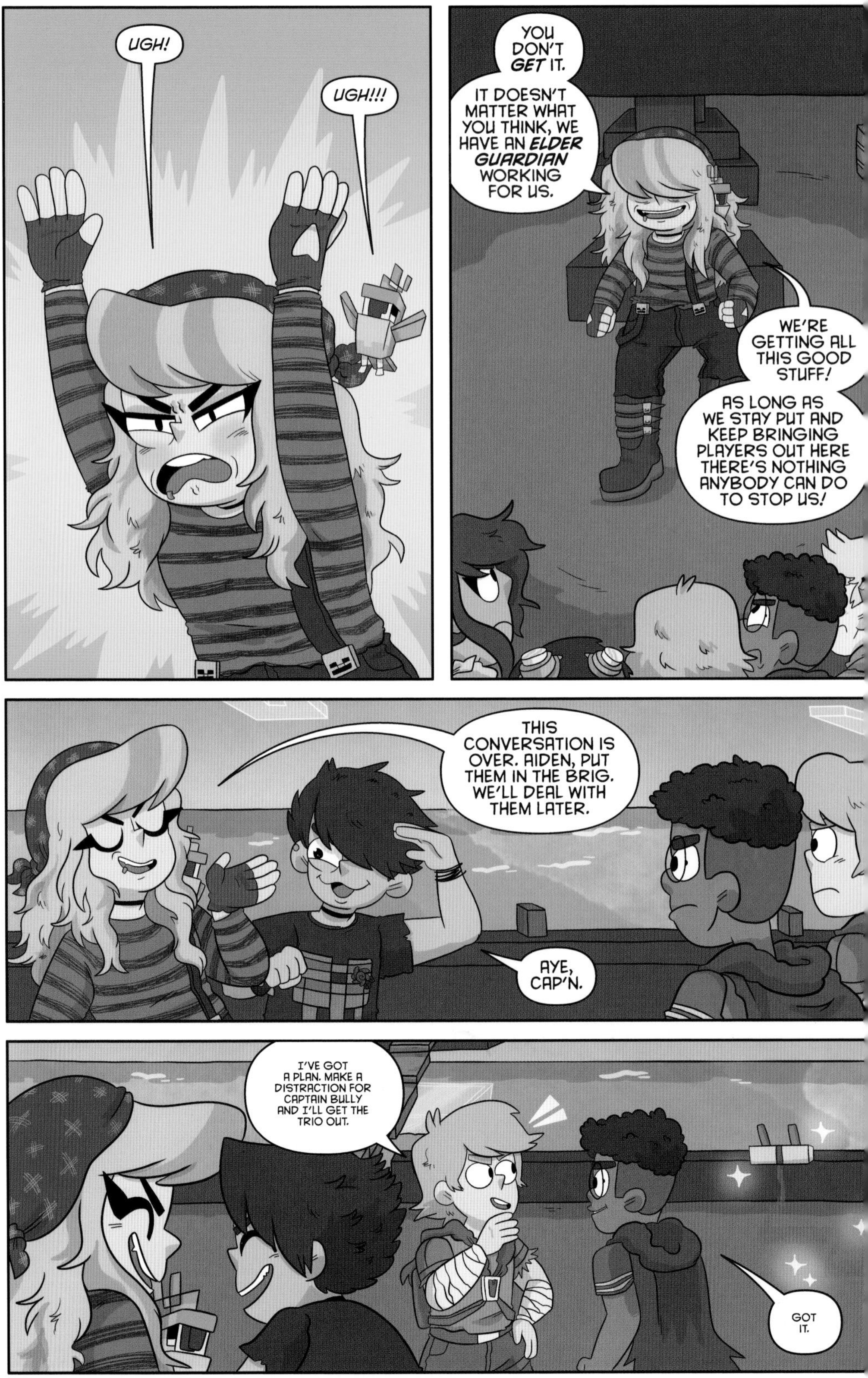
UGH!
UGH!!!
YOU DON'T GET IT.
IT DOESN'T MATTER WHAT YOU THINK, WE HAVE AN ELDER GUARDIAN WORKING FOR US.
WE'RE GETTING ALL THIS GOOD STUFF!
AS LONG AS WE STAY PUT AND KEEP BRINGING PLAYERS OUT HERE THERE'S NOTHING ANYBODY CAN DO TO STOP US!
THIS CONVERSATION IS OVER. AIDEN, PUT THEM IN THE BRIG. WE'LL DEAL WITH THEM LATER.
AYE, CAP'N.
I'VE GOT A PLAN. MAKE A DISTRACTION FOR CAPTAIN BULLY AND I'LL GET THE TRIO OUT.
GOT IT.

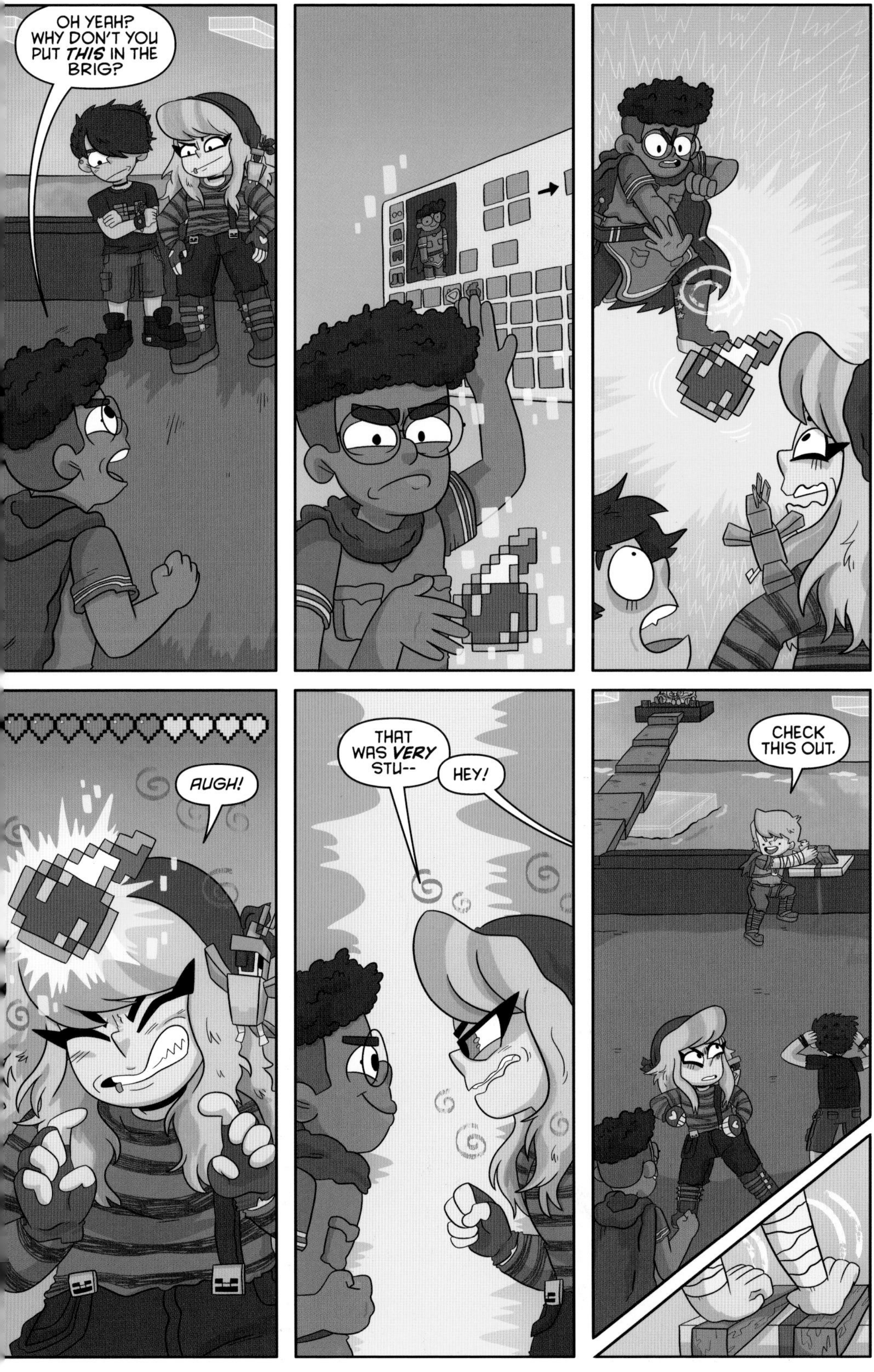
OH YEAH? WHY DON'T YOU PUT *THIS* IN THE BRIG?
AUGH!
THAT WAS **VERY** STU--
HEY!
CHECK THIS OUT.

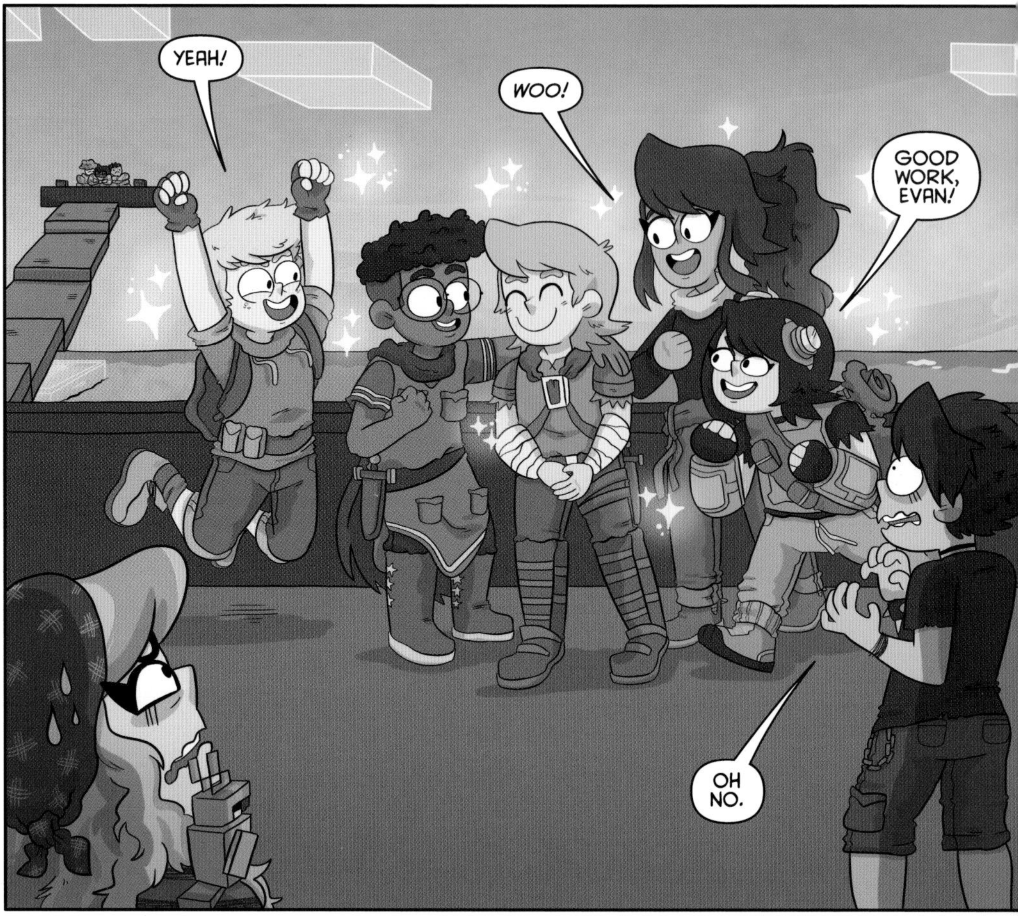
YEAH!
WOO!
GOOD WORK, EVAN!
OH NO.

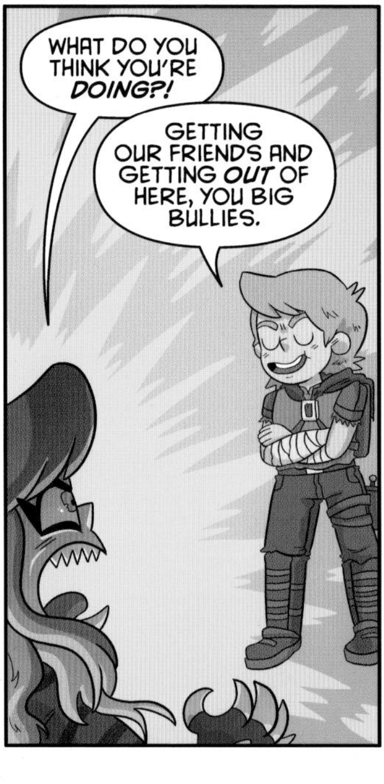
WHAT DO YOU THINK YOU'RE *DOING?!*
GETTING OUR FRIENDS AND GETTING *OUT* OF HERE, YOU BIG BULLIES.

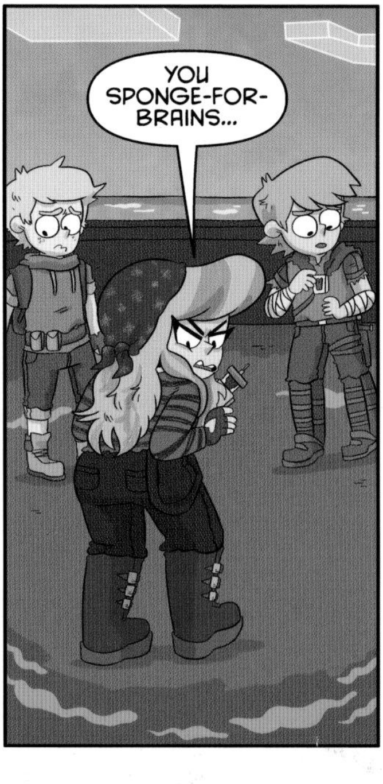
YOU SPONGE-FOR-BRAINS...

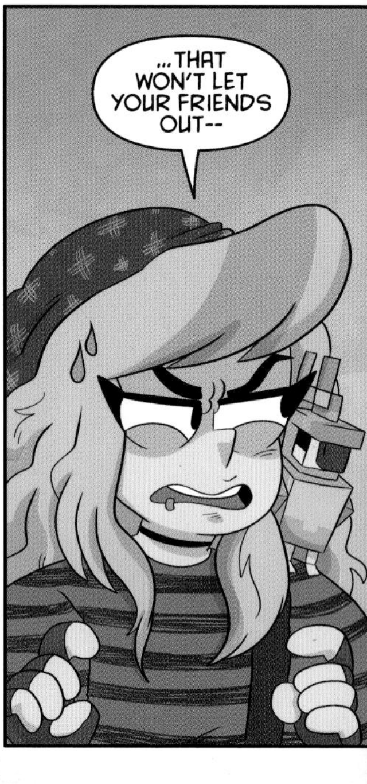
...THAT WON'T LET YOUR FRIENDS OUT--

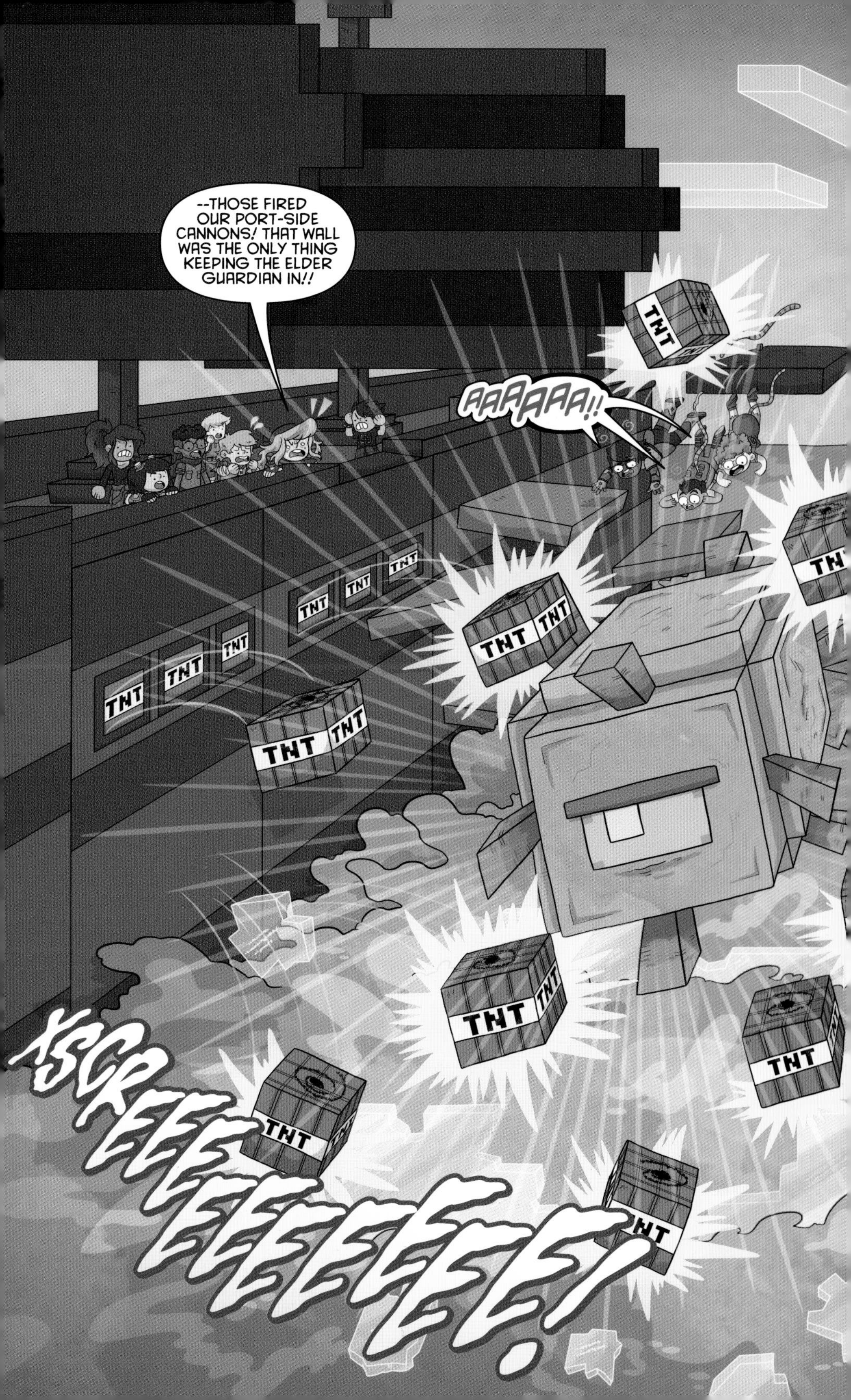
--THOSE FIRED OUR PORT-SIDE CANNONS! THAT WALL WAS THE ONLY THING KEEPING THE ELDER GUARDIAN IN!!
AAAAAAA!!
TNT
XSCREEEEEEEEEEEE!

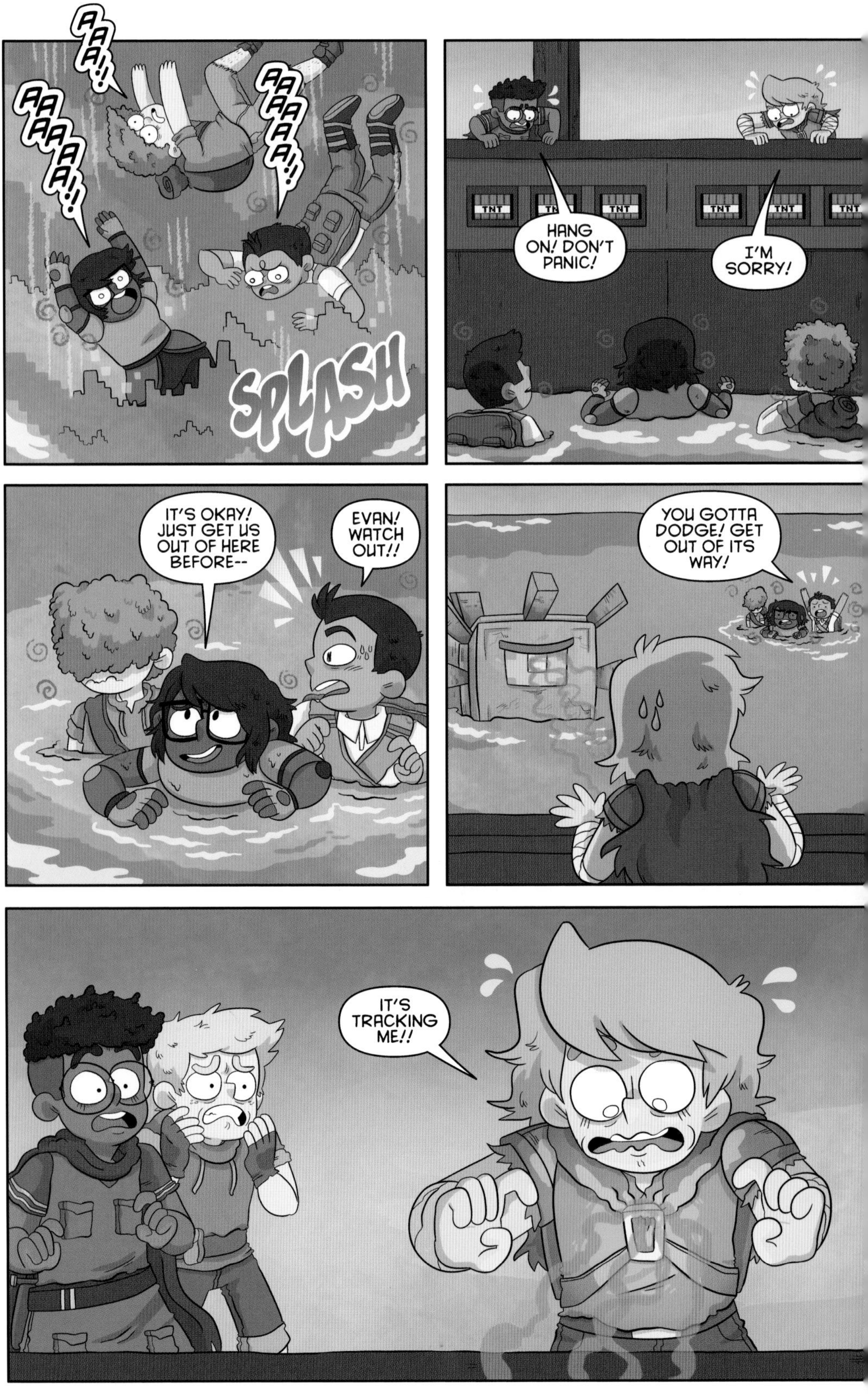

AAAA!!
AAAAAA!!
AAAAAA!!
SPLASH
HANG ON! DON'T PANIC!
I'M SORRY!
IT'S OKAY! JUST GET US OUT OF HERE BEFORE--
EVAN! WATCH OUT!!
YOU GOTTA DODGE! GET OUT OF ITS WAY!
IT'S TRACKING ME!!

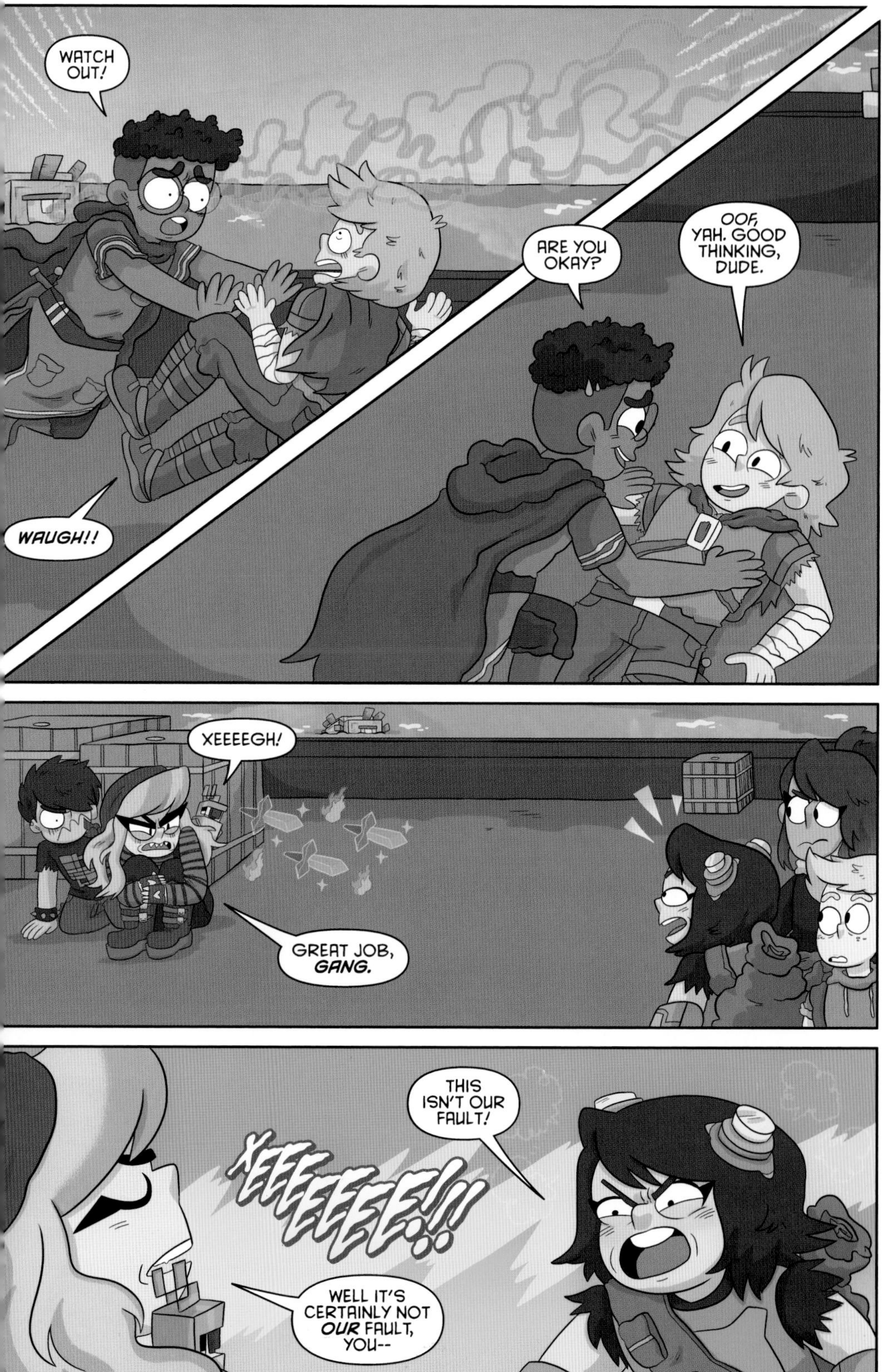
WATCH OUT!
WAUGH!!
ARE YOU OKAY?
OOF, YAH. GOOD THINKING, DUDE.
XEEEEGH!
GREAT JOB, GANG.
THIS ISN'T OUR FAULT!
XEEEEEEE!!!
WELL IT'S CERTAINLY NOT OUR FAULT, YOU--

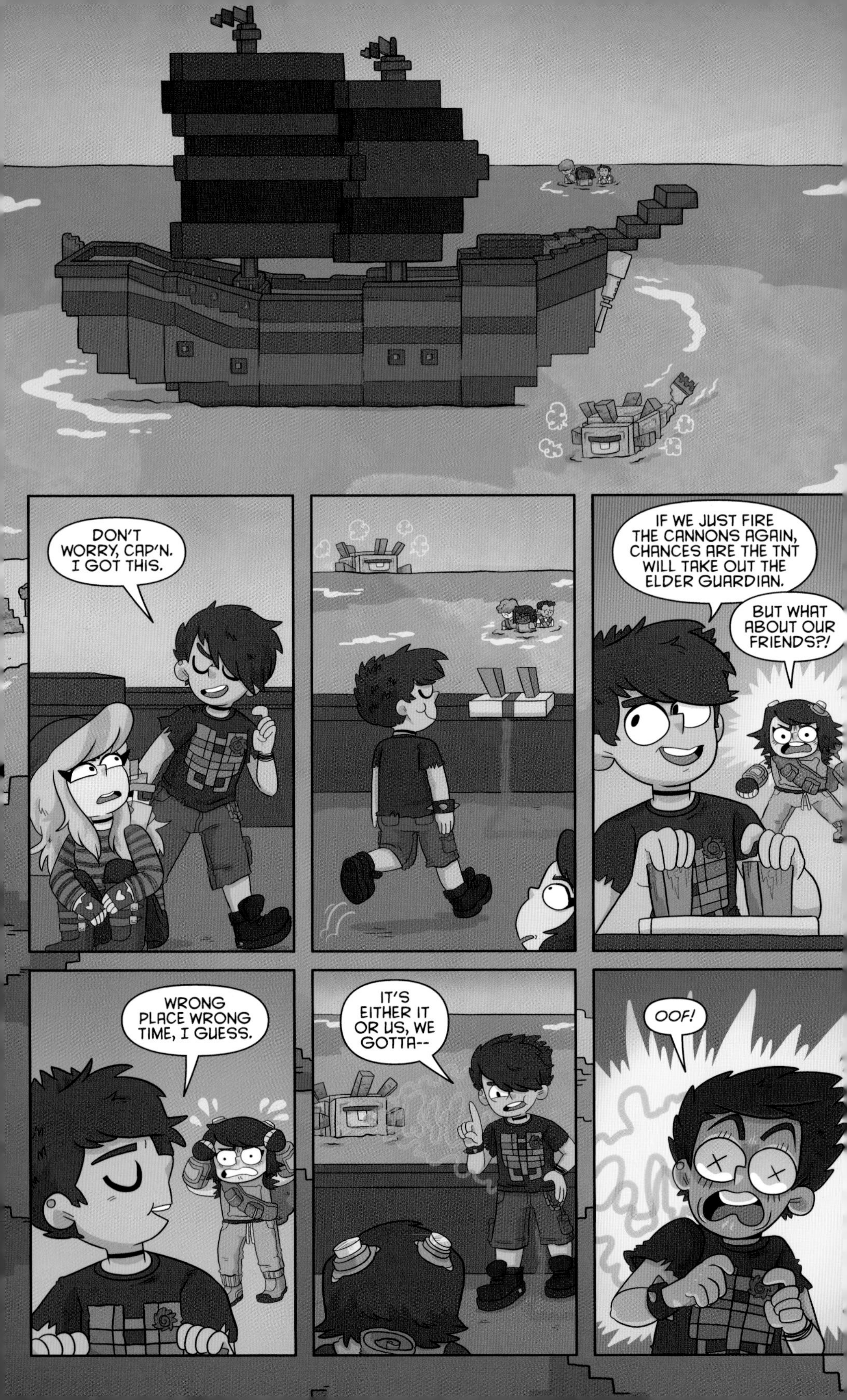
DON'T WORRY, CAP'N. I GOT THIS.
IF WE JUST FIRE THE CANNONS AGAIN, CHANCES ARE THE TNT WILL TAKE OUT THE ELDER GUARDIAN.
BUT WHAT ABOUT OUR FRIENDS?!
WRONG PLACE WRONG TIME, I GUESS.
IT'S EITHER IT OR US, WE GOTTA--
OOF!

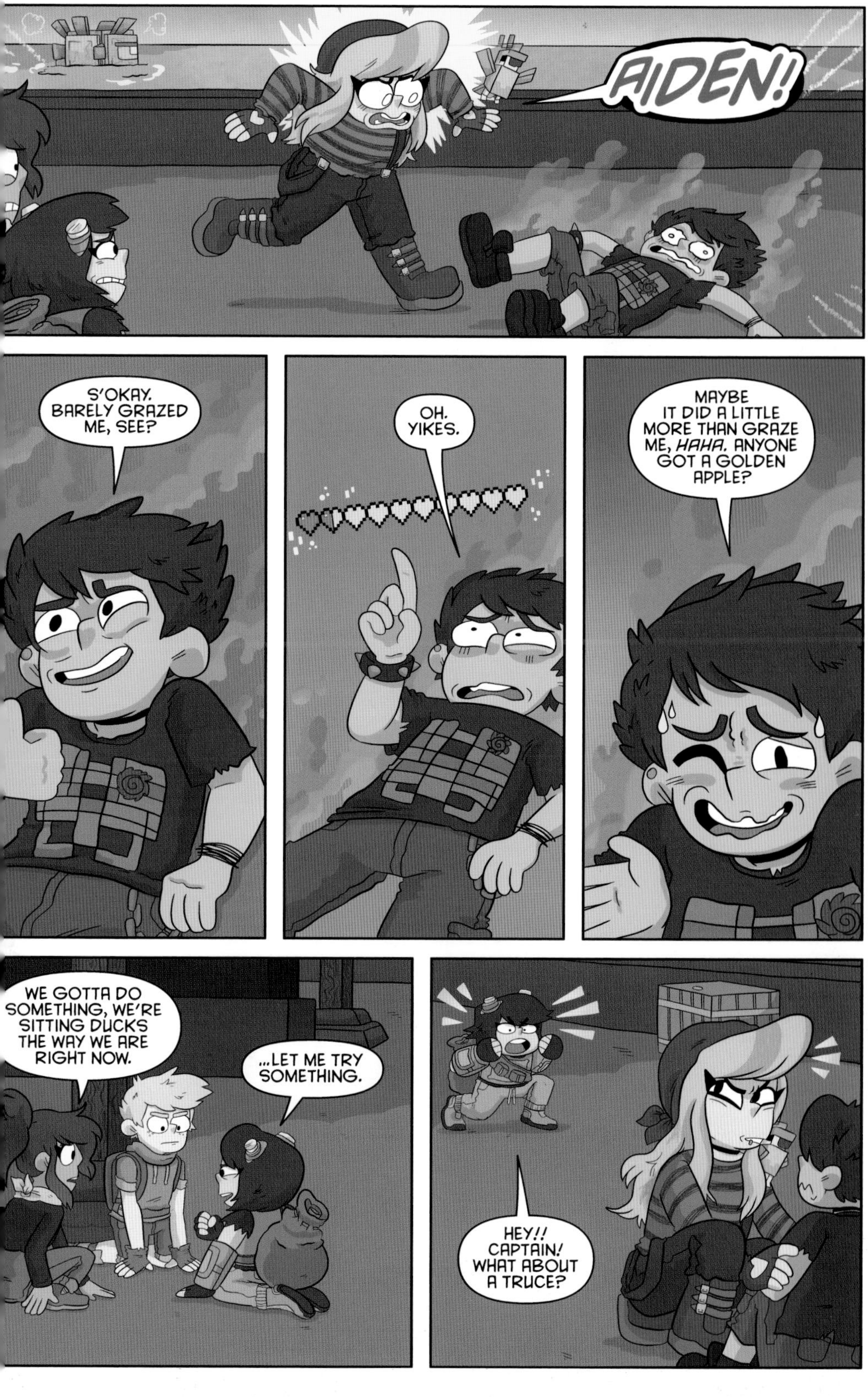
AIDEN!
S'OKAY. BARELY GRAZED ME, SEE?
OH. YIKES.
MAYBE IT DID A LITTLE MORE THAN GRAZE ME, *HAHA.* ANYONE GOT A GOLDEN APPLE?
WE GOTTA DO SOMETHING, WE'RE SITTING DUCKS THE WAY WE ARE RIGHT NOW.
...LET ME TRY SOMETHING.
HEY!! CAPTAIN! WHAT ABOUT A TRUCE?

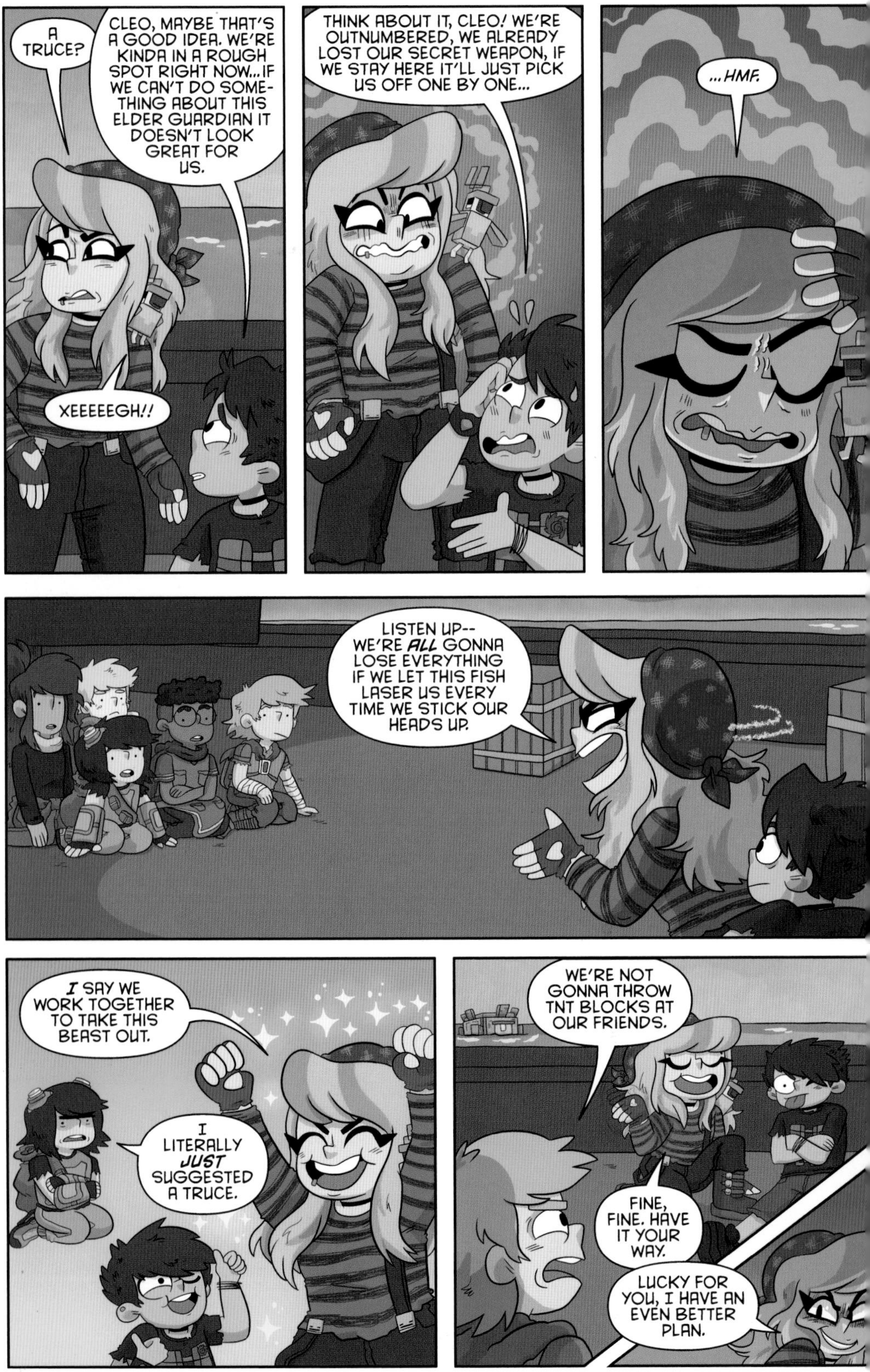
A TRUCE?
CLEO, MAYBE THAT'S A GOOD IDEA. WE'RE KINDA IN A ROUGH SPOT RIGHT NOW... IF WE CAN'T DO SOMETHING ABOUT THIS ELDER GUARDIAN IT DOESN'T LOOK GREAT FOR US.
XEEEEEGH!!
THINK ABOUT IT, CLEO! WE'RE OUTNUMBERED, WE ALREADY LOST OUR SECRET WEAPON, IF WE STAY HERE IT'LL JUST PICK US OFF ONE BY ONE...
...HMF.
LISTEN UP-- WE'RE *ALL* GONNA LOSE EVERYTHING IF WE LET THIS FISH LASER US EVERY TIME WE STICK OUR HEADS UP.
*I* SAY WE WORK TOGETHER TO TAKE THIS BEAST OUT.
I LITERALLY *JUST* SUGGESTED A TRUCE.
WE'RE NOT GONNA THROW TNT BLOCKS AT OUR FRIENDS.
FINE, FINE. HAVE IT YOUR WAY.
LUCKY FOR YOU, I HAVE AN EVEN BETTER PLAN.

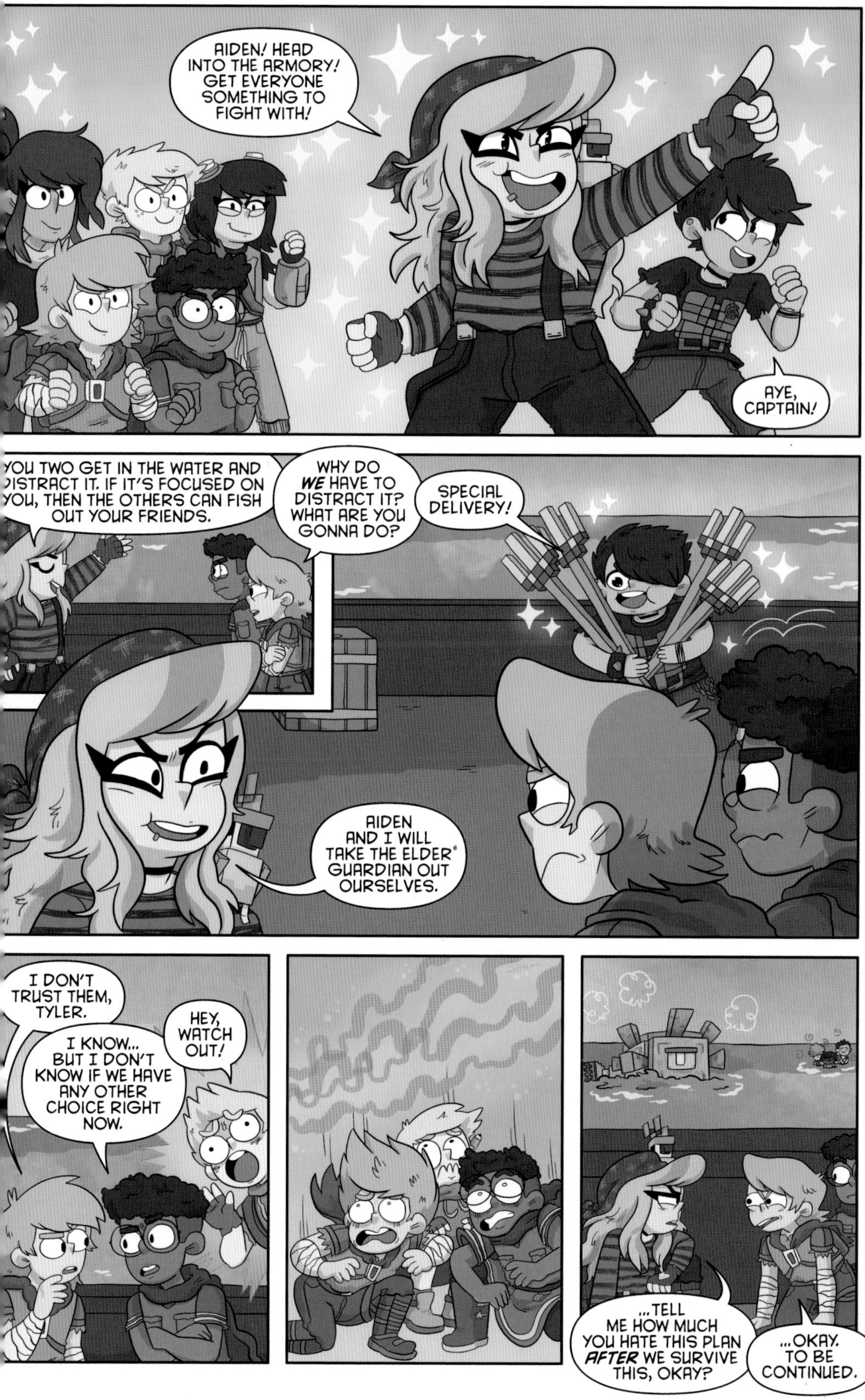
AIDEN! HEAD INTO THE ARMORY! GET EVERYONE SOMETHING TO FIGHT WITH!
AYE, CAPTAIN!
YOU TWO GET IN THE WATER AND DISTRACT IT. IF IT'S FOCUSED ON YOU, THEN THE OTHERS CAN FISH OUT YOUR FRIENDS.
WHY DO *WE* HAVE TO DISTRACT IT? WHAT ARE YOU GONNA DO?
SPECIAL DELIVERY!
AIDEN AND I WILL TAKE THE ELDER GUARDIAN OUT OURSELVES.
I DON'T TRUST THEM, TYLER.
I KNOW... BUT I DON'T KNOW IF WE HAVE ANY OTHER CHOICE RIGHT NOW.
HEY, WATCH OUT!
...TELL ME HOW MUCH YOU HATE THIS PLAN *AFTER* WE SURVIVE THIS, OKAY?
...OKAY.
TO BE CONTINUED.

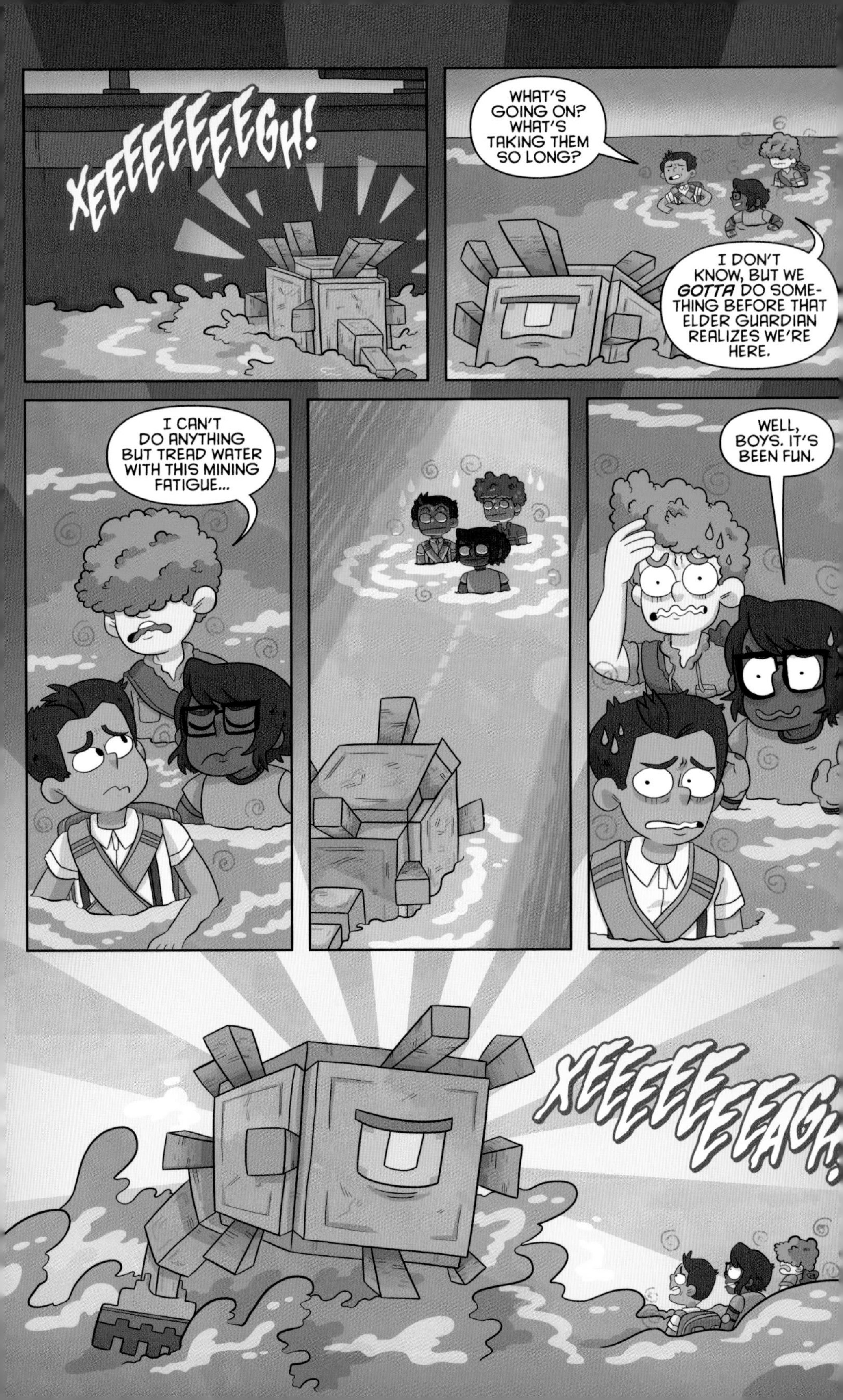
XEEEEEEEEGH!
WHAT'S GOING ON? WHAT'S TAKING THEM SO LONG?
I DON'T KNOW, BUT WE *GOTTA* DO SOMETHING BEFORE THAT ELDER GUARDIAN REALIZES WE'RE HERE.
I CAN'T DO ANYTHING BUT TREAD WATER WITH THIS MINING FATIGUE...
WELL, BOYS. IT'S BEEN FUN.
XEEEEEEEAGH!

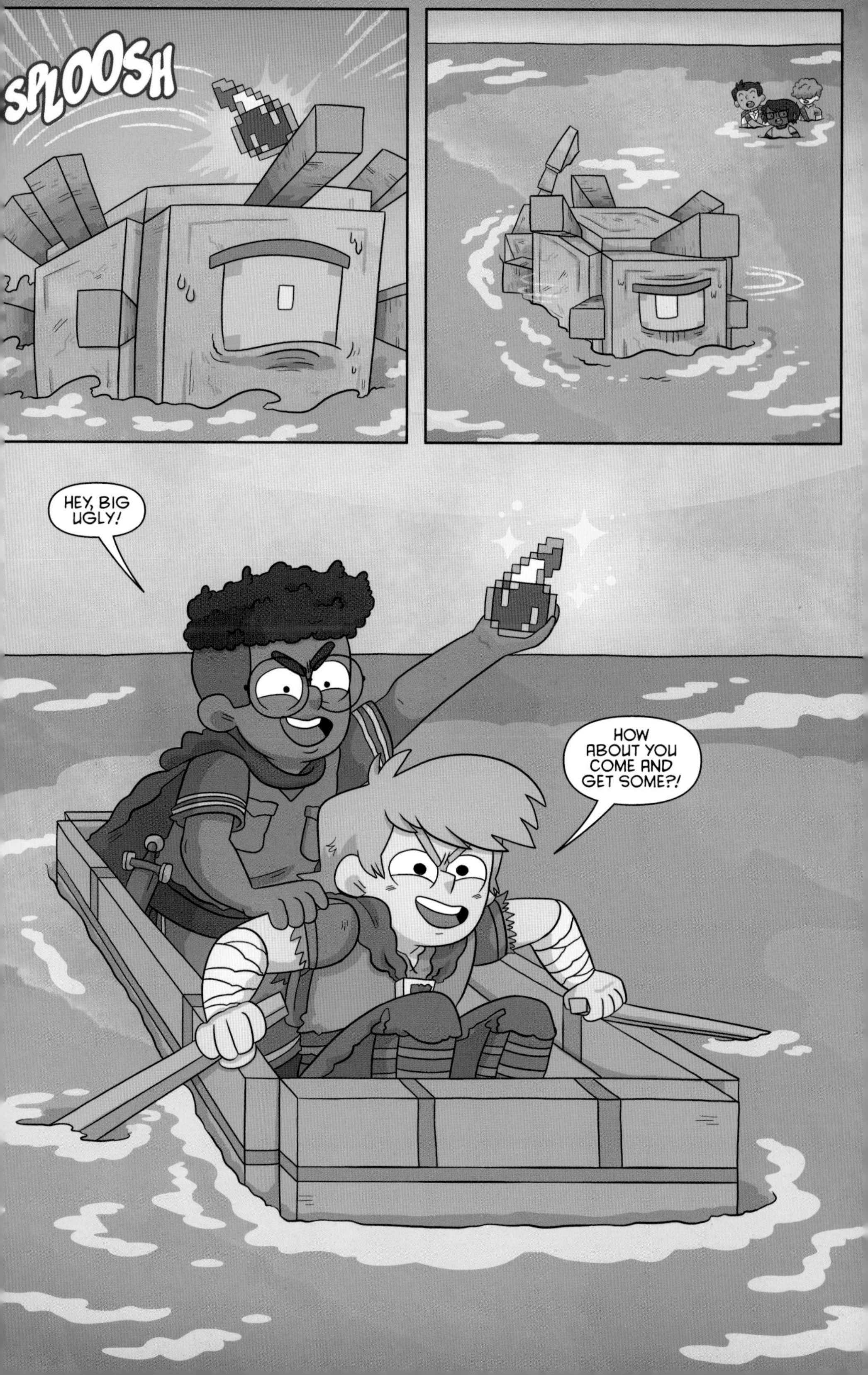
SPLOOSH
HEY, BIG UGLY!
HOW ABOUT YOU COME AND GET SOME?!

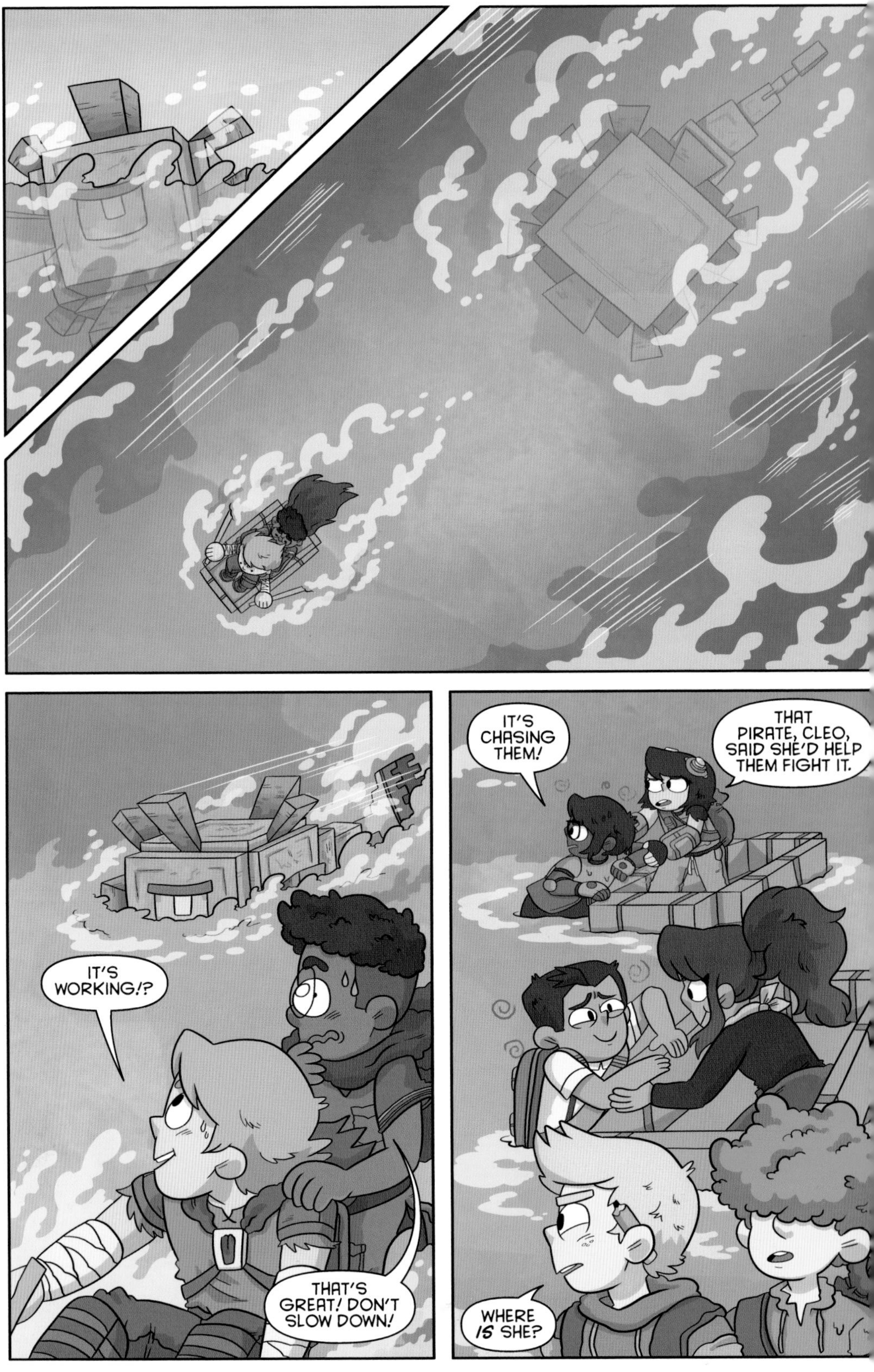

IT'S WORKING!?
THAT'S GREAT! DON'T SLOW DOWN!
IT'S CHASING THEM!
THAT PIRATE, CLEO, SAID SHE'D HELP THEM FIGHT IT.
WHERE *IS* SHE?

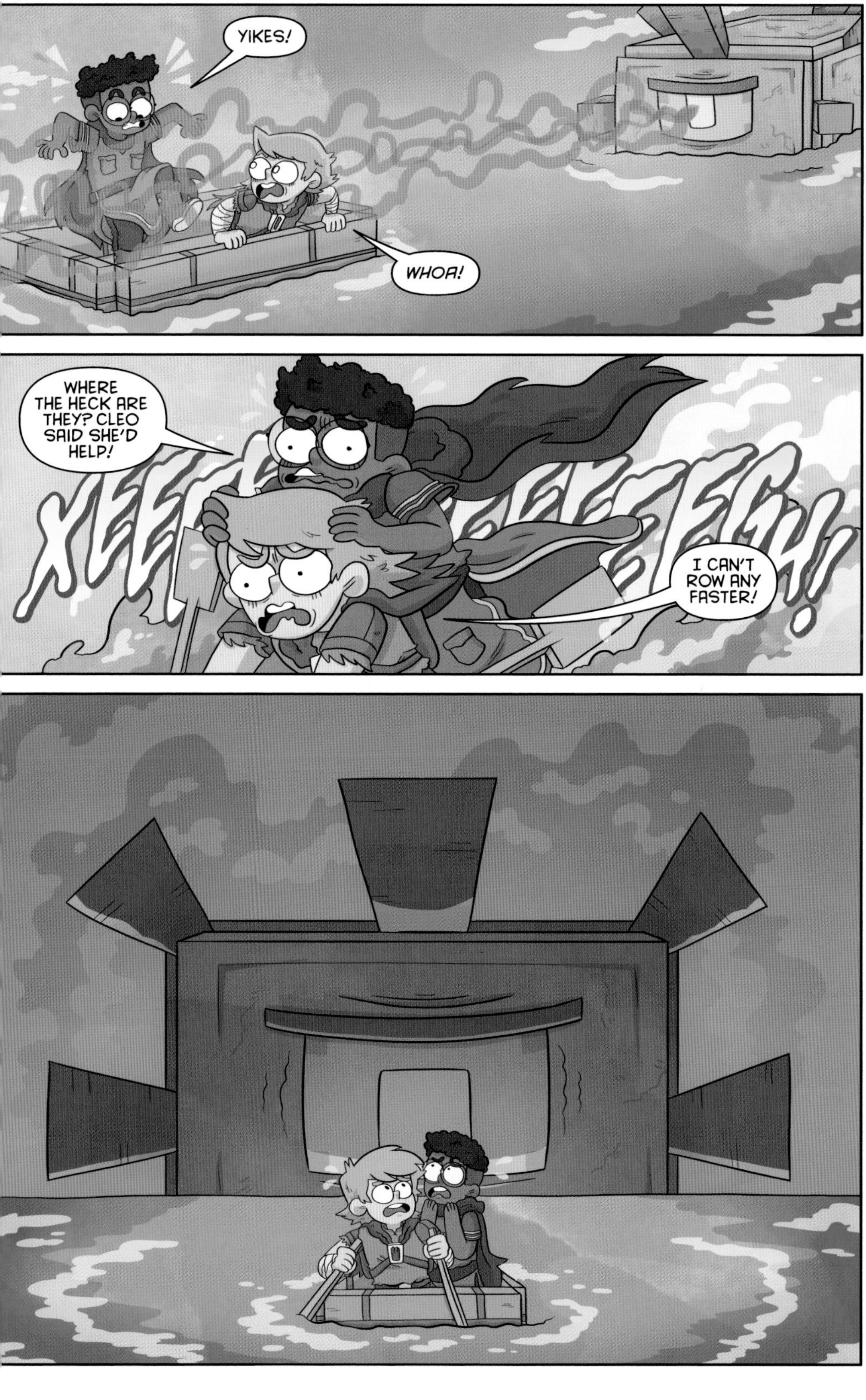
YIKES!
WHOA!
WHERE THE HECK ARE THEY? CLEO SAID SHE'D HELP!
I CAN'T ROW ANY FASTER!

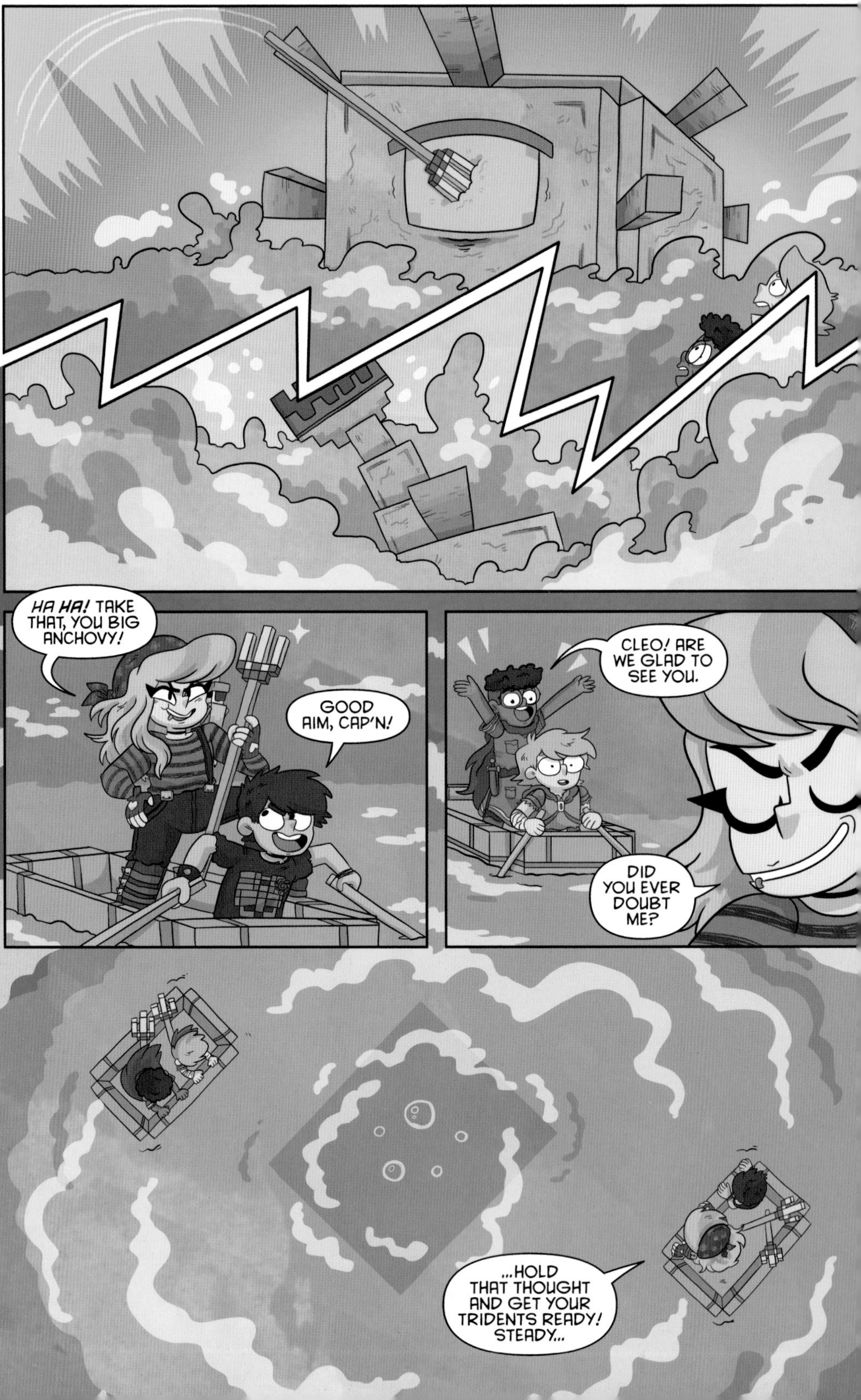

HA HA! TAKE THAT, YOU BIG ANCHOVY!
GOOD AIM, CAP'N!
CLEO! ARE WE GLAD TO SEE YOU.
DID YOU EVER DOUBT ME?
...HOLD THAT THOUGHT AND GET YOUR TRIDENTS READY! STEADY...

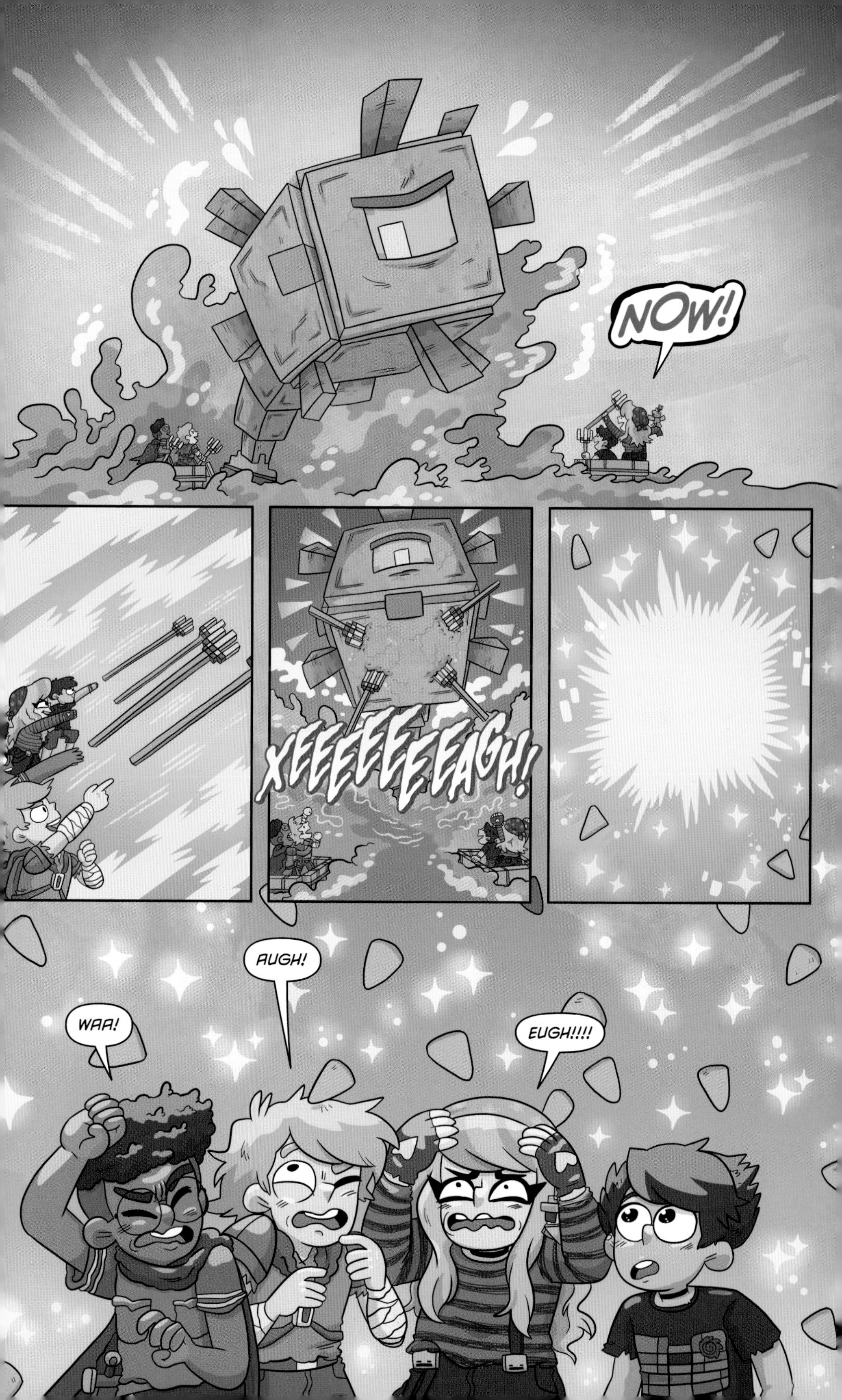
NOW!
XEEEEEEEEAGH!
WAA!
AUGH!
EUGH!!!!

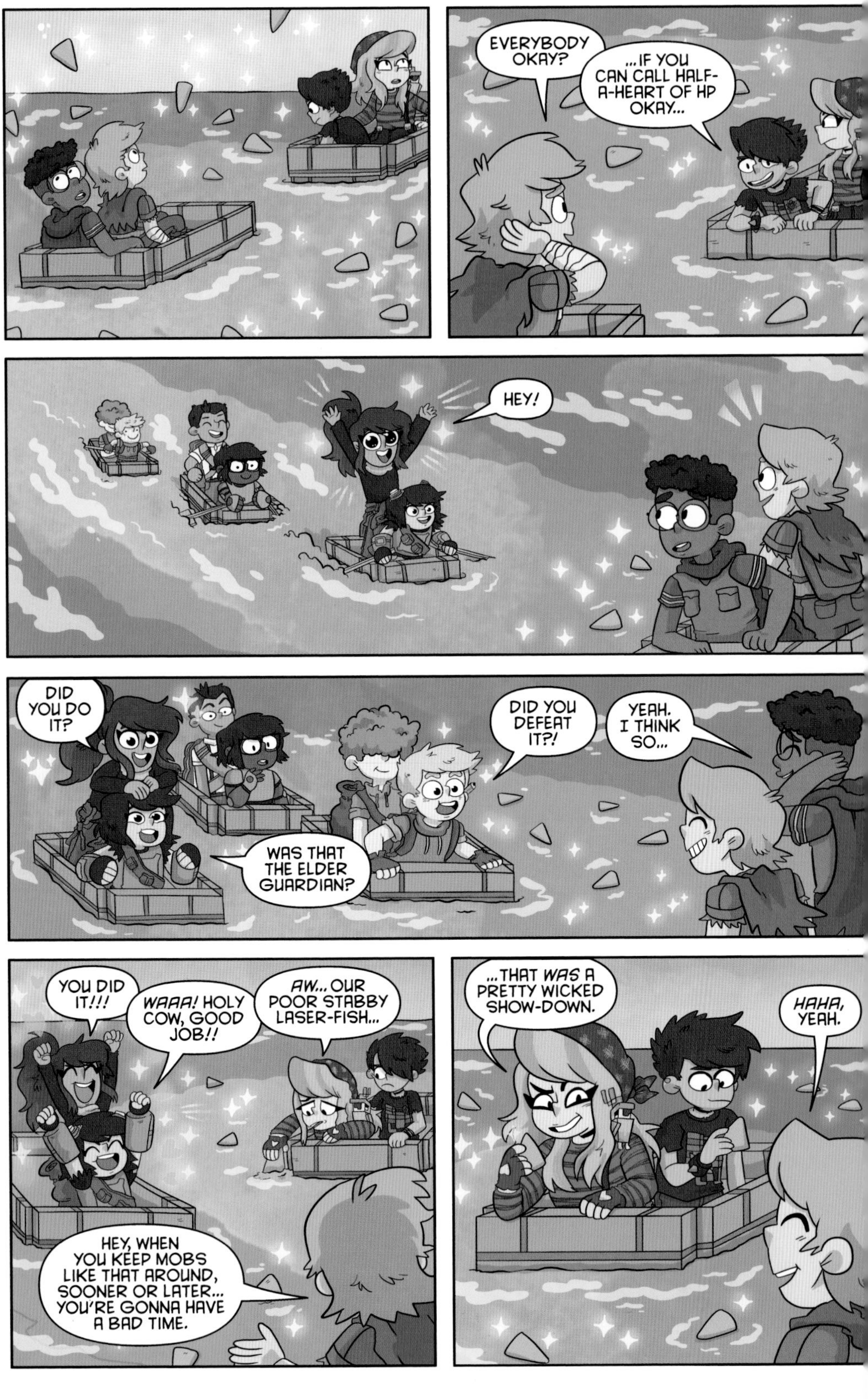
EVERYBODY OKAY?
...IF YOU CAN CALL HALF-A-HEART OF HP OKAY...
HEY!
DID YOU DO IT?
WAS THAT THE ELDER GUARDIAN?
DID YOU DEFEAT IT?!
YEAH. I THINK SO...
YOU DID IT!!!
WAAA! HOLY COW, GOOD JOB!!
AW... OUR POOR STABBY LASER-FISH...
HEY, WHEN YOU KEEP MOBS LIKE THAT AROUND, SOONER OR LATER... YOU'RE GONNA HAVE A BAD TIME.
...THAT WAS A PRETTY WICKED SHOW-DOWN.
HAHA, YEAH.

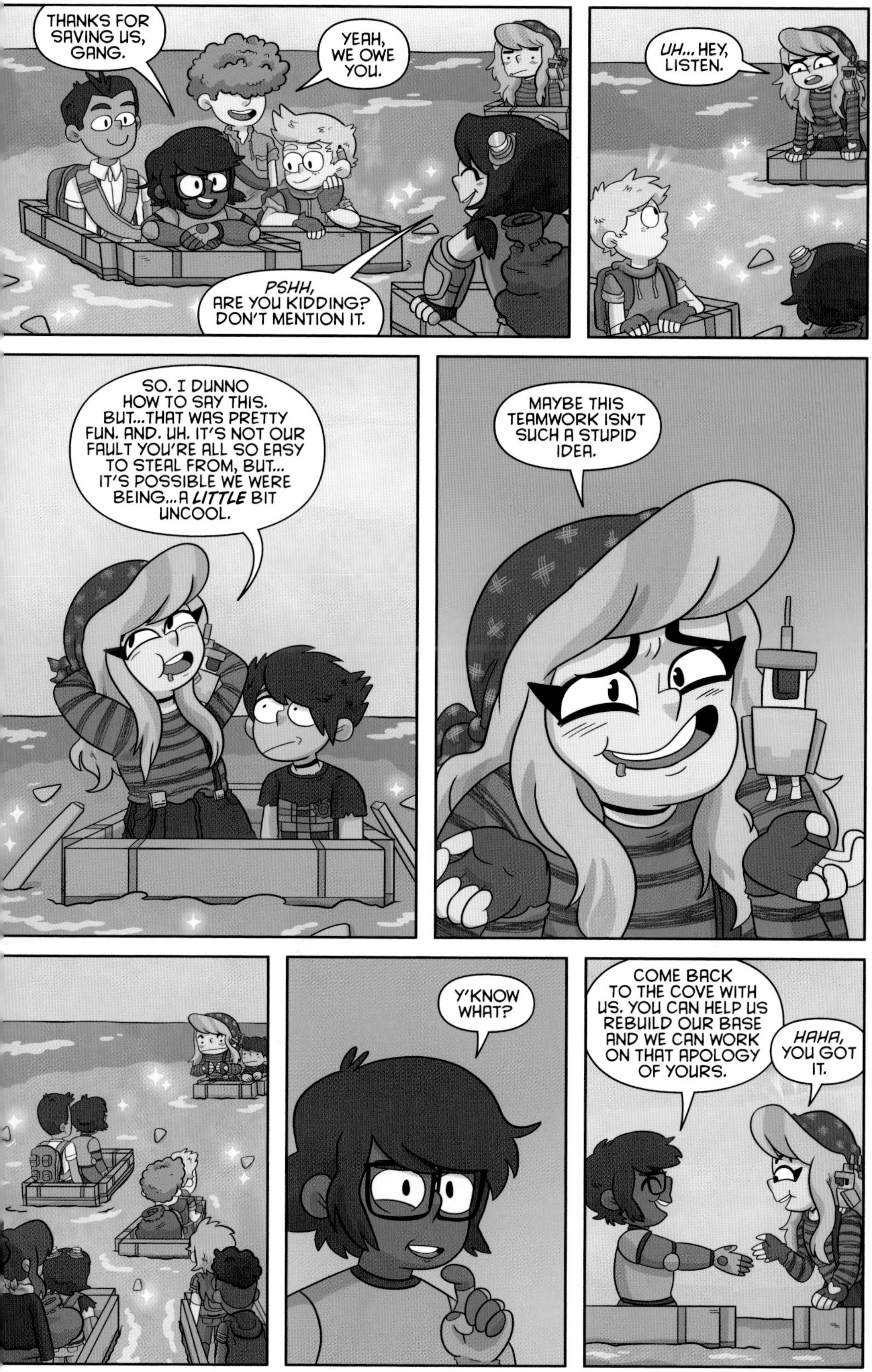
THANKS FOR SAVING US, GANG.
YEAH, WE OWE YOU.
*PSHH,* ARE YOU KIDDING? DON'T MENTION IT.
*UH...* HEY, LISTEN.
SO. I DUNNO HOW TO SAY THIS. BUT...THAT WAS PRETTY FUN. AND. UH. IT'S NOT OUR FAULT YOU'RE ALL SO EASY TO STEAL FROM, BUT... IT'S POSSIBLE WE WERE BEING...A *LITTLE* BIT UNCOOL.
MAYBE THIS TEAMWORK ISN'T SUCH A STUPID IDEA.
Y'KNOW WHAT?
COME BACK TO THE COVE WITH US. YOU CAN HELP US REBUILD OUR BASE AND WE CAN WORK ON THAT APOLOGY OF YOURS.
*HAHA,* YOU GOT IT.

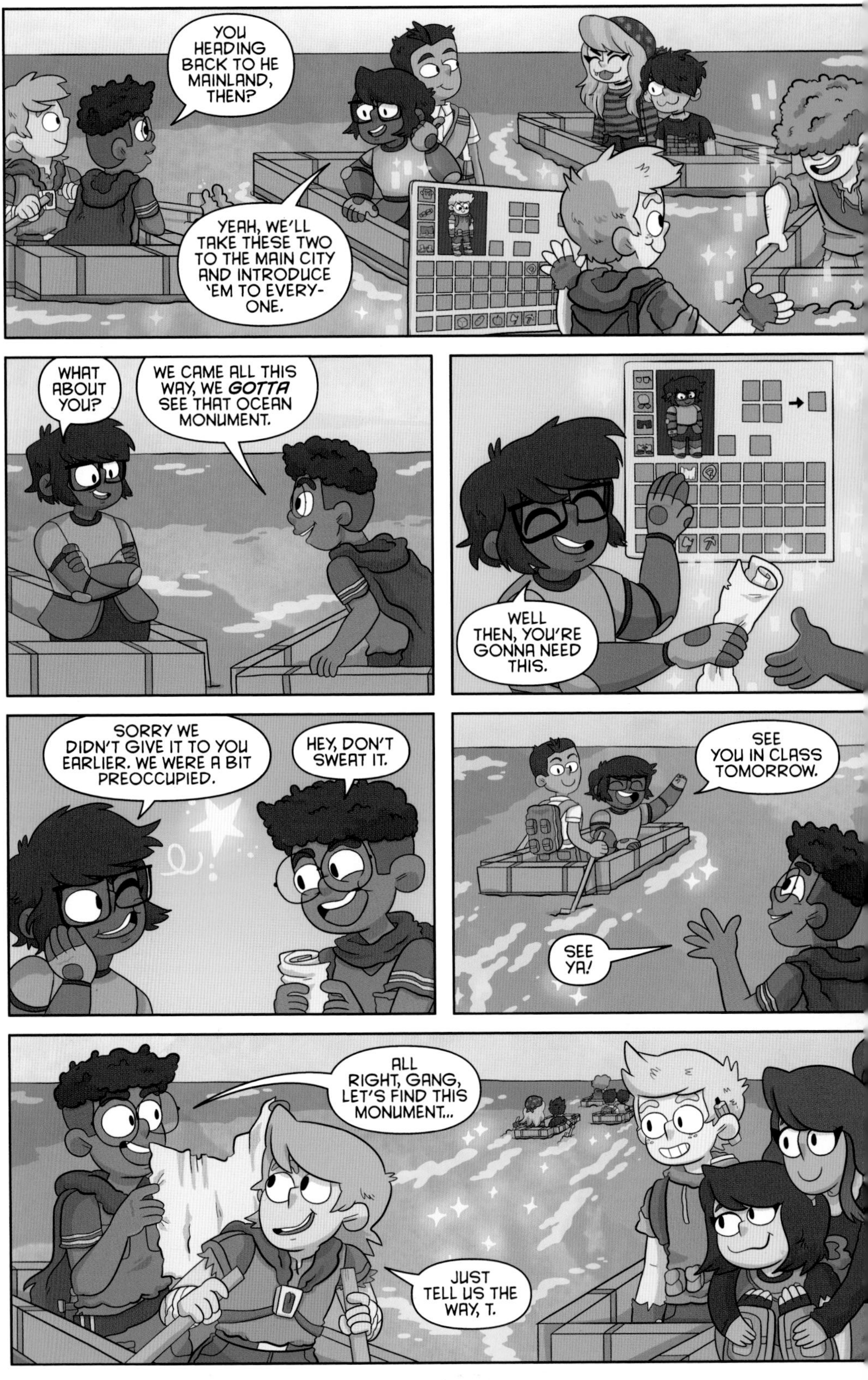
YOU HEADING BACK TO HE MAINLAND, THEN?
YEAH, WE'LL TAKE THESE TWO TO THE MAIN CITY AND INTRODUCE 'EM TO EVERY-ONE.
WHAT ABOUT YOU?
WE CAME ALL THIS WAY, WE *GOTTA* SEE THAT OCEAN MONUMENT.
WELL THEN, YOU'RE GONNA NEED THIS.
SORRY WE DIDN'T GIVE IT TO YOU EARLIER. WE WERE A BIT PREOCCUPIED.
HEY, DON'T SWEAT IT.
SEE YOU IN CLASS TOMORROW.
SEE YA!
ALL RIGHT, GANG, LET'S FIND THIS MONUMENT...
JUST TELL US THE WAY, T.

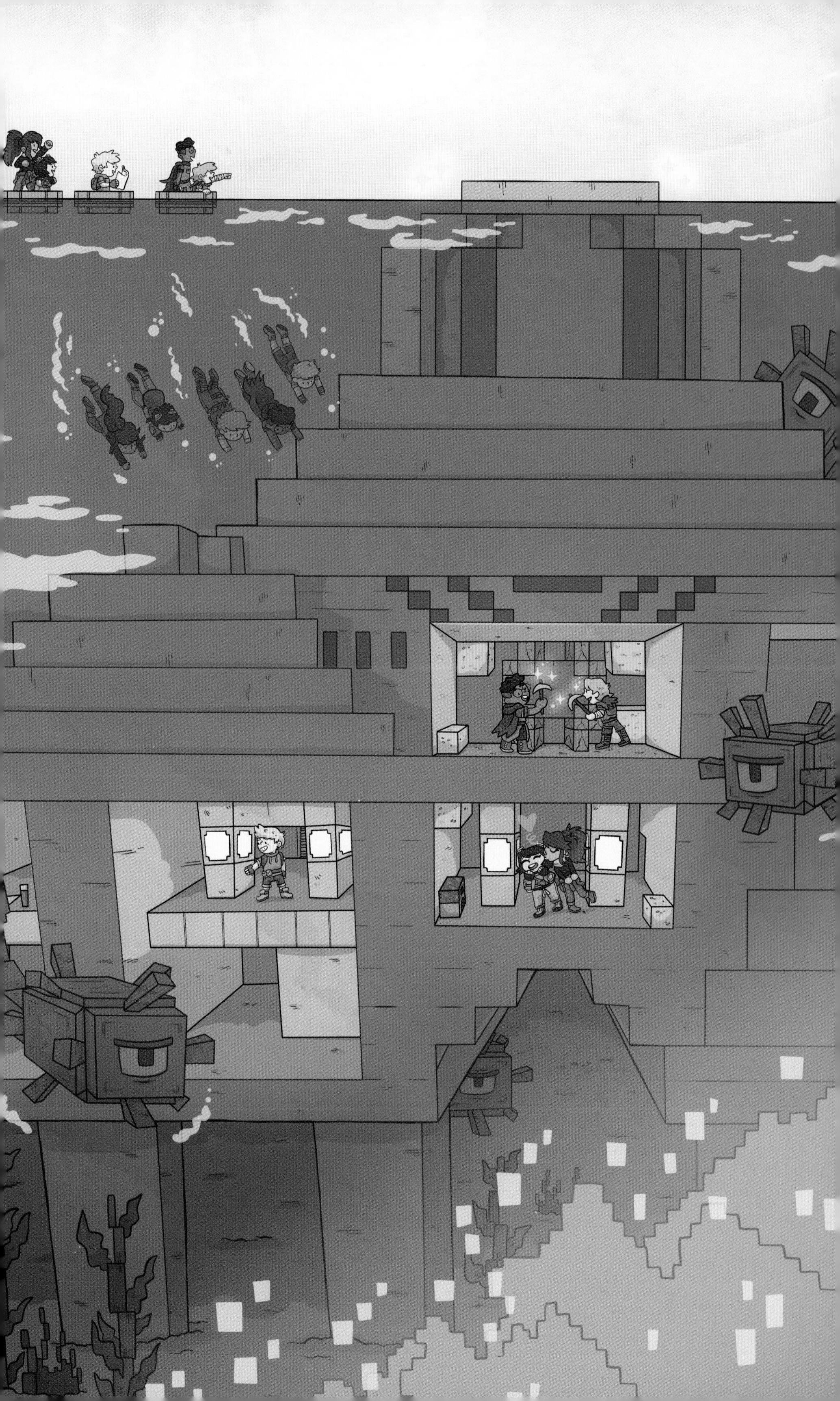

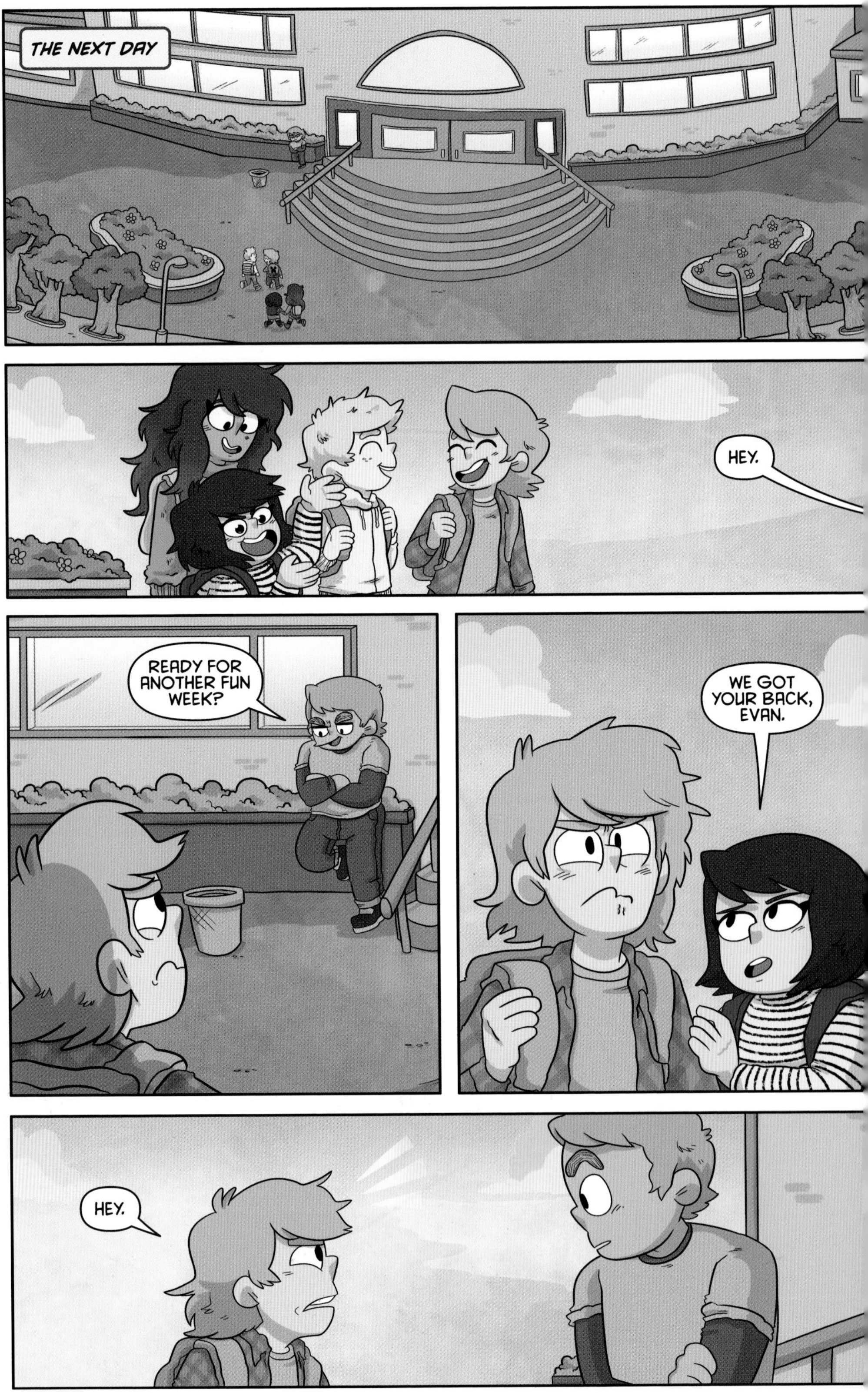
THE NEXT DAY
HEY.
READY FOR ANOTHER FUN WEEK?
WE GOT YOUR BACK, EVAN.
HEY.

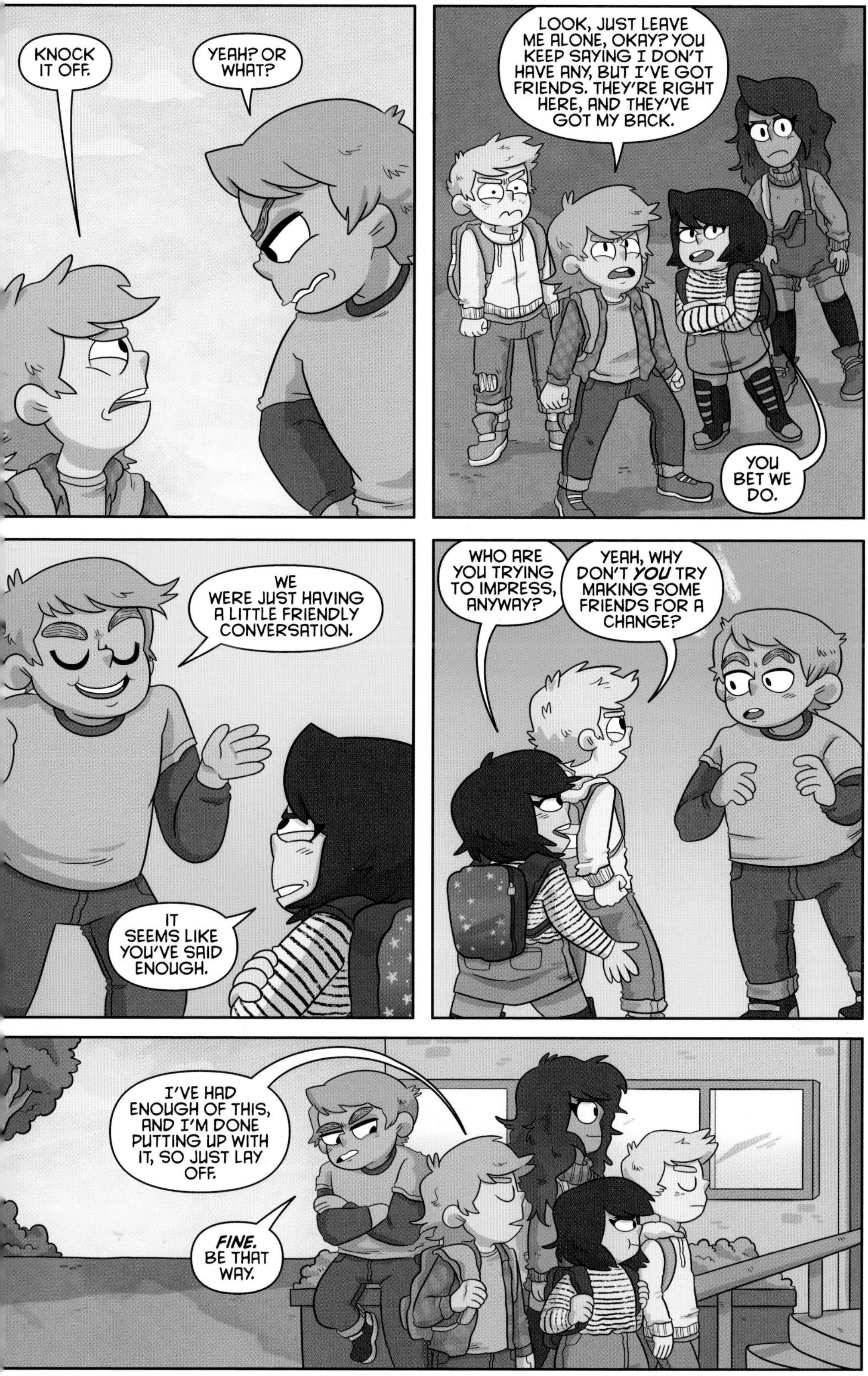

KNOCK IT OFF.
YEAH? OR WHAT?
LOOK, JUST LEAVE ME ALONE, OKAY? YOU KEEP SAYING I DON'T HAVE ANY, BUT I'VE GOT FRIENDS. THEY'RE RIGHT HERE, AND THEY'VE GOT MY BACK.
YOU BET WE DO.
WE WERE JUST HAVING A LITTLE FRIENDLY CONVERSATION.
IT SEEMS LIKE YOU'VE SAID ENOUGH.
WHO ARE YOU TRYING TO IMPRESS, ANYWAY?
YEAH, WHY DON'T *YOU* TRY MAKING SOME FRIENDS FOR A CHANGE?
I'VE HAD ENOUGH OF THIS, AND I'M DONE PUTTING UP WITH IT, SO JUST LAY OFF.
*FINE.* BE THAT WAY.

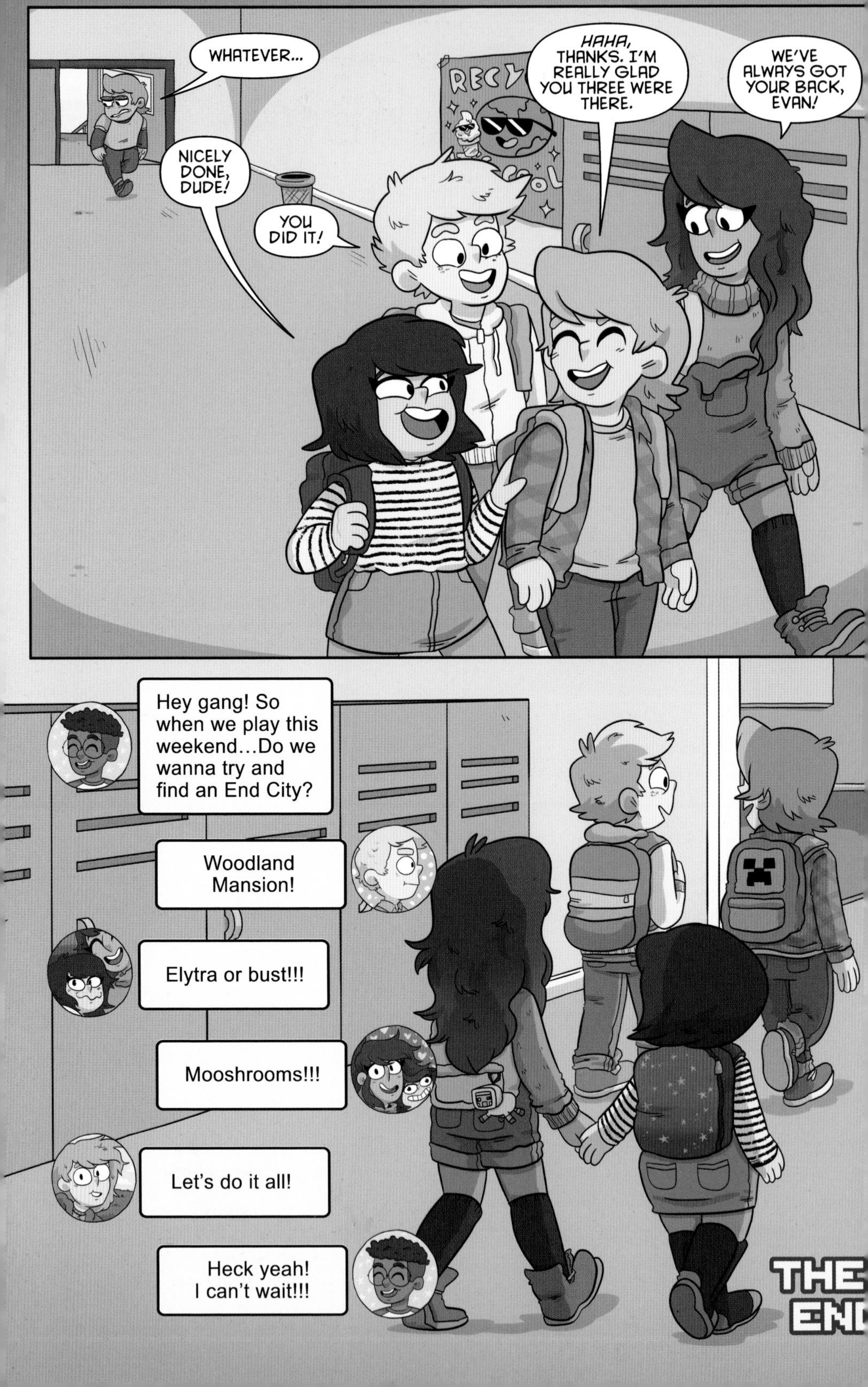
WHATEVER...
NICELY DONE, DUDE!
YOU DID IT!
HAHA, THANKS. I'M REALLY GLAD YOU THREE WERE THERE.
WE'VE ALWAYS GOT YOUR BACK, EVAN!
Hey gang! So when we play this weekend…Do we wanna try and find an End City?
Woodland Mansion!
Elytra or bust!!!
Mooshrooms!!!
Let's do it all!
Heck yeah! I can't wait!!!
THE

# MINECRAFT™
## SKETCHBOOK

COMMENTARY BY
### SARAH GRALEY

CLEAR TOP

YELLOW STRIPE

BLUE

YELLOW

## CHARACTER DESIGN

As this is a sequel, I already had the main cast of characters designed! But as time had passed since I had worked on the first book, I wanted to revisit and familiarize myself with the cast by redrawing everyone.

With every book I work on, I like to draw the whole cast and all their outfits that'll appear in the book, print out a big version and hang it above my desk before starting any pages! That way, if I'm not sure what a particular outfit should look like, I can just look up and check. (There's a very big cast in the Minecraft book, so there are a lot of fun looks to keep track of!)

Sfé did introduce three new characters to design, though! One school bully and two mean pirates! I was asked to give the pirates mall-punk fashion with a pirate flair, and as someone who dressed similarly to mall-punks growing up, I really enjoyed this challenge!

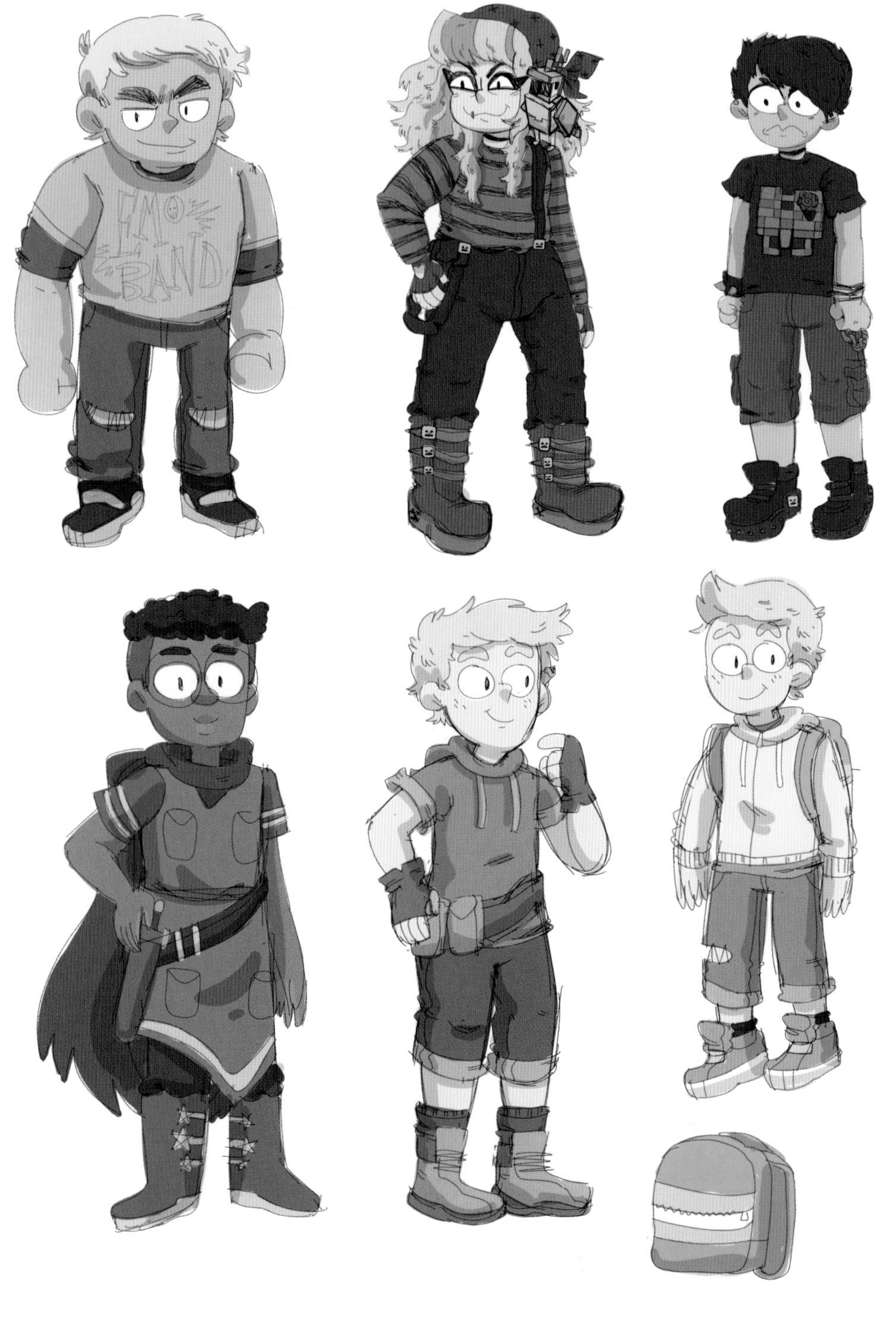
EMO BAND

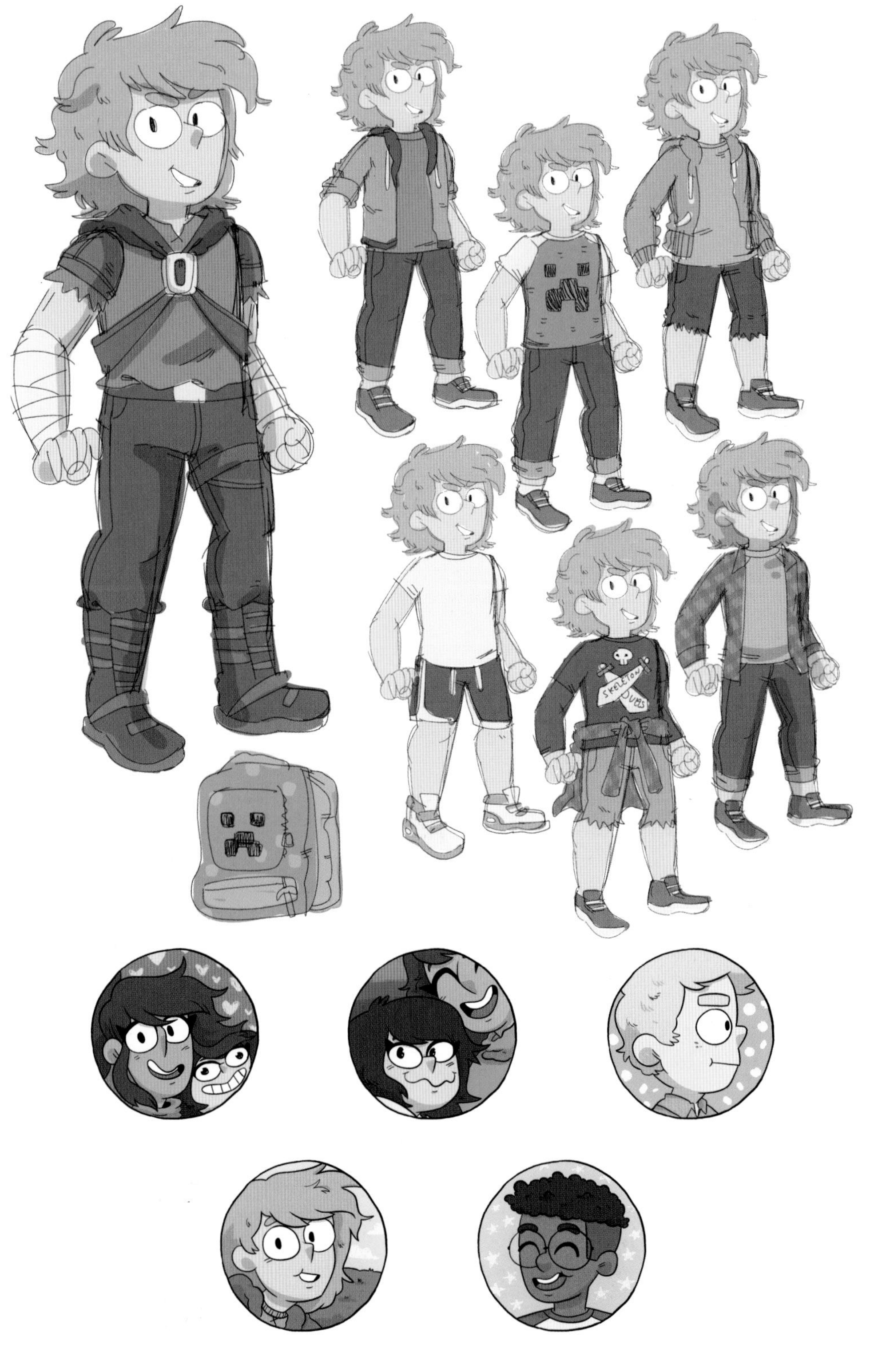

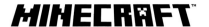

When coming up with the cover for the book, I'll pitch several different ideas! After some back and forth, we'll figure out the best cover to proceed with and any other minor tweaks that will make the cover even better before I start drawing!

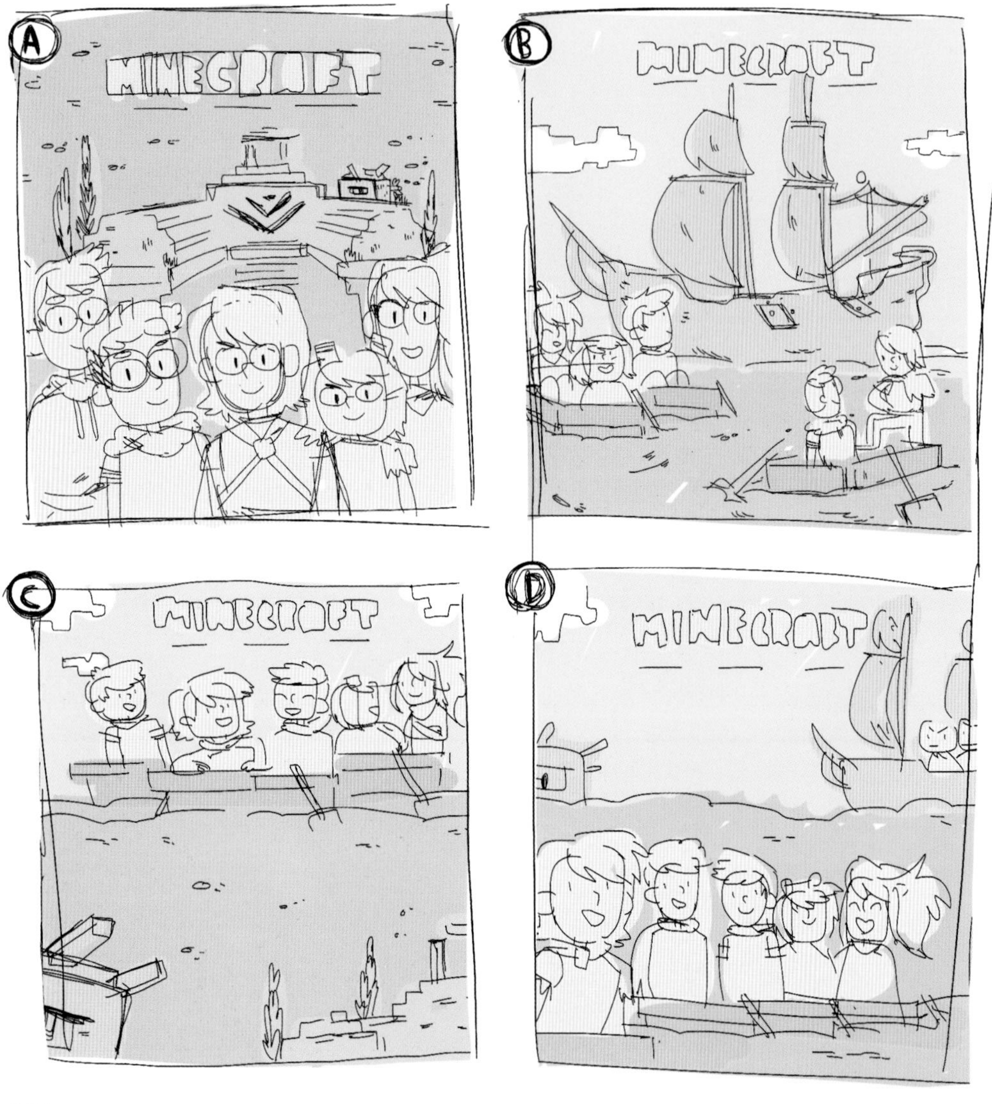
A
B
C
D

## 1 Rough cover pencils

My first idea played off the cover of Volume One, using a similar set up but with the background relating to the story of Volume Two! The other ideas all focused heavily on the sea adventure, including elements like the Pirate Ship, the Ocean Monument, and the Elder Guardian!

Cleo and Aiden's big Pirate Ship is one of the most exciting parts of the book, so it made sense to have it on the cover of the book!

## 2 Rough cover pencils

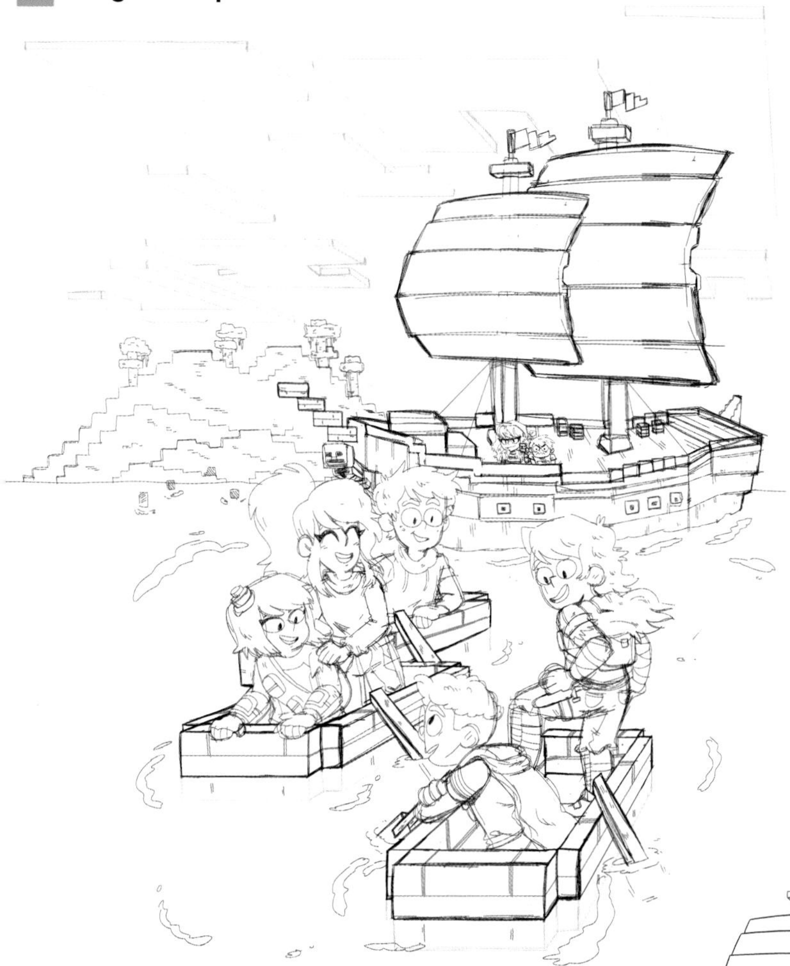

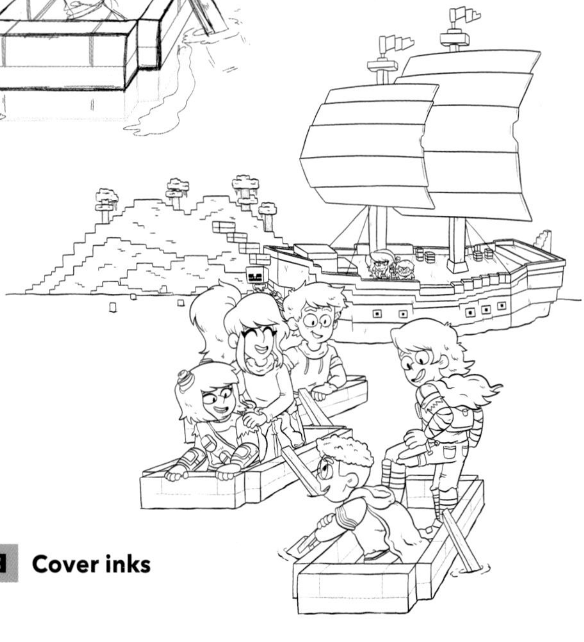

## 3 Cover inks

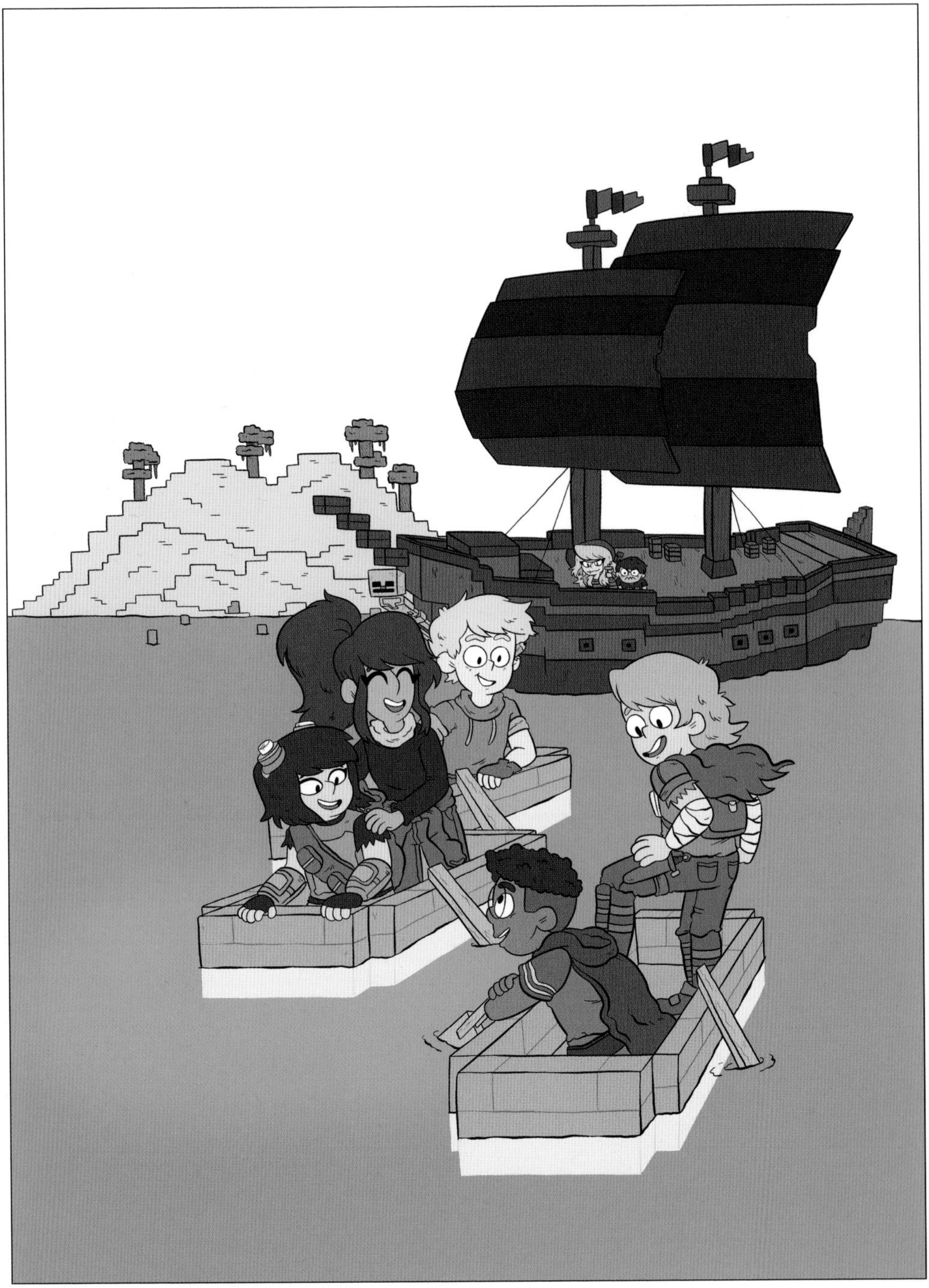

**4** **Cover with flat color**

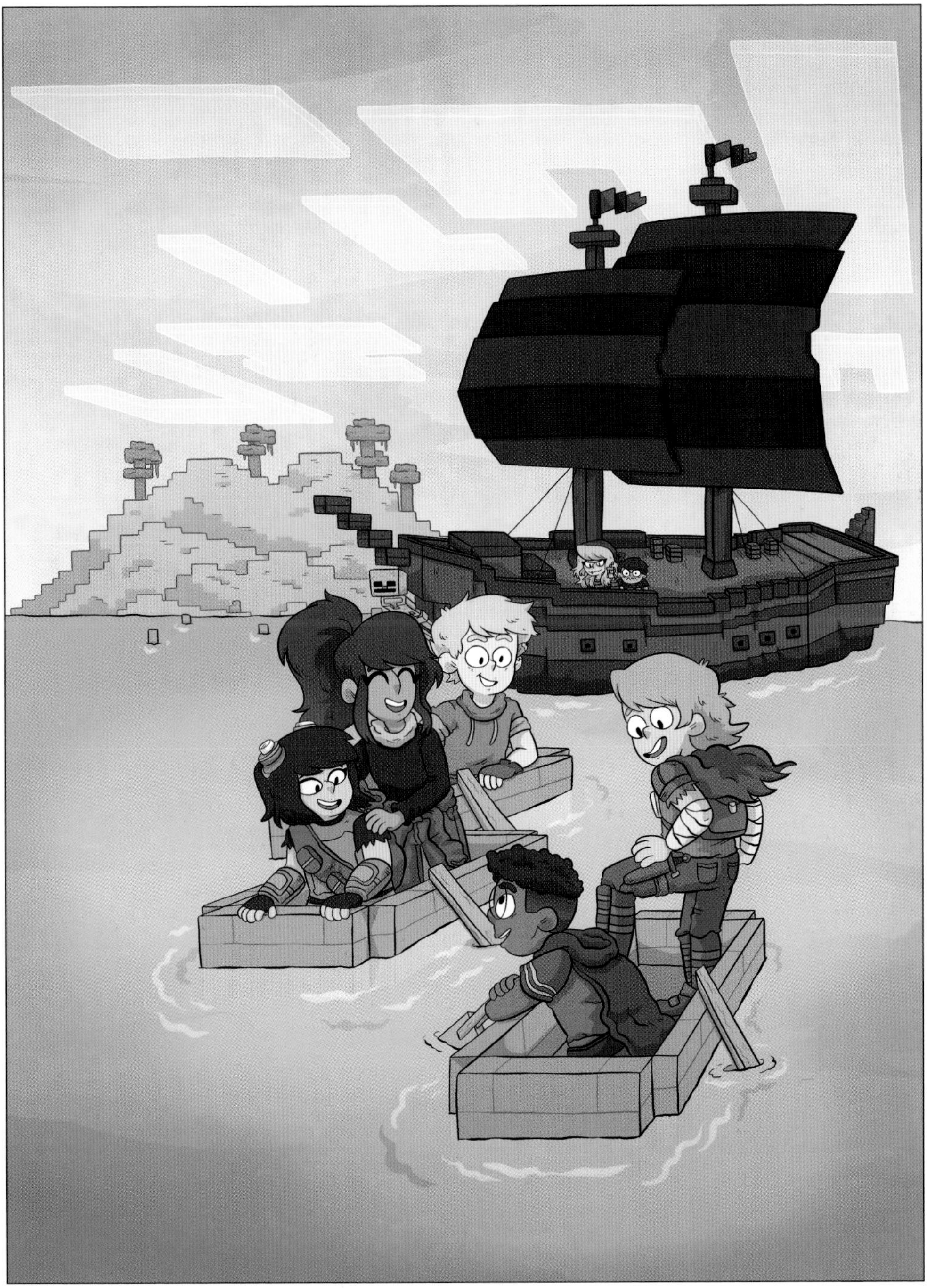

5 Final colored cover

Before starting pencils, I'll usually draw rough layouts for each page of the script. As you can see—these drawings are super scrappy! This step helps me to figure out where all of the panels will go and lets me start thinking about general character expressions before I dive into anything more concrete.

After the penciling and inking stages, my color assistant, Stef, steps in—he fills the final inked black and white lineart with flat colors before passing it back to me for the final coloring steps!

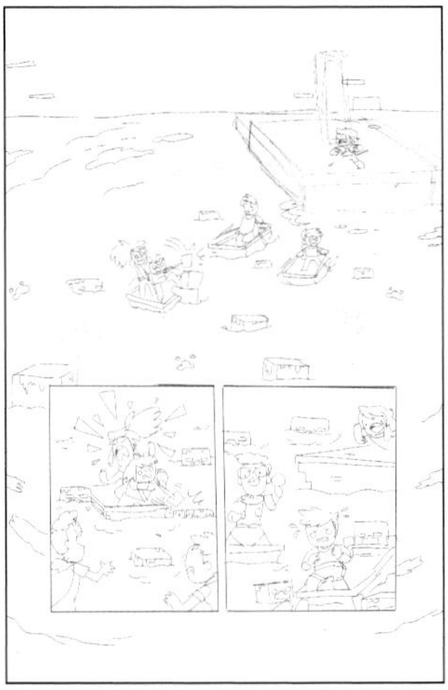

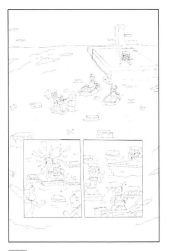

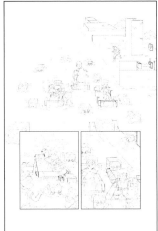

**1 Rough pencil layout**

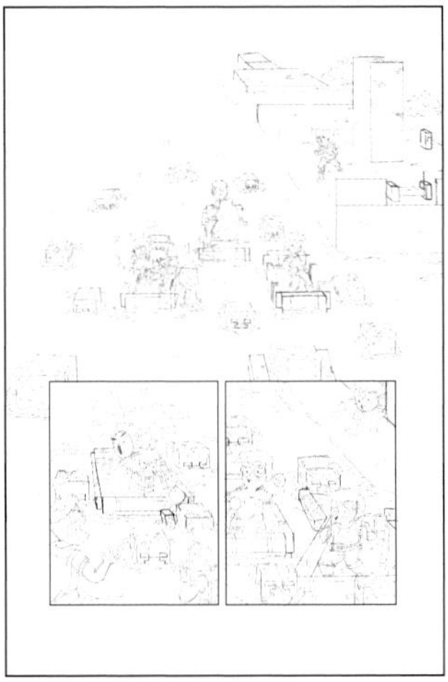

**2 Pencils**

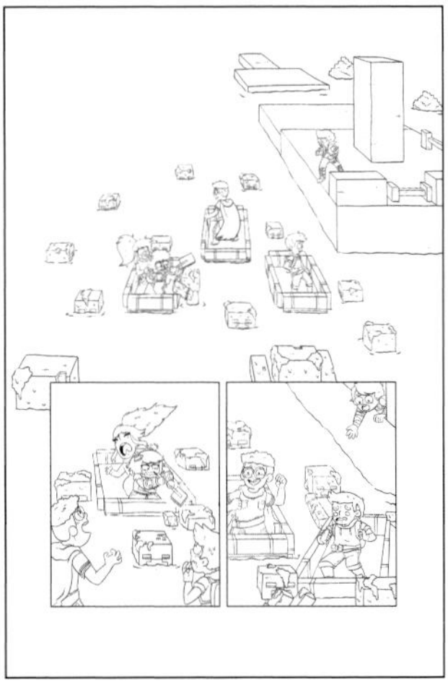

**3 Inks**

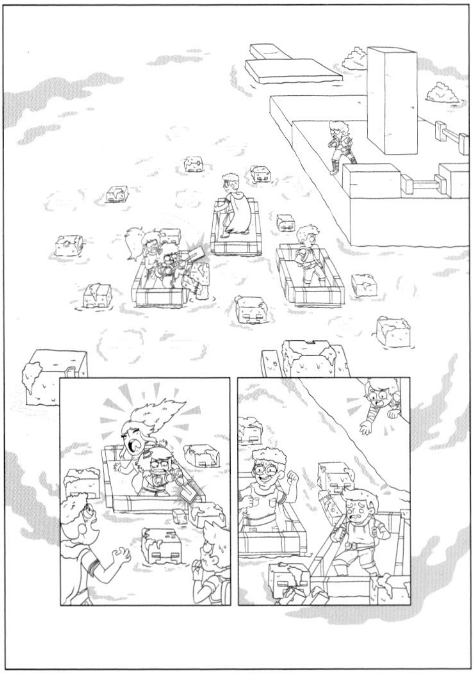

**4 Detailed inks**

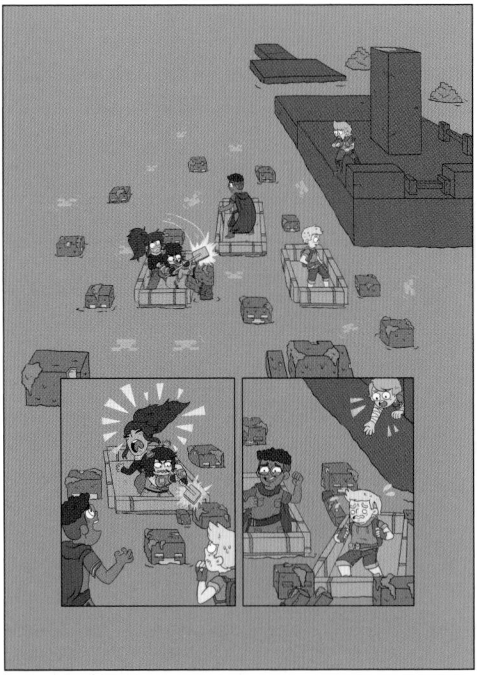

**5 Flat colors**

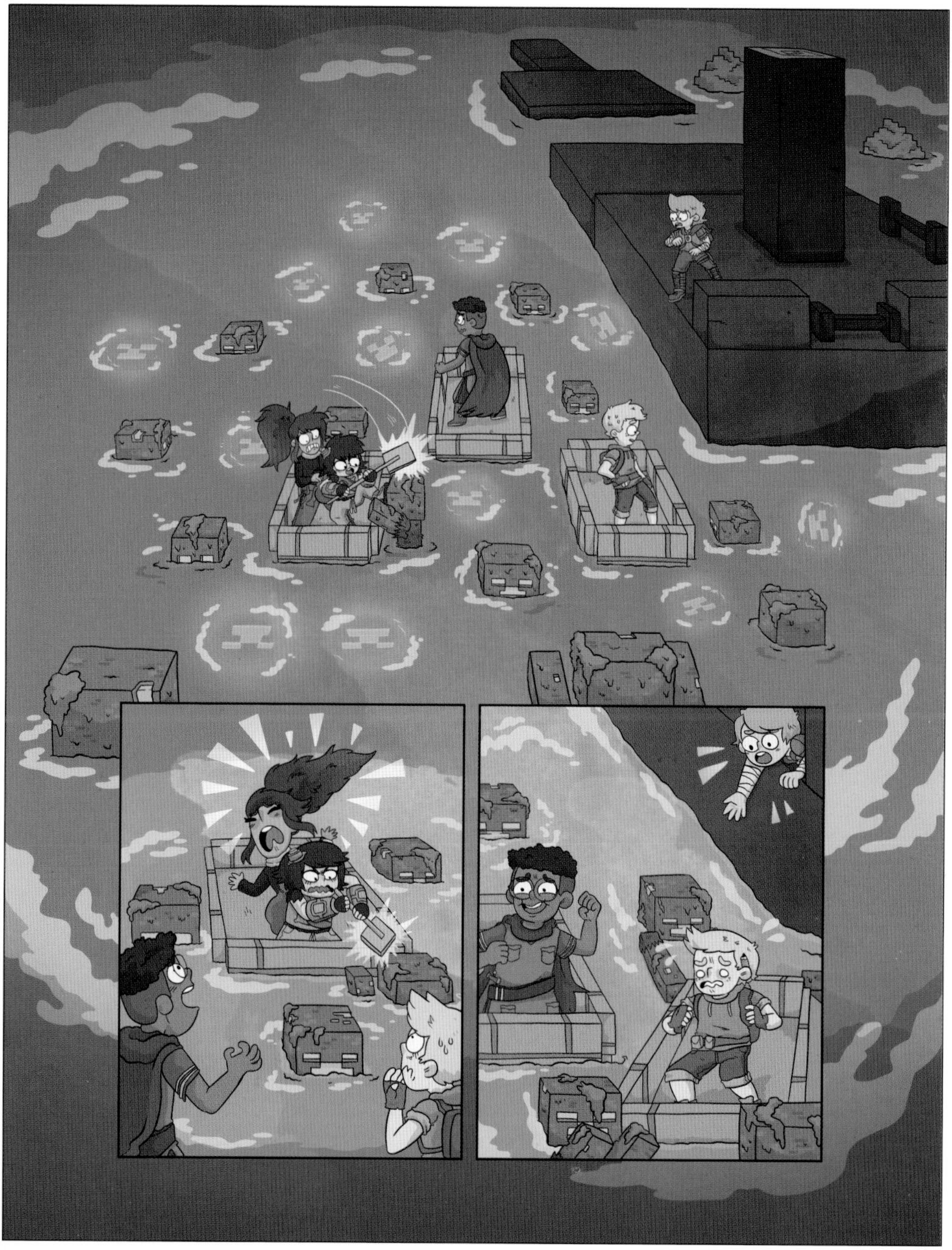

## 6 Final colored page

I then add more detailed coloring work like adding lighting effects and shading. This is one of my favorite stages, as you can see the final artwork start to really come together!

This is one of my favorite pages from the book! With the spooky atmosphere and the glowing faces of the Drowned, this was definitely a fun page to work on and one I looked forward to drawing after reading the script! I love all things spooky, and the Drowned are 100% haunting!

# MORE SERIES YOU MIGHT ENJOY!

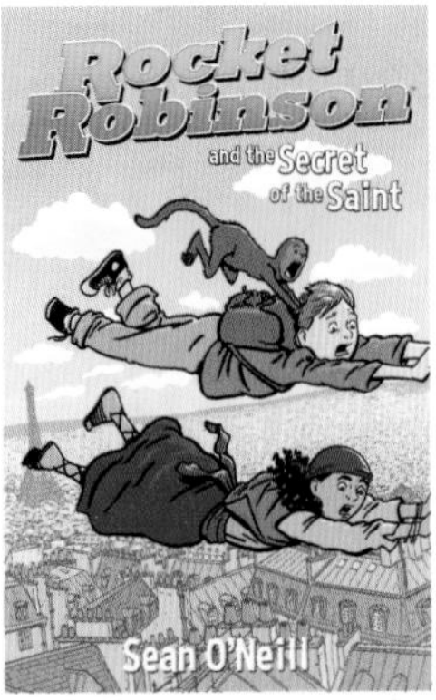
Rocket Robinson
and the Secret of the Saint
Sean O'Neill

### *ROCKET ROBINSON* — SEAN O'NEILL

Cairo, 1933—The Egyptian capital is a buzzing hive of treasure-hunters, thrill-seekers, and adventurers, but to 12-year-old Ronald "Rocket" Robinson, it's just another sticker on his well-worn suitcase. The only son of an American diplomat, Rocket travels from city to city with his monkey, Screech, never staying in one place long enough to call it home, but when Rocket finds a strange note written in Egyptian hieroglyphs, he stumbles into an adventure more incredible than anything he's ever dreamt of.

| | | |
|---|---|---|
| Rocket Robinson and the Pharoh's Fortune | ISBN 978-1-50670-618-4 | $14.99 |
| Rocket Robinson and the Secret of the Saint | ISBN 978-1-50670-679-5 | $14.99 |

---

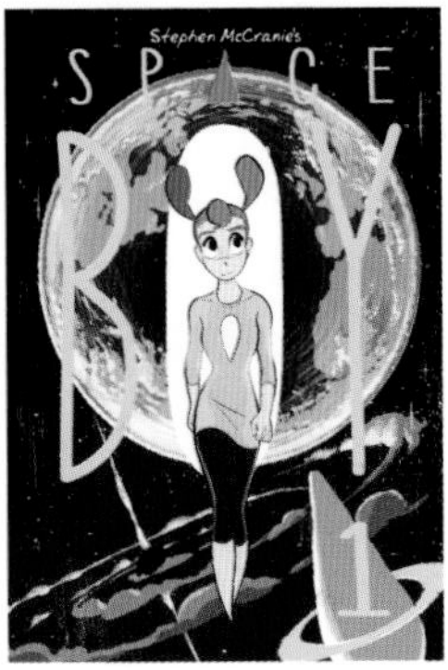
Stephen McCranie's
SPACE BOY
1

### *STEPHEN MCCRANIE'S SPACE BOY* — STEPHEN MCCRANIE

Amy lives on a mining colony out in deep space, but when her dad loses his job the entire family is forced to move back to Earth. Amy says goodbye to her best friend and climbs into a cryotube where she will spend the next thirty years frozen in a state of suspended animation, hurtling in a rocket toward her new home. Her life will never be the same, but all she can think about is how when she gets to Earth, her best friend will have grown up without her.

| | | |
|---|---|---|
| Volume 1 | ISBN 978-1-50670-648-1 | $10.99 |
| Volume 2 | ISBN 978-1-50670-680-1 | $10.99 |
| Volume 3 | ISBN 978-1-50670-842-3 | $10.99 |
| Volume 4 | ISBN 978-1-50670-843-0 | $10.99 |
| Volume 5 | ISBN 978-1-50671-399-1 | $10.99 |
| Volume 6 | ISBN 978-1-50671-400-4 | $10.99 |
| Volume 7 | ISBN 978-1-50671-401-1 | $10.99 |
| Volume 8 | ISBN 978-1-50671-402-8 | $10.99 |

---

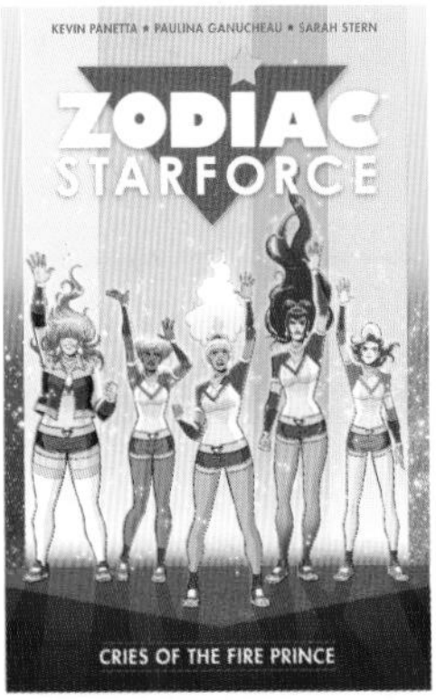
KEVIN PANETTA • PAULINA GANUCHEAU • SARAH STERN
ZODIAC STARFORCE
CRIES OF THE FIRE PRINCE

### *ZODIAC STARFORCE* — KEVIN PANETTA, PAULINA GANUCHEAU

An elite group of teenage girls with magical powers have sworn to protect our planet against dark creatures . . . as long as they can get out of class! Known as the Zodiac Starforce, these high-school girls aren't just combating math tests. They're also battling monsters! But when an evil force infects leader Emma, she must work with her team to save herself and the world from the evil Diana and her mean-girl minions!

| | | |
|---|---|---|
| Volume 1: By the Power of Astra | ISBN 978-1-61655-913-7 | $12.99 |
| Volume 2: Cries of the Fire Prince | ISBN 978-1-50670-310-7 | $17.99 |

---

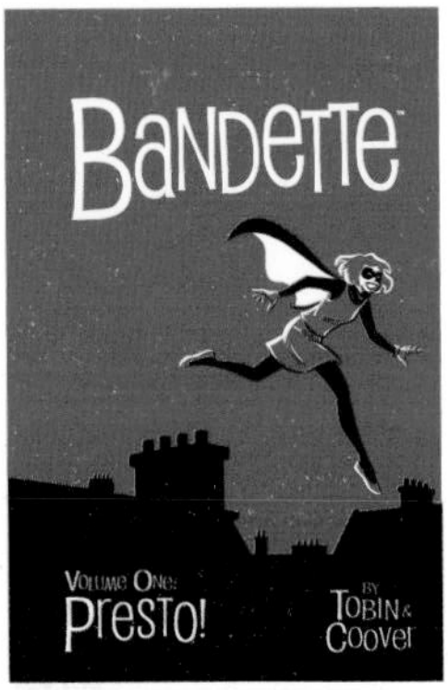
Bandette
Volume One:
Presto!
By
Tobin & Coover

### *BANDETTE* — PAUL TOBIN, COLLEEN COOVER

A costumed teen burglar by the *nome d'arte* of Bandette and her group of street urchins find equa fun in both skirting and aiding the law, in Paul Tobin and Colleen Coover's enchanting, Eisne nominated series! But can even Bandette laugh off the discovery of a criminal plot against her lif

| | | |
|---|---|---|
| Volume 1: Presto | Hardcover ISBN 978-1-61655-279-4 | $14 |
| | Paperback ISBN 978-1-50671-923-8 | $1 |
| Volume 2: Stealers, Keepers! | Hardcover ISBN 978-1-61655-668-6 | $ |
| | Paperback ISBN 978-1-50671-924-5 | |
| Volume 3: The House of the Green Mask | Hardcover ISBN 978-1-50670-219-3 | |
| | Paperback ISBN 978-1-50671-925-2 | |
| Volume 4: The Six Finger Secret | Hardcover ISBN 978-1-50671-926 | |